THE LOST SHEEP

BRANDT DODSON

HARVEST HOUSE PUBLISHERS

EUGENE, OREGON

Cover photos © Krzysztof Bednorz; Kirk Johnson; Jeremy Edwards / iStockphoto

Cover by Garborg Design Works, Savage, Minnesota

THE LOST SHEEP
Copyright © 2007 by Brandt Dodson
Published by Harvest House Publishers
Eugene, Oregon 97402
www.harvesthousepublishers.com

Library of Congress Cataloging-in-Publication Data
Dodson, Brandt, 1958-
   The lost sheep / Brandt Dodson.
    p. cm. — (Colton Parker mystery; #4)
  ISBN-13: 978-0-7369-2140-4
  ISBN-10: 0-7369-2140-0
  1. Parker, Colton (Fictitious character)—Fiction. 2. Private investigators—Fiction. 3. Fathers and daughters—Indiana—Indianapolis—Fiction. 4. Indianapolis (Ind.)—Fiction. 5. Kidnapping—Fiction. I. Title.
  PS3604.O33L67 2007
  813.'6—dc22

2007002496

Printed in the United States of America

07 08 09 10 11 12 13 14 15 / RDM-SK / 12 11 10 9 8 7 6 5 4 3 2 1

PRAISE FOR BRANDT DODSON
AND THE COLTON PARKER MYSTERY SERIES...

ᏋᎦ

Book one... *Original Sin*

"Brandt Dodson's writing combines two of the best traditions of the private eye novel: a clean, laconic style and plotting based on believable human emotions and reactions."

TERENCE FAHERTY, SHAMUS AWARD WINNER, AUTHOR OF *KILL ME AGAIN*

"*Original Sin* reads like it was plucked from the police files, and Colton Parker is the kind of hard-nosed, bloodhound P.I. you'll want to follow from case to case. Brandt Dodson has delivered a strong, intriguing first novel."

MARK MYNHEIR, FORMER HOMICIDE DETECTIVE AND AUTHOR OF
ROLLING THUNDER AND *FROM THE BELLY OF THE DRAGON*

"*Original Sin* is a terrific read, packed with characters—both savory and otherwise—you couldn't forget if you tried. I'm looking forward to the next book!"

JOHN LAURENCE ROBINSON, AUTHOR OF THE JOE BOX MYSTERIES:
SOCK MONKEY BLUES AND *UNTIL THE LAST DOG DIES*

"I loved *[Original Sin]*. A friend sent it to me as a gift. I had others in front of it...so I figured it would be a month or two till I read yours. Then I teased myself with the first chapter. Oops. From there, I was hooked and raced through the whole thing in a day and a half."

ERIC WILSON, AUTHOR OF *EXPIRATION DATE* AND *THE BEST OF EVIL*

"This is a terrific beginning to what promises to be a great series of mysteries with a touch of inspiration." Rating: 4 ½ daggers

JERI NEAL, THE ROMANCE READERS' CONNECTION

"*Original Sin* is the first in a series that promises a bright future. Fans of Robert Parker's Spenser series will feel right at home. Recommended."

ASPIRING RETAIL MAGAZINE

"I love a good mystery, and *Original Sin* by Brandt Dodson has all the elements of a good mystery; a PI the reader can identify with, and a believable cast of characters and a plot that's right out of the daily paper. Highly recommended!"

LINDA HALL, AWARD-WINNING AUTHOR OF *DARK WATER*

"The bottom line: a very readable novel well deserving of the proverbial two thumbs up. Can't wait for Colton Parker's next case!"

ROBERT, FROM A REVIEW FROM THE HARVEST HOUSE WEBSITE

"I picked up *Original Sin* and found myself unable to put it down after reading the first page. I loved the characters and the straightforward writing. The author gave me a greater world of feelings and emotions for Colton Parker. I'm ready to read number two…right now!"

JULIE, FROM A REVIEW FROM THE HARVEST HOUSE WEBSITE

"I like what Brandt Dodson presents in *Original Sin;* a mystery/crime novel with a witty and guilt ridden protagonist. The added conflict with his daughter puts Colton on a human level where we get his struggle with his humanity and his failures…The writing is tight and moves quickly…I can't wait for book number two!!"

LINDA MAE BALDWIN FOR THE ROAD TO ROMANCE

Book two…*Seventy Times Seven*

"*Seventy Times Seven* deals with forgiveness and the consequences of lack of forgiveness. If Robert Parker's Spenser ever needed help in Indianapolis, Colton would be the man for the job."

ASPIRING RETAIL MAGAZINE

"I love this author and his unique, descriptive style of writing. He brings you into the character's world with such clarity and skill that the result is breathtaking. I want good things for Colton Parker and I hope that the next book in this series helps him see some light at the end of his very dark tunnel of grief. This book is a winner for both mystery and inspirational fans."

THEROMANCEREADERSCONNECTION.COM

"Crisp. Wry. Honest. P.I. Colton Parker is as unexpected as a bullet hole in a brand new Brooks Brothers suit. You're gonna like this gumshoe!"

CLINT KELLY, AUTHOR OF *SCENT*

"You can't resist cheering for this guy and hoping that he'll solve both his case and his personal dilemmas. This was a story that I didn't want to put down until I reached the conclusion…Looking forward to the next novel in this series. Keep 'em coming!"

RICK BARRY, AUTHOR OF *YODER'S WAR*

Book three….*The Root of All Evil*

"Characters of depth, a driving plot, and powerful pacing make *The Root of All Evil* a great read and author Brandt Dodson a favorite."

ALTON GANSKY, AUTHOR OF *CRIME SCENE JERUSALEM* AND *FINDER'S FEE*

"Have you ever picked up a book and within the first five pages you know it's a winner? That's the way it is with Brandt Dodson's *The Root of All Evil*…Armchair Interviews says: Catch your breath… and then read on."

ARMCHAIRINTERVIEWS.COM

"Dodson just keeps getting better. This one has everything a classic hard-boiled PI mystery should: murderous biker gangs, corrupt politicians, and the wealthy who'll stop at nothing to get even wealthier…I highly recommend this series to any mystery fan."

RONALD FROM MICHIGAN AT AMAZON.COM

To Christopher and Sean.
No father has ever been more proud.

Acknowledgments

Jeff and Ruby Goldberg: Thank you for reviewing a work in progress. Your suggestions, as always, are on target.

Bob and Linda Lenn. Ditto. And for sharing your anniversary celebration. When can we move in?

The members of First Christian Church, for your very kind and enthusiastic support.

My friends at Welborn Clinic and the Deaconess Wound Services, for your encouragement and support.

To the many bookstore owners, managers, and staff, for their unwavering support. This would not be possible without you.

Nick, for your patient editing.

Thanks to all the professionals at Harvest House Publishers. All of you make this a true pleasure. And,

To Karla.

CHAPTER ONE

I like to do a lot of different things. Playing poker with my friends, listening to the music of Benny Carter, and enjoying a good steak.

Sitting in a police station on a cold November evening isn't one of them.

"Sounds like she's run away."

"Thanks for clearing that up," I said.

"I'm a cop," Wilkins said. "Clearing things up is what I do."

Harley Wilkins, captain of detectives with the Indianapolis Police Department, was seated at his desk with his hands resting on top of his head. The fluorescent lighting reflected off his black skin.

"Can you put out an AMBER Alert?" I asked. I was sitting alongside his desk with my right leg crossed over my left. My right foot was bouncing.

He shook his head. "Sorry, Colton. That's for abductions only." He glanced at my foot. "Relax, okay? We'll find her."

I stopped bouncing. "Sure. Sorry."

"Any idea when the call came in?"

"No. I got home a little before three thirty—that's about the time she gets home from school—and checked for messages as soon as I got in the house."

"You always do that? Check for messages as soon as you get home?" He was drinking a can of Sprite.

"I'm not a cop anymore, Harley. I eat what I kill. If a piece of business wants to reach me, I've got to be available."

"Right." He took a long, slow drink from the can. "Were there any other messages? Something that might have come in after Callie's call? Maybe a message from someone you know? Someone who could let you know what time they left their message? It might help us to pin down when she called."

I gave him a look that told him I knew my job. At least as an investigator, if not as a father.

He finished the last of the Sprite and tossed the empty can into the receptacle under his desk. "You want some coffee or something?" he asked.

"No."

"Tell me again what she said."

I sighed. "I got home at about three thirty. I checked for messages and heard Callie's voice say, 'Daddy, please don't try to find me. Please.'"

He leaned back in his seat and studied me. "Were there any background noises? Something we can use to help pin down her location?"

I tried to rub the strain from my eyes. "I didn't pick up on any."

"Okay. We'll have the lab examine your answering machine. If anything shows up, I'll let you know."

"Thanks," I said.

Wilkins continued to study me the way cops do even when they don't know they're doing it.

"You sure you don't want some coffee or something?" he asked again. "You look beat."

"Yeah, sure," I said, on second thought. "Coffee would be good."

He left for the coin-operated machine that stood outside the squad room, abandoning me to my thoughts. It was nearly six thirty, and everyone else had already gone home, leaving the squad room as empty as I felt.

Callie blamed me for her mother's death. It was an issue that had divided us for the better part of two years. Yet over the past few months, she had seemed to be coming around. She had even gotten involved in soccer again, leading me to believe we had turned a corner. Yet here we were, with me sitting in a police station and her being somewhere she wasn't supposed to be.

My foot was beginning to bounce again. I uncrossed my legs and stuck them straight out ahead of me.

As soon as I discovered Callie had left home, I called the Shapiros, Anna's parents. Since Anna's death, they had been increasingly involved in their granddaughter's life. This latest episode would upset them, but they had to know. I told them that Callie had run away and that I was already working to find her. I told them about my planned visit with Wilkins and tried to sound as encouraging to them as Wilkins was trying to sound to me. I even caught myself using some of the same tactics. But the tone of their comments made it clear that I hadn't been any more successful with them than he had been with me.

"Here we go," Wilkins said, returning to the squad room. He was carrying a couple of lidless Styrofoam cups and set one in front of me as he dropped his ample frame into his chair. "Now, tell me again what the message said."

I sighed. "Harley, I—"

"Humor me, Colton. Just tell me again what she said."

Harley was a good cop. And he was doing the good-cop thing. Asking for the story again was a tried-and-true way to uncover discrepancies. Not that he was expecting any. Not in this case. But he kept digging, prying, trying to find anything that might point him in a direction where none seemed to exist.

"She said, 'Daddy, please don't try to find me. Please.'"

He eased back in the chair with his coffee in one hand while he stroked his chin with the other. "Most runaways don't call and leave messages."

"I'm aware of that," I said, hearing the edginess in my voice. "But kidnap victims don't get the chance."

He continued stroking his chin in thought. "Have there been any problems?"

"Things haven't been right since Anna died."

"How long has that been?"

"Almost two years."

Wilkins wasn't taking notes. He didn't need to. He just wanted to keep me talking until I said something he could use. Something I probably wouldn't even realize I had said. After all, I wasn't thinking as clearly or with as much detachment as he was. Callie wasn't his daughter.

"But you told me earlier that things have been getting better."

"I thought they were. She'd gotten back into soccer, and her grades were beginning to improve." I rubbed my eyes. "She even seemed to be happier, Harley. Not happy, just happier."

I drank some of the coffee. Wilkins drank some of his.

"She's playing for a different school now," Wilkins said. "Any problems there?"

"None I'm aware of. She did have a boyfriend, and that ended, but she seemed to have bounced back pretty quickly."

"After losing your mother, losing a boyfriend just doesn't compare," he said.

"And Mary's been spending time with her. Giving her pointers." I drank more coffee. Wilkins took advantage of the silence.

"On boyfriends?" He smiled.

As a Chicago cop, and later as an FBI agent, I had often employed the tactics Wilkins was using. But now that I was on the receiving end, I realized just how lame they were.

"Why don't you stick to law enforcement and leave the humor to the professionals?" I said.

"Right. Sorry," he said. "Does Mary know she's missing?"

"I called and left her a message."

Mary Christopher was a former colleague from my days with the FBI. Since Anna's death, she had filled the role of surrogate mother. She had also begun to fill a hole in my heart.

"Has she returned your call?"

"No. The bureau sent her to Chicago to testify at a trial. She did some of the legwork for the case here in Indianapolis."

There was a lapse of silence as Wilkins paused to blow on his coffee.

"I searched her room," I said, breaking the silence. "I went through her closet, desk, old yearbooks, anything that might help me get a handle on why she left."

"I understand," he said.

"I found a photo of some guy I don't know and the address of a friend."

"Was the man in the photo her old boyfriend?" Wilkins asked.

I shook my head. "No. I've never seen this guy. No name, just a picture."

"Do Anna's parents know?" Wilkins asked.

"Yeah. I called them before I came here."

"And?"

I sighed. "And they were upset to say the least."

"With you?"

"I don't think so," I said. "They understand that Anna's death has thrown all of us over the edge and that it's going to be a rocky climb back to the top."

"Does your mother know?" he asked.

"I called but she and her husband are on an extended cruise to the Mediterranean. They aren't expected back for a couple of weeks."

My mother had been a prostitute and had given me away shortly after I was born. Although I had established contact with her and was trying to put the past behind me, our relationship was tenuous at best.

"She and her husband are trying to work out their problems," I said.

"Probably best that they don't know," he said. "Sounds like they have enough to work on."

Wilkins blew on his coffee again.

"Can you put out an APB?" I asked.

"Now *that* I can do." He moved forward in the chair. "I'll need a description. And if you've got one, a picture would help. I'll copy it and get it to the roll call stations."

I pulled a photo from my wallet and gave it to him. I told him how tall she was and how much she weighed. I told him what she had been wearing when she left for school. I also gave him my answering machine.

"DOB?" he asked.

I told him, and he wrote it down.

"She's fifteen?" he asked.

"As of last month."

There was another brief period of silence as he studied me again. Not in an accusatory way, but in an *I could be you* way.

"My daughter ran away once," he said. "Tore my ex and me apart. But she came home in forty-eight hours. Most of them do, you know."

"Most of them do. But that means some of them don't. And the longer they're gone…"

"Yeah. I know," he said. "By the way, if she has a cell phone, we can—"

"She doesn't."

"Okay." He stood from his desk. "When I first started on the department, we used to let these things ride for twenty-four hours. But now I can get this thing on the wire right away."

He was trying to be cheerful, upbeat. I appreciated his effort, but it didn't help.

"Sit tight," he said, gently slapping me on the back. "I'll get this picture and your answering machine down to the lab.

Wilkins left me alone again. I glanced around. Photos of spouses, children, and grandchildren sat on most of the desks. Photos that represented loved ones who were waiting at home.

Daddy, please don't try to find me. Please.

It was a request I would ignore. Unless I found her, and found her in time to save her from whatever or whoever lured her away, I would have no reason to go home. Or maybe even to go on.

CHAPTER
TWO

Informing Wilkins of Callie's disappearance was the first step of a plan that I was formulating on the fly. The second step was to meet with Stacey Newton.

I left IPD and drove toward the south side of town. According to the address I had found in Callie's room, Stacey lived on a side street just off of Meridian, the main north-south artery in Indianapolis. Finding her house didn't take long.

It was an older model Cape Cod, with a small front porch, a neat lawn, and shimmering white siding that appeared to be new. A dormant rose bush decorated one side of the house.

After knocking on the door, I was greeted by a pleasant-looking woman who appeared to be in her late thirties. Her hair was copper colored and fashionably done. She was dressed in khaki Dockers and a plaid blouse.

"Yes?" She was smiling.

"My name is Colton Parker," I said. "I'm Callie Parker's father."

"Oh." She continued smiling.

"Callie is missing," I said.

The smile remained for a second longer, then quickly morphed into something more appropriate to the situation.

"I'm so sorry, Mr. Parker," she said, opening the door and stepping aside. "Won't you come in?"

I stepped into a home that seemed warm and inviting. The air was permeated with a pleasant after-dinner aroma.

"Michael," she said, turning to a man who was sitting in a recliner and watching television, "this is Colton Parker. He's Callie's father."

The man turned a quarter turn before standing and extending a hand.

I shook it.

"He says that Callie is missing," the woman said.

The man glanced at his wife. "Missing?"

"She's run away," I said. "I know that Callie and Stacey are friends, and I wanted to talk with Stacey to see if she might know something."

"I'll get her," the woman said, moving toward the rear of the house.

After his wife left the room, Michael said, "When did you discover she had run away?"

"This afternoon. She didn't come home from school."

He crossed his arms and looked at his feet for a moment before saying, "Are you sure she's run away?"

"She left a message. Victims don't often get a chance to do that."

"Right." He gave me a sheepish grin. "I guess that would be logical, wouldn't it?"

"Here she is," the woman said, ushering an attractive fifteen-year-old into the room.

Stacey was tall with thick brown hair that was braided. Like most kids her age, she was dressed casually, wearing jeans and a polo shirt. She also wore braces that didn't look necessary.

"Stacey," her mother said, "this is Callie's dad. He says Callie's run away from home, and he wants to ask you some questions."

"Run away?" She shook her head in disbelief. "Wow. That's a bummer."

"Bummer," I said.

The woman said, "Yes."

Michael continued to stand with his arms crossed.

"Has she said anything lately," I asked, "that might have indicated where she could have gone?"

The girl paused to think before slowly shaking her head. "No. If she did, I can't remember."

"Has she been acting unusual lately?" I asked.

"Would you like to go into the dining room, Mr. Parker?" Stacey's mother asked. "It's more comfortable in there."

"It is," Michael said, reinforcing his wife's offer.

The three of us went into the dining room and sat while Stacey's mother went into the kitchen. She returned carrying a half-full pot of coffee, which I assumed was left over from dinner, along with some cups and a plate of Girl Scout Thin Mints. After setting everything on the table, she sat opposite me and alongside her daughter. Michael was sitting at one end.

"Has Callie been acting unusual lately?" I repeated.

Stacey glanced at her mother. "Well...yeah, kind of."

The woman poured me a cup of coffee. "Cream? Sugar?"

"Just black," I said.

She set the cup on a saucer before sliding it toward me. She gestured toward her husband with the coffeepot. He shook his head.

"How?" I asked.

The girl glanced at both parents this time. "Me and Callie used to be good friends."

"*Callie and I,* dear," her mother said.

The girl continued. "Anyway, lately, she's been kind of...distant."

"How?" I asked.

Stacey shrugged. "Just...standoffish. Like there's somewhere else she'd rather be."

"Has she been acting like this for long?" I asked.

The woman reached for a thin mint and then raised the plate of cookies toward me.

"No, thank you," I said.

"Since right after school started," Stacey said. "Since she got to be friends with Wendy."

"Wendy?"

The girl nodded. "Wendy Wells."

"Do you and Wendy get along?" I asked.

"Stacey gets along well with everyone, Mr. Parker," her mother said, biting into the cookie.

"Doris, let the man talk," Michael said.

Stacey glanced again at both parents.

"Do you?" I repeated.

She slowly shook her head. "We don't have problems, but that's because I stay away from that crowd."

"What crowd?" I asked.

"The Goth crowd," Stacey said. "There aren't many of them, but they stand out."

Despite her mother's death and the troubles it had wrought, Callie hadn't shown any inclination toward anything that might be considered extreme. Always a middle-of-the-roader, she tended to shy away from politics of any stripe, even refusing to run for student council.

"And Wendy is part of this crowd?"

The girl nodded. "They're into vampires, witches, that kind of stuff. You know?"

"Sure," I said.

"Callie hasn't started dressing like them, but she's starting to talk like them."

"How many *thems* are there?"

She shrugged.

"More than ten?" I asked.

"Probably less."

"Do you know any of the others?" I asked.

Stacey's mother sighed. "Mr. Parker. Stacey has already said that she doesn't hang with that crowd."

The girl glanced again at her mother. "I know Tony Mason, but not well."

"Who's he?" Michael asked.

Stacey lowered her eyes toward the table and shrugged. "We had some classes together last year," she said. "But then he dropped out again."

"So he doesn't go to school with you anymore?" I asked.

Her head was still down, her eyes still focused on the table. "He still comes around. I see him hanging around the yard sometimes, trying to talk to some of the girls."

"He talk to Callie?"

The girl nodded. "Yeah. He'd talk to both of us. A lot."

I looked at both parents. Michael kept his eyes focused on his daughter. His wife's eyes had shifted to my still-full cup.

"Would you like something else?" she asked. "We have wine, tea—"

"I'm fine, thanks," I said. "Does this Goth crowd tend to stay together?" I asked Stacey.

She rolled her eyes. "Oh, yeah."

"You said you're not part of the crowd. Does that mean it was unusual for Tony to want to talk with you?"

She shrugged again. "Yeah, I guess so."

"Stacey is a very outgoing, sociable girl, Mr. Parker," her mother said. "Although I can't say I approve of this Tony, I can certainly understand why he would want to talk with her. Can't you?"

"Of course," I said.

Stacey's face reddened.

"What did he want to talk about?" I asked.

She shrugged. "Just stuff. How we're doing, school, sports, stuff like that."

"Where can I find Tony?" I asked.

One hand began to fidget with the other. "He asked me out once. He wanted to go to Binky's."

Her mother paled.

"Binky's? The pool hall on Madison?" I asked.

The girl nodded.

"Do you know where he lives?"

The girl shook her head.

"I might know," Michael said, rising to leave the table.

"Stacey," her mother said, "I don't want you hanging around a boy like that."

The girl said nothing.

"That kind of boy is no good. He's no good for anything but trouble."

All pretenses had vanished. There was nothing left for me to say or do except to wait for Michael's return.

"Here it is," he said, coming back to the table with a booklet that bore the Thomas E. Benton High School logo. He sat and nodded toward his wife. "Doris is active in the PTO. This lists all the names of the students, along with the parents' addresses and phone numbers. This year's book isn't out yet, but…" he began flipping through the pages.

"He won't be in there," the girl said.

Michael quit flipping, and we all focused our attention on her.

"He doesn't live with his parents."

"How about Wendy?" I asked. "Do you know where I can find her?"

The girl shook her head. "I don't know where Wendy is. She dropped out of school last month."

Her mother paled again. Michael flipped to the *W*s.

"Here it is," he said. "Anderson and Barbara Wells."

I pulled a spiral notebook from inside my jacket and flipped it open. "Address?"

He gave it to me.

After recording the address, I replaced the notebook and pulled out the photo I had found in Callie's room.

"Is this Tony?" I asked.

The girl looked at the photo and shook her head. "No. That's not him," she said.

"Who is it?" I asked.

"I don't know, Mr. Parker. But he gives me the creeps."

"How's that?" I asked.

She glanced at her parents again. "I've seen him in Tony's car. He acts like he's Tony's boss or something."

"His boss?"

"He rides in the back, and Tony drives. When Tony comes and talks to us, he keeps looking back at the car. When it's time to go, the man lights a cigarette and Tony leaves. Sometimes he'll even leave in the middle of a sentence."

"Has this man ever talked to you?"

She shook her head.

"Callie?"

The girl nodded. "Yeah. He really likes her."

CHAPTER THREE

The mid-November air had grown decidedly chillier since I arrived, and a layer of crust had already begun to form on my windshield.

So far, I knew that the boy who might be a link in finding Callie liked to play pool at Binky's and had asked Stacey Newton, a girl who was outside his normal social circle, for a date. I also knew that his name was Tony Mason, and that he wasn't the man in the photo I had found in Callie's room. But I also knew the two were connected in a way that sounded very much like an employer and an employee. I had also learned that Tony's boss had an apparent affinity for Callie.

According to Stacey, Wendy was a dropout and very much into Tony's crowd. That made her a very strong link to Tony, who was a strong link to the man in the photo. Things were beginning to gel.

After clearing the ice, I drove to the address I had been given for Wendy and found a house very much like the one I had just left—a two-story Cape Cod with a small front porch and a couple of pine trees in the yard. It seemed every bit as inviting as the previous one, but in this case there was no pretense. Anderson and Barbara Wells didn't offer Thin Mints. They extended a plate of hot apple crisp.

"So you don't know where Wendy is?" I asked, eating the last bite from my plate.

"Not a clue," Anderson said with a tinge of frustration in his voice. "We haven't heard from her since she dropped out of school last month."

I was sitting at someone else's dining room table for the second time that evening. Husband and wife were sitting opposite me.

"Do you think that your Callie and our Wendy are together?" Barbara asked.

The woman asking the question was considerably older than Stacey's mom. This woman and her husband looked to be closer to sixty. Both of them had indicated that Wendy was adopted, and their home and the manner in which they spoke of their daughter showed that they had lavished her with love and attention.

"Possibly," I said.

"Maybe if you find your daughter, you'll find ours too," Wendy's father said.

"If Wendy is with Callie, I'll find her."

In fact, I was hoping that Wendy *had* left with Callie. Running away is an act of disappearance. A very difficult thing to do, even for the street savvy. When more than one person is involved, particularly more than one teenager, the difficulty rises exponentially.

"I'm sorry to have to ask you this," I said, "but Wendy seems to have gotten into the wrong crowd. Has she ever given you any trouble before?"

Tears filled Barbara's eyes. Anderson reached to clasp both of her folded hands with one of his. His hand was big and callused and misshapen from years of manual labor.

"She's never given us anything *but* trouble," he said. "Just one thing after another."

His wife dabbed at her eyes with a napkin and nodded her head in agreement. Her husband put his arm around her.

"Like what?" I asked.

"We adopted Wendy when she was about seven years old. The adoption agency told us that if we wanted an infant, it could take years." He paused to look at his wife and gave her a gentle squeeze.

"So we adopted Wendy. But we knew almost from the beginning that she had problems."

"How so?"

"For starters, she was always in trouble at the group home. Always getting into one thing or another. But she just seemed like the right child for us. You know? Just…like she needed what we could offer."

"Love," his wife said.

"Right," he echoed. "Love. And a home. A place to belong. The kinds of things all kids need."

"But she continued to get into trouble," I said.

"Yes sir. She continued to get into trouble. First, there were the notes from the teachers. Then, visits to the principal's office. Then, as she got older, there was detention. Then, suspension." He shook his head. "We can't tell you the number of times she's had to stay after school."

"And the drinking," his wife added. "Always drinking."

"Which is something we could never understand," he said. "We don't drink. We don't even have the stuff around."

"When she dropped out of school, did she give an explanation?"

Both shook their heads.

"She had been very upset for a couple of weeks before she left," Anderson said.

"What about?"

He shrugged. His wife shook her head. "We don't know," she said. "She would never confide in us. Kept us in the dark most of the time."

"Unless she wanted money," he said. "Never had a problem asking for that."

"Has she?"

"What?" Anderson asked.

"Asked for money?"

"No. We haven't heard from her since she ran away."

"Some friends of ours saw her a couple of weeks after she left, but we haven't heard anything since then," the woman said.

"Where did they see her?"

"A place called Binky's. A pool hall on Madison," Anderson said.

"Do your friends hang out there?"

Anderson shook his head. "No. I shoot a little and have a pool table in the basement." He paused. "I can't think of a single day when she expressed any interest in it."

"Did she ever mention Callie?"

"No," the man said, glancing at his wife, who indicated her agreement.

"I've been told," I said, being cautious to not reveal Stacey's identity, "that Wendy has gotten into the Goth crowd."

"You mean dressing in black with spiked hair and an earring in her nose?" the man asked.

"That's what I mean," I said.

He chuckled—not in amusement, but in irony. "She didn't get into the Goth crowd, Mr. Parker, she invented it. She's always liked scary movies, goblins, that sort of thing. Halloween was always bigger than Christmas."

"She was wearing all black when she was just a child," the woman said. "Then, as she got older, she came home with that awful thing through her nose." She paused to fold the napkin she had been using to dab at her eyes. "We made her take it out."

"We were trying to do the right thing," the man said.

"Sure," I said.

"But after that, it was all downhill," the woman said, completing her thought.

"We filed a police report," the man said, "but they said that since she was eighteen, she had the right to live anywhere she wanted."

"Eighteen?"

"She was held back a couple of years," the woman said.

I pulled the photo from my jacket. "Ever see this man?" I asked, sliding it across the table to the couple.

Both shook their heads.

"We never met any boyfriends. She always kept them away from the house. Like she was ashamed of us," Anderson said.

"Nothing to be ashamed of here," I said.

CHAPTER FOUR

The dawn of morning light, which had so pleasantly begun the day, had now shifted to the full blackness of night. I left the Wells' home and was immediately enveloped in darkness.

I still didn't have an identity for the man in the photograph, but I did know that Binky's was coming into play. It was one of the common links between Wendy and Tony.

The pool hall was located on the very near south side of Indianapolis on Madison Avenue, a main artery that led directly from the downtown area. Binky's was part of a three-building strip mall that also housed a small grocery store and a New Age shop that sold crystals and incense. I was able to reach the place inside of five minutes.

Instead of entering the pool hall right away, I decided to stay in my car and watch to get a feel for the establishment and the clientele it attracted. In only a few minutes, I saw several drug deals go down without any concern for the fact that I was watching. I also saw several hookers go into the building but never come out.

Having gotten a sense of the place, I got out of my car and went into the hall.

The room was dimly lit, with four pool tables standing in the center of the room and four times as many men playing at them. There was a room in the back, and from where I stood, I could see several pinball machines and a soft-drink dispenser. A few men were playing pinball. Beyond the game room, a narrow stairway led to the second floor.

The clacking sound of pool balls and the occasional *thump* as they landed in the pockets competed with the *ding-ding* of the pinball machines.

"Five dollars a game, no weapons, and you gotta rerack the cues when you're done," a voice to my right said.

I saw a bald, weathered-looking man sitting behind a cage similar to the type I used to see at bank tellers' stations. A sign that read Cash Only was taped to the wall over the man's head.

"Cash," he said.

"I'm not here to play," I said. "I want to ask some questions."

"Then you need to get going, pal. We don't make money answering questions."

I reached into my jacket for the photo as the man kept a wary eye on my hand.

"Know this guy?" I asked, sliding the photo in the pass-through of the cage.

Before he could look at the photo, a sudden noise erupted from the floor. Four men who were playing together at one of the tables were beginning a heated argument over a game that had gone sour. One of the men had backed away from the table and had his cue in hand. The man in the cage cast a narrow-eyed look in their direction.

"It don't matter," he said. "I done told you to—"

Someone from the floor cursed, and the group began shoving each other.

"Excuse me," the bouncer said, sliding from behind the cage.

He moved toward the group as he pulled a cue from one of the wall-mounted racks. He rapped it hard on the table, and the men ceased their shoving.

"Out! Now!"

The men stood motionless for a moment before the largest of the four, the one with the cue, approached the bouncer. Before he could close the distance, the bouncer swung his cue with a backhand that would have set Wimbledon on its ear. He struck his would-be attacker in the face, forcing the man backward and causing him to drop his weapon.

Then, like any family who will fight among themselves but unite against an outsider, the remaining three men jumped the bouncer, taking him to the floor.

The man who had been struck with the cue wiped blood from his nose as he stooped to pick up his weapon.

I retrieved the photo and crossed the floor.

"Let's see how you like it," the man said, swinging the stick high over head like an executioner about to decapitate his victim.

Before he could bring it down, I drove a straight right into his chest. He exhaled sharply and fell backward against the pool table, where he slumped to the floor, dropping his cue.

I turned my attention to the tussle on the floor and pulled one of the men off the bouncer. The man swung at me but missed. The group dynamic had emboldened him to believe he had skills he did not possess. He swung again, and I blocked the blow with ease, hitting him with a right hook. He collapsed.

As I turned to pull another one of the men off the bouncer, the first man was on his feet and approaching me.

He swung at me with a sloppy right, and I hit him again with a straight left to the chest followed by a right hook to the head. He went down again.

The two men on the floor had the bouncer pinned when I heard the click of a knife. I pulled my Ruger from its holster and put the barrel in the ear of the man who had the blade.

"Drop it," I said.

He hesitated.

I cocked the hammer.

"Please?"

He dropped the knife. I told him and his partner to get off the bouncer.

The rest of the room was quiet, with all eyes trained on me and the man with the gun barrel in his ear. The other two men were beginning to get to their feet. The bouncer rose to his.

"Get out," he said to the men.

The four of them hesitated, glanced at the Ruger, and began to move toward the door. The largest of the four let his shoulder brush hard against mine as he passed. After the men were out the door, I holstered the gun.

"Get on with it," the bouncer said to the others in the hall. "There ain't nothin' to see."

As the others slowly began to resume their play, I sat on the edge of the table where the four men had been arguing. The bouncer went to the back room and came back with two cans of Coke. He put one against his battered face and handed the other to me.

"Thanks," he said.

I popped the top on the can and took a long, slow drink. "Sure."

"Those guys come in here about once a month. They always get into some sort of argument, but this is the first time it's turned violent."

"Why do you let them come in?"

He grinned. "Business. People like to play. I like to make money. It's the way the world works."

"They play rough," I said.

"Yep. Might not let them come in here anymore. I don't need the money that bad."

We were silent for a moment as the hall began to refill with the active sound of pool and pinball.

"You own the place?" I asked.

"Naw. I just manage it. But I get a piece of the take."

At five dollars a game, his piece of the take wouldn't be enough to keep him alive. That began to explain the extra activity I had seen in the lot.

"I saw some stuff in the lot that might force this place to close," I said.

He turned to look directly at me. "You a cop?"

I shook my head. "Like I said, I have a few questions. I'm trying to find someone."

"Who?"

I pulled the picture from my pocket and showed it to him. "Know this guy?"

The bouncer's eyes narrowed as he held the picture out to full arm's length.

"He's been in here a few times."

"What's his name?" I asked.

"Don't know."

"Does he come in here regularly?"

He shook his head and rubbed the can across his face again.

"Does he come in here often?"

"Yeah, I'd say he comes in here a lot. Just not regular. You know?"

"Sure."

"If I had to depend on him, this place wouldn't be in business long."

"Know where I can find him?"

He shook his head. "Not directly. He hasn't been in here in a while. But I know someone who might know." He looked at me with an expression that made it clear he didn't want trouble.

"I can forget everything I saw," I said. "All I want is to find this guy."

"Why? What's he done to you?"

"My daughter's missing," I said. "And I want her back."

CHAPTER FIVE

According to the bouncer, Tony Mason was the person most likely to know the man in the photo and was living in a four-apartment complex at the corner of Raymond and Meridian streets. From what I could see on the mailbox, Mason lived in apartment C, located on the northwest corner of the second floor. The apartment appeared dark, as did all of the others.

I climbed the stairs to the second floor and knocked on the door of apartment C. There was no answer, so I knocked again, and again I received no reply.

Callie was missing. I didn't know where she was or with whom. But the man in the photo seemed to be the likely suspect, and the bouncer had seen Tony with the man on several occasions. That meant that Tony was also a likely suspect, and where Callie was concerned, *likely* was good enough.

I pulled the Ruger from inside my jacket and tried the door. It was locked, so I kicked it in. It gave way with ease.

As soon as I was in the apartment, I began to grope for a light switch. I didn't like the feeling of standing silhouetted in the doorway of an apartment that just might have someone in it despite its unattended appearance.

I found the switch and flicked on the light. Seeing that no one was home, I holstered my gun and repositioned the door.

I glanced around the apartment before slipping on a pair of latex gloves.

It was an efficiency apartment with a tattered curtain that separated the kitchen area from the rest of the room. A heavily stained sofa sat along one wall beside a dilapidated recliner, an end table that supported a brass lamp, and a CD rack that held a pile of CDs. A TV sat on a cart along the opposite wall, and to the left, a computer was set up on a computer table. The linoleum on the floor was old and worn.

I crossed over to the computer and flicked on the CPU and the monitor. While I waited for the system to boot up, I began to search the room.

Mason had a penchant for fringe music. Most of the CDs featured artists who were heavily into the Goth style of black clothing, body piercings, and facial expressions that revealed their hopelessness and despair. They billed themselves under names such as Black Lung, Blood Drive, and Sludge.

"Benny Carter, eat your heart out," I said in homage to the world's greatest jazz musician.

I fingered the dingy curtain that partially covered the cooking area before opening it to reveal the kitchen.

A short counter of tile with yellowing grout separated equally short rows of upper and lower metal cabinets. The sink was full of dishes, and a roll of Bounty was impaled on a vertical towel holder off to one side.

"The quicker picker-upper," I said, opening the refrigerator.

Tony had a taste for alcohol. I counted four six-packs and two wine coolers. In addition to the booze, I found a half carton of eggs, a pound of bacon, a moldy package of opened Cheddar, and three jars of mustard. I closed the refrigerator and searched through the cabinetry. Besides a few dishes, mostly plastic cups from various restaurants and some heavily used silverware, there were two boxes of Pop Tarts and a half-empty box of Frosted Flakes.

A tall, metallic cabinet stood next to the kitchen. I opened it and found several black shirts, a couple pairs of jeans, a pair of tennis shoes, and a pair of boots.

I closed the cabinet and continued to search the room.

I opened the single drawer in the computer table and found some printer paper and an ink cartridge but nothing else.

In the drawer of the end table, I found a small notebook and an envelope containing a check stub. The stub was for two weeks' pay and had been issued by the Sunshine Inn. The stub was almost two weeks old.

I read a notation in the notebook.

Tuesday 5:00 p.m. J. Bigelow.

Which Tuesday? Tomorrow? And what kind of meeting was it? And where was it going to be held? And who was J. Bigelow?

I flipped through the notebook. Except for the cryptic message, it was empty. I tucked the notebook and the check stub into the pocket of my jacket.

I glanced around the room. There was no cable connection, wireless hardware, or satellite hookup. The only high-tech item I saw was the computer, which had finally booted up.

I sat down at the desk and began by working my way through the list of Mason's favorite websites. My hope was to find something that would give me a better understanding of him and of the man whose photo I had found in Callie's room.

A cursory glance at his bookmarks revealed that Tony had a taste for pornography. Lots of it. But I found other things in his list that were even more disturbing.

Six sites that Tony had bookmarked centered on Satanism. I chose one of the sites at random and left-clicked the link.

The computer was slow to respond, and the hard drive made a grinding noise. But after a bit, the monitor filled with a red pentagram set against a black background. Several other icons then appeared, all miniature pentagrams, and they seemed to float around the periphery of the larger satanic symbol.

I clicked on the About Us icon, and a lengthy essay appeared. I began reading it and immediately recognized the commentary as an introduction to devil worship for the uninitiated. From what I was seeing, I was clearly one of the uninitiated.

The writer began by recounting some of the history of Satanism and then slid into a short piece about its many followers ("Could be your next door neighbor, your child's teacher, your physician— we're everywhere"). This was followed by a brief bit about some of the rituals involved. The writing concluded by explaining that the authors did not believe in Satan as an existing personality. Instead, they saw him as a focal point for those who did not appreciate the public persona of Christianity and who felt that any maneuver to force a moral issue on anyone was reprehensible. The devil didn't exist, they said. But as a rallying point for those who opposed any-thing the group considered anti-choice, he clearly did.

I closed that window and opened another that was labeled Our Tenets.

In this section, the group seemed to indicate that "might makes right." According to their thinking, they believed that mercy was a sign of weakness and that no one should avoid taking revenge when wronged by someone else. Strong threads of antisocial behavior were woven throughout the commentary.

A cursory inspection of a couple of the other websites indicated entirely different beliefs. Clearly, some Satanists *did* believe in the existence of Satan and welcomed his future rise to power as a persona who understood the true meaning of the world and who would not hesitate to exert his power over it. This was in stark contrast, they said, to the hypocrisy of pasty-faced Christians, who were eagerly waiting to be saved.

Despite the differences between the satanic groups, both seemed to be committed to power and violence.

I closed the bookmarks and began a review of Mason's word pro-cessing software.

I found several essays that were similar to the ones I had already read but that also seemed to echo the anti-establishment thrust of the sixties. Tony was opposed to war but believed all "weaklings" should be "annihilated." He was opposed to the "class system," but he was entrenched in his belief that "power should be given to the power-less" to "exert their will over their oppressors." He was not opposed to using anyone for anything.

I backed out of his software and opened his e-mail.

He had a few messages in his Inbox, but all of them seemed to be spam or invitations to visit other pornographic sites. Some of them had been in his computer for over a week. Either he hadn't been home, or he was loath to check his e-mail.

I backed out of his computer and shut it down, and it ground to a slow and painful halt.

"Need to be careful, Tony," I said. "This stuff will infect more than your computer."

CHAPTER SIX

I had set up another answering machine before I had left for IPD headquarters. When I arrived home that evening, I checked to see if I had any new messages. The red light was blinking, and the message counter said I had three. I hit the play button, and the series of messages began to play.

"Colton, I just heard."

It was Dale Millikin. He had been Anna's pastor prior to her death. Although the man meant well, he seemed to need to interject himself into all areas of my life, particularly into my relationship with Callie. I appreciated his intent, but I often resented his intrusion.

"Call me as soon as you get home."

The call ended. His voice sounded weak.

I glanced at the clock. It was a few minutes after eleven.

The second message began to play.

"Colton, it's Frank. Any news on Callie? Corrin and I are just sick. Call us when you get in. We don't care how late it is."

Frank and Corrin Shapiro had become the parents I never had. From the time it was clear that Anna and I were serious, they had taken me into their family with a grace I had never experienced. Though we'd experienced some bumpy times, Anna's death had drawn us closer.

Before the final message began to play, I turned the volume of the recorder to maximum and went into the kitchen to make coffee. It was going to be a late night, and I would need the caffeine.

"Colton, it's Mary."

I stopped midstance.

"It's nine o'clock, Chicago time. I just got your message. I've been in court all day, and then we had to go to the office to prepare for tomorrow. Call me as soon as you get home regardless of the time."

She gave me her room and telephone numbers, and I wrote them down on a memo pad that I kept magnetically attached to my refrigerator. After starting the coffee, I dialed her room. She answered on the first ring.

"It's me," I said.

"You okay?"

"As well as can be expected."

"Any news?"

I told her all that I knew.

Since Anna's death, Mary and Callie had grown quite close. Although soccer was their common bond, their relationship had been fueled by something more than their joint love of the sport. Mary had no children, and Callie had no mother. Each filled a void in the other's life.

I had a void too. A painful one. And the sound of Mary's voice soothed the hurt.

Anna's death had inverted my world. Needs were no longer supplied, and desires were no longer met. I became the walking wounded. My attraction to Mary was beginning to develop in ways for which I hadn't been prepared.

When relationships are forged out of a need to assuage an aching heart, they carry with them the seed for future trouble. I was attracted to Mary. But I wanted the attraction to spring from the right things. If the relationship was to last, it would have to be planted in the right time.

Almost two years had passed since Anna had died, and I hadn't thought it was planting season until Mary began seeing another federal agent. I hadn't liked it, and when the relationship failed, I was glad.

"I didn't want to bother you, Mary. You've got enough on your—"

"Hogwash!"

"—mind."

"You think the guy in the picture is behind her disappearance?" she asked.

"I don't know. But since his picture was in her room, he becomes a possible link."

"You going out again tomorrow?"

"Yep."

"I can't leave here yet," she said.

"I know."

"When I get out of this, I'll give you a hand."

"I know."

Neither of us said anything for a moment. The silence between us was one of the things that attracted me to Mary. She was comfortable in her own skin and didn't see the need to fill the air with mindless chatter.

"Where you off to next?" she asked.

"I'm going to try the Sunshine Inn. I found a check stub in Tony's apartment. I don't know if it'll lead to much, but it's a thread I've got to pull."

"Have you talked to Millikin?"

"Not yet. He called, but I was out."

"Call him, Colton."

After Anna's death, Mary had begun having long talks with Millikin. They had met during Anna's funeral, and the meeting had placed Mary on a spiritual quest of her own. Before long she began seeking him out, and she soon became a Christian. Though not as intrusive as Millikin, Mary often brought up the topic of her newfound faith.

"Not tonight, Mary. I'm not in the mood for sermonizing."

She sighed. "He does tend to do that, doesn't he?"

"Yes."

"But he can help. He has insight into Callie. He's spent a lot of time with her."

"I'll call him," I said. There was more silence. "When will you be back?"

"I don't know. I have to go back on the stand tomorrow and possibly again the day after. But it shouldn't last long. We have these guys bound up pretty tight."

"I miss you," I said, allowing the words to come forth without the benefit of a filter.

I had spoken from the heart. The seed was sown. Colton Parker was becoming the Johnny Appleseed of love—and opening himself to rejection.

"I miss you too," she bounced back without hesitation.

"We probably need to talk when you get back," I said.

"If you want."

"I want."

Just a few hours before, I had been fighting with four thugs in a pool hall. Now I was talking to a beautiful woman on the night my daughter had run away from home. But life can do that to you sometimes. It can cast you into the tempest when you least expect it and then pull you to shore by the kindest of hands.

My relationship with Mary was a long time in coming, and I was glad to have my feelings for her out in the open. But for now, all of that would have to wait.

The tempest was calling, and Callie was out there somewhere. And that meant I had work to do.

CHAPTER SEVEN

I awoke at half past five, draped over my recliner. I couldn't remember when I had fallen asleep, but from the way I felt, it clearly hadn't been very long ago.

After spending most of the night—and a pot of coffee—mulling over the problem, I felt as if my body desperately wanted to remain in the chair. But I willed myself to get moving despite the creaks and groans of joints that had been misaligned over the course of a restless night.

After a shower and a change of clothes, I left the house at six thirty. By seven, I was on the west side of town in the lobby of the Sunshine Inn. I poured myself a cup of their complimentary coffee before dinging the bell on the registration counter.

The inn was located off of I-465, the highway that encircles the Circle City, and seemed to be a reasonably nice place, considering that someone like Tony worked there. The lobby furniture was clean and in good repair; several potted plants were well positioned throughout the nicely lit area, and a stack of recent magazines dotted the various tables that stood about the room. Before I could ding the bell a second time, a pleasant-looking man of about thirty came from the back office. He was wearing a green vest over a white shirt and had sandy-colored hair that was closely cropped. His white plastic name tag identified him as Jason.

"Can I help you?" he asked.

"Sure, Jason," I said. "I'm looking for a coworker of yours. Or maybe he's a friend. His name is Mason. Tony Mason."

The man's faced turned color faster than a chameleon on a tie-dyed shirt.

"Problem?" I asked.

"What do you want with *him?*"

"I want to talk with him," I said.

"He's not a friend," he said.

"But he *is* a coworker," I said, "and I still want to talk with him."

The man was about to speak, but he hesitated with his mouth open. "Are you the police?"

"Why?" I asked. "Is he doing something that would interest them?"

Jason crossed his arms. Although I couldn't see his lower body because of the counter, I could clearly tell he was bouncing his foot.

"Tony does a lot of stuff." He gave me the once-over. "You sure you're not a cop?" he repeated.

I assured him I wasn't.

"Then why are you looking for Tony?"

"Personal," I said.

He stopped bouncing long enough to think about whether he wanted to talk with me.

"He quit," he said.

The check stub I had seen had been dated for the previous pay cycle.

"When?"

"Couple of days ago."

"Did he say why he wanted to quit?" I asked.

Jason huffed. "He just quit," he said. "And he did it just like that." He snapped his fingers. "He just didn't show up. Just left me holding the bag."

"No reason given?"

"None. And that's just rude."

"The nerve," I said.

He folded his arms across his chest again.

"So, getting back to my previous question," I said, "was he doing something that the police might be interested in knowing about?"

He pursed his lips. "Maybe. I'm not sure if I should say. I don't want to get into trouble."

"If you know something," I said, "and don't tell me, I'll tell the police when I find out."

His expression changed, and he uncrossed his arms. "But I didn't do anything," he said.

"Maybe, maybe not. But you know what he's doing, and that makes you an accessory."

He frowned as he thought about his predicament.

"And if I tell you, am I okay?"

"In my book, sure." I didn't see a need to tell him that my book didn't count for much.

He crossed his arms again, though less defiantly this time, and resumed bouncing on his foot. "He was running women in and out of here."

"Women of the night? At the Sunshine Inn?"

He nodded vigorously.

"By himself?"

He rolled his eyes. "Well, how am I supposed to know that?"

"Because you work with him?"

He huffed. "Just because you work with someone doesn't mean you know all about him."

"Tell me what you do know, and I'll take it from there. Okay?"

He frowned again.

"Okay?" I repeated.

He bounced a bit more. "He used to tell the women what rooms they could use. Vacant rooms. He'd tell me to not say anything if I knew what was good for me. Sometimes, when the evening was over, he'd give me money for my trouble."

"Any meetings ever held here?" I asked, recalling the memo I found in the notebook.

"Meetings?" He paused to think. "No. I don't know about any meetings. What kind of meetings?" His brow furrowed.

"Nothing. Probably not important. Did he mention any names? Did he call any of the girls by name?"

He paused to think again. "No."

I showed him the picture of Callie that Wilkins had photo-copied.

"Recognize her?"

He looked at the picture and shook his head.

I showed him the photo of the man. He shook his head again.

"Does *Wendy* ring a bell?"

"No."

"Does Mason have any pay coming to him?" I asked.

The man shrugged. "I don't know," he said.

"Could you check, please?" I asked.

Jason remained motionless for a moment before acquiescing and leaving to go to the back office. Waiting at the counter, I finished the coffee I had poured earlier, refilled the cup, and grabbed a com-plimentary cookie from a nearby tray.

"He has almost a full check coming to him," he said, returning from the office, "but we can't give it to you."

"I don't want it," I said.

"Oh?"

I shook my head. "Nope."

"What do you want?"

"I want to talk with him," I said, repeating my earlier statement.

"Oh," he said, again. "Well then, you probably want to know where he is."

I searched Jason's face for signs of humor. There weren't any.

"Uh-huh," I said slowly, not wanting to tax him. "That would be helpful."

"Well, he hangs with a pretty rough crowd."

"Birds of a feather," I said.

"Exactly."

"So who's in this tough crowd?"

He shrugged. "I don't know their names. I just know they're a rough bunch. Tattoos, piercings," he shuddered. "Just a rough bunch." He paused. "Tony's a ladies' man."

"Sure. Someone has to be."

"Right. Anyway, he likes the ladies. All of them. But there's this one who just can't let go. Know what I mean?"

"I'm trying to," I said.

He glanced toward the back room before leaning across the counter.

"He used to see this dancer at the Lucky Dice. But then he up and dumped her."

"No way," I said.

He nodded vigorously again. "And she can't get past it. Still carries a torch."

"And you think she might know where he is?"

"I know she does."

"How do you know that?"

"She's my sister."

CHAPTER EIGHT

I drove to the Lucky Dice. Two red dice appeared on the hand-painted marquee. According to Jason, his sister was a dancer at the bar, but she was often there earlier in the day, doubling as the manager. He called her before I left the inn and told her I'd be coming. When I arrived, I found a blue Dodge Caravan parked alone in the lot. It had a bumper sticker that read Dancing—America's Other Sport.

I parked next to the van and entered the bar.

After allowing my eyes to adjust to the sudden darkness, I saw a raised platform that served as a stage. Two aluminum poles rose from the center of the platform, a large disco ball floated overhead, and a string of lights ran from one end of the stage to the other. At the moment, neither the lights nor the poles were in use.

A series of tables sat along the periphery of the room, and several stools stood along the lower edge of the platform. Anyone who sat on them would be looking up at the dancer on the stage. A bar ran along one end of the room.

"Hello," I called out.

"In here," a feminine voice said from a room that was left of the bar.

I followed the voice into the back office and found a pretty red-head sitting at a desk with a pencil stuck behind her ear. One hand held a cup of coffee, and the other was poised over a calculator.

"You the guy that talked to Jason?" she asked.

"Yes."

"He's a good kid," she said. "He's my older brother, but I've got to look out for him."

"Sure."

She used her foot to push a chair toward me. "Have a seat," she said.

The woman was young, probably in her mid-twenties, and was dressed in a pinstriped blouse and jeans.

"My name's Pam. What do you want to know about Tony?"

"I want to know where I can find him," I said.

"Why? What's he done to you?" She sipped the coffee.

"Not the same thing he's done to you," I said.

Her eyes narrowed over the rim of the cup. "Your wife?"

I shook my head. "My daughter."

"Oh." She set the coffee down. "How old is your daughter?"

"Fifteen."

She leaned back in her chair. It creaked.

"Jason told me that Tony was running a prostitution ring out of the inn," I said.

"And you think he's got your daughter doing that?"

"Be best for him if he doesn't," I said.

She snorted and shook her head before letting out an expletive. "He just keeps getting them younger and younger."

She opened the drawer of her desk and took out a pack of cigarettes. She half shook one from the pack before extracting it with her lips and lighting it with a lighter. When the cigarette was lit, she dropped the pack into the drawer and pulled the cigarette from her mouth with her thumb and forefinger. She exhaled, and a large plume of smoke swirled about her head.

"Jason told me you might know where he is," I said.

She shrugged. "I know where he lives. But that doesn't mean he spends all his nights there."

"Corner of Raymond and Meridian?"

Her eyes locked on mine for a moment. "You've been there?"

"Last night."

She took another long drag before exhaling. She suddenly seemed much older.

"I was in love with him," she said.

"According to Jason, you still are."

She snorted in disgust. Her eyes became red-rimmed. "Tony's a few years younger than me. He dropped out of high school for a while, went back, and then dropped out again." She took another drag on the cigarette. "What will you do if you find him?"

"*When*, not if. And that depends on him."

She slid the cigarette into her mouth and inhaled deeply. She exhaled through her nose, leaving the cigarette to dangle between her moving lips as she talked. "What if your daughter's not with him?"

I shrugged. "Then she's not."

"What if she is?"

"Then we have business."

"You mean you're going to kill him."

I said nothing.

Her laughter was absent of humor.

"I'll find him," I said. "But the sooner I find him, the better for all of us."

She pulled the cigarette from her mouth again. Ash had accumulated on the tip. She flicked it into a plastic ashtray. "There have been others, you know. Your daughter isn't the first."

"The others aren't my responsibility," I said.

"He gets them all, sooner or later." Her eyes were alive with defiance. "He wants all of them."

"Why doesn't he want you?" I asked.

The question visibly jolted her. The look of defiance turned into anger—before contorting into pain. She lowered her eyes. "I was in love with him."

"You still are," I said.

She shrugged. "But he didn't want it." She stood and spun around with her arms extended. "Take a look. Men fill this place every night, paying good money to see this." She sat down again. "He could have had it for free." She bit her lower lip as her eyes fell to the floor again. "There was no challenge, I guess. Men want what they can't have."

"Sure," I said.

I showed her a picture of Callie.

"I don't know her."

I showed her the photo I had found in Callie's room.

She shook her head. "No. Sorry." She crushed out the cigarette.

I looked at my watch. Callie had been gone for more than seventeen hours.

"I want him," I said.

The red-rimmed eyes gave way to full-blown tears. She wiped them from her eyes with the back of both hands. "If he isn't at home, you can probably find him at Binky's."

"Been there," I said.

She shook her head. "No. I mean Binky's. Not the pool hall."

I hadn't known if there was really a Binky or not. And until now, I hadn't cared. But as she gave me the address, I suddenly developed a new interest in the man.

CHAPTER NINE

Binky lived on the south side of Indianapolis in a small house off Shelby Street.

The house had white siding, as most of the houses along Shelby did, and a small, screened porch along the front. The lawn was reasonably well maintained.

I knocked on the door and was greeted by a large man in an outlandishly colorful bathrobe. He had a cup of coffee in one hand and a piece of toast in the other. If ever a man could look like Al Capone without actually being Al Capone, it was Binky.

"Yeah?"

"My name is Colton Parker," I said. "I need to talk to you about Tony Mason."

"What about him?" He bit into the toast.

"My daughter is missing, and I think he knows something about it."

He sipped some of the coffee. "What's that got to do with me?"

"I'm told you might know where I can find him."

"You a cop or something?"

"Worse. I'm an angry father."

He grinned and bit off another piece of toast. "What makes you think I care?"

"Because I sat in front of your pool hall last night and watched enough drug deals going down to put the Medellin Cartel to shame. You know everything that goes down on the south side, Binky, and if I don't get some cooperation from you, I'm going to hand you over to every law enforcement agency in the state."

Men like Binky can stay in business only as long as graft is being paid. His grin revealed his sense of security.

"And if that doesn't get it done," I said, "I'll hand you over to somebody who will."

The grin vanished. Men like Binky also have enemies. And graft doesn't do much with them.

"Who did you say you was?" he asked.

"Colton Parker."

He slipped the last bite of toast into his beefy face and pushed open the screen door.

"Why didn't you say so? Come on in."

Given the appearance of its owner, I was surprised to find that the house was surprisingly sedate. No outlandish furniture, no high-tech electronic equipment, and no evidence to indicate the man was anything other than a moderately successful, law-abiding business-man.

I sat on a sofa, next to the recliner where Binky sat, and watched as the portly pool hall operator downed the last of the coffee and patted his mouth dry with a paper napkin.

"Now," he said, "tell me about your daughter."

"She's run away."

"Sorry to hear that." He feigned interest.

"And I think she's run away with your friend."

He edged forward on his seat. "Let's get this clear, straight up. Tony Mason is not my friend."

"Sure," I said. "And you don't sell drugs to little kids."

He waved a pudgy finger at me. "I don't sell nothing except a good game of pool."

"Are you telling me you don't know where Mason is?"

He spread his arms and tried to look truly hurt. "What is this? I let you into my home and try to help you find your daughter, and you accuse me of dealing in drugs? And lying?"

"I don't care if you're selling pot to the pope," I said. "All I want is my daughter back."

He lowered his arms and narrowed his eyes. "Then what?" he asked.

"Then you and I are through."

He glanced at my jacket.

In my anger, I had forgotten who I was talking with and how his chosen lifestyle had necessitated certain precautions.

I stood and removed my jacket, along with my shoulder holster. I raised the T-shirt I was wearing and allowed him to see my bare chest. Despite the graft he had shelled out, he could never be completely certain that he could buy off everyone.

"Okay," he said.

I sat.

"Tony does some work for me. But he has a taste for some stuff I'm not into."

"Little girls?" I asked.

"I don't know about that. I really don't. And I'm being straight up with you."

"What's he do for you?"

The man hesitated.

"Binky, I already showed you I'm not wired."

He leaned forward on the edge of his seat. His bathrobe gaped open to reveal a hairy chest. "You need to forget what you saw going on in front of my pool hall."

"What do you care? You're buying enough protection."

"I'm buying enough. Don't you worry about that. I just want to make sure you forget." He leaned forward even further. "You getting me?"

"Sure," I said. "I've forgotten already. Like I said, all I want is my daughter. And I've got to find Tony to do that. Do you get me?"

He waved a hand dismissively. "Okay then. We got an understanding?"

"We do," I said.

"I had to let him go."

"Why?"

His face became inflamed, and his voice rose instantly. "Because he's a sick little…" He paused to take a deep breath. "Because he's a sick…individual."

"How?"

"He's violent. Dark."

"And that's why you let him go?"

He shook his head. "No, I let him go because he's a danger to my business. I can pay to keep the cops from snooping around my place when drugs are involved, but I can't pay enough if someone like him is on the premises."

"I've been to his apartment," I said.

"And you didn't find him?"

"I wouldn't be here if I did."

Binky settled back on the recliner and rubbed a big hand on his bloated belly. "The guy's trouble," he said.

I showed him the photo. "Know this guy?"

"No."

"How about someone named Bigelow. J. Bigelow. Does that ring a bell?"

His face contorted. He slid forward again. "Where'd you hear that name?"

"Why?"

"J. Bigelow is Janus Bigelow." His eyes narrowed. "Some people call him Binky."

CHAPTER TEN

I told Binky I'd heard his name in conjunction with Tony's while I was at the pool hall but couldn't remember who had said it. He bought the lie, and I left his place with plans to return and tail him later in the day. According to the note I found in Tony's apartment, he had a meeting at five p.m. Tuesday, and if the meeting was for this particular Tuesday, I had a chance to find Tony.

But in the meantime I had other errands to run, and the first would take me to Callie's school.

I reached Thomas E. Benton High ten minutes after leaving Binky's and entered the building as the morning session was beginning to transition toward the lunch hour.

I found the principal's office just inside the main door and to the right. A middle-aged woman wearing a red blouse and blue slacks was sitting behind an elevated counter. She had a pair of silver-framed glasses suspended from her neck, and she raised her head to look at me when I approached.

"I'd like to speak with the principal," I said.

"Do you have an appointment?"

"No."

"What is this regarding?"

I told her.

She seemed perturbed as she sighed and rose from her chair. Within a minute, she reappeared.

"Principal Evans will see you."

"Imagine that," I said. "Me, asking to see the principal."

She dropped her ample backside into the chair as she ignored my subtle attempt at humor.

When I entered Evans' office, he was seated behind his desk but stood and extended his hand as I approached him. He was a pleasant-looking man with a round face and receding hairline. He smiled, revealing that his demeanor could be just as pleasant.

"Porter Evans," he said as I shook his hand. "My secretary said your daughter has run away." He motioned for me to have a seat.

"Yes." I sat in a chair that was in front of his desk.

"Have you notified the police?" he asked, settling himself into his chair.

"Yesterday evening, after she didn't come home."

He folded his hands and rested them on his desk. "Callie has not been a problem, Mr. Parker. We had great hopes that she was recovering from her mother's death."

"Has she been involved in anything unusual?"

He paused to think and then shook his head.

"What about Wendy Wells?" I asked.

The light went out of his eyes.

"Has Callie been seen with her?" I asked.

"If she has, I'm not aware of it."

"I spoke with another student," I said, "and she seemed convinced that Callie and Wendy are friends."

"If she is, I haven't seen it."

I showed him the photo. "Know this man?"

He leaned forward and studied the picture. "Yes and no."

"Yes and no?"

He settled back in his chair. "I've seen the face around campus once or twice. But I don't know him. Whoever he is, he hasn't been around enough to arouse too much suspicion."

"How about Tony Mason?"

He frowned. "That boy—man, actually—is trouble. First he's in school, and then he's out. Sometimes he's out for a year or two. He was finally expelled—we'd had enough."

"What was he expelled for?" I asked.

Evans stood and closed the door to his office. "Laura is a temp," he said. "I'd just as soon she not hear any of this."

He resumed his position behind the desk, easing backward in his chair and resting his arms on top of his head. "It all began when Tony started coming to school dressed in black clothing. Capes, that sort of thing."

"Goth?"

He nodded. "Yeah, I guess you could call it that. But for him, it went beyond a taste in fashion. He began bringing books to school that dealt with vampirism, death, the occult…things like that. It wasn't long before we started seeing some of the other kids doing the same." He sighed. "We heard that he was getting very heavily involved in role playing. He even started calling himself *Bela*."

"Bela? As in Lugosi?"

The principal shrugged. "I think so, but I'm not sure he was thinking that deeply. From what I could tell, he just thought it sounded vampirish."

"What happened next?"

"He started coming to school with increasingly bizarre taste in clothing and began to make inappropriate advances to some of the students and teachers. He was a distraction, and frankly, many of the teachers were concerned he might be a threat. When he got into trouble the last time, we decided it was best for all concerned that he be expelled."

"What trouble did he get into?"

"He assaulted a teacher."

"What about the kid's parents," I said. "How did they handle his actions?"

"What parents? Tony was living with his grandmother, and she was very elderly. Too elderly to be involved in his life."

"Was?"

He gave me a *you know* glance.

"Oh," I said.

"Yeah. Maybe if things had been different..."

"Sure," I said. "Maybe if things had been different."

CHAPTER ELEVEN

I left the school and drove the five minutes to my house, stopping long enough to get multiple copies made of Callie's picture and of the unknown man's photo I had found in her room. I paid extra in order to get digital copies made from the originals. The plan I had come up with the night before included dispensing multiple copies of both photos to as many people as I could. And digital copies were going to make that possible.

After leaving the originals with the store clerk, I drove to my place and parked curbside in front of my duplex.

My house sat on the periphery of Garfield Park, a south side Indianapolis landmark. I had purchased the home and soon found a renter for the other side. In fact, it was with my tenant that I needed to speak.

Pat Rengle had moved from Encino when her daughter's marriage had failed. Although Tricia was well into her early thirties and had begun another relationship, Pat felt the need to be close to her daughter in her time of distress. Once she moved to Indianapolis, she found work as a hairdresser and was known to be quite good.

Pat was a short, round woman who preferred Day-Glow orange hair, hoop-style earrings, and turquoise jewelry. As flamboyant as they come, she wore her emotions and her heart for all to see.

"Have a seat," she said, motioning me toward a sofa.

Her side of the house was outlandishly decorated, yet clean and quiet. A small birdcage containing a parakeet stood on one side of the room, and a large aquarium sat on the other.

"What's up, Colton?" she asked nervously as she sat next to me. "The rent's been paid. Is there a—"

I held up a hand and smiled. "There's a problem, but not with you. Callie's run away from home."

She recoiled. "Run away?"

"Yes."

"Why?"

I shrugged. "I don't know yet. But I'm going to need your help."

"You've got it. What do you want me to do?"

"She called before she ran away. I've got to be out looking for her, so I was wondering if you'd mind checking my answering machine every hour and calling me if Callie calls."

She slapped one knee. "Well, sure. I'd be happy to do that. Listen, that little girl was the first one in the neighborhood to speak to me. I love her like she's my own."

I thanked her and told her where I kept a spare key.

She blushed and grinned. "Colton, I already know about the key."

"You do?"

"I saw Callie get it once when she had locked herself out. In fact, I just used it."

"For what?"

"To let your preacher in. He was sitting in his car waiting for you to come home, and the man just looked plumb sick. So I let him in. I hope that was okay."

When I entered my half of the house I found Dale Millikin sitting in my recliner, wrapped in a blanket. He was sweating, and his face was pale.

"Dale, what are you doing here? You need to be home in bed."

He sniffled. "I hope you don't mind, Colton. Your neighbor let me in."

"I don't mind," I said. "But you should still be home."

"I've been waiting for you to call, but you never did."

I slipped out of my jacket and holster and tossed them onto the sofa opposite the recliner.

"Sorry, but I've been pretty busy."

"I can imagine."

"You want something to drink?" I asked.

The man was visibly shaking under the blanket. "Something hot would be nice."

I went to the thermostat and raised the temperature from sixty-eight to seventy-four. The mid-November weather was taking a nosedive, but I often kept the house cooler than most because I didn't have the income of most.

"I think I've got some hot chocolate. Will that work?"

"That would work just fine."

A few minutes later, Millikin and I were sitting in the living room with cups of hot chocolate. I filled him in on what I knew so far.

"If she left a message, Colton, there's still hope."

"Yeah," I said. "That's what I thought too." I blew on the chocolate before drinking.

"Have you given any consideration to what you'll do when you find her?"

"Sure. I'm going to bring her home."

Millikin hadn't yet drunk any of the hot chocolate. Instead, he wrapped the blanket tightly around himself. "How are you going to do that?"

I sipped at the beverage and winced as it burned all the way down. "I'll tell her to get in the car."

"What if she doesn't want to?"

"It isn't up to her, Dale. I'm her father. I know what's best for her."

He nodded his head. "No doubt." He glanced at the mug of hot chocolate sitting on the end table next to his chair. "But that doesn't mean she's going to recognize that."

"Clearly," I said. "If she did, she wouldn't have run away."

He poked an arm through an opening in the folds of blanket and grabbed the mug. "That brings me to my question. What if she says no?"

"I bring her home anyway."

"And what if she runs away again?" He sipped the hot chocolate.

"Then I bring her home again."

"And then what?"

"You got me, Dale. What?"

Despite the man's illness, he was able to keep his cool. He smiled. "Sorry, Colton. I tend to make my points in roundabout ways."

"Sure. But my question remains. What do I do about it? I can't duct tape her to the wall every time I have to leave the house."

"Of course not. You can't make her do anything she truly doesn't want to do. And why would you?"

"Because I want what's best for her?" I asked, downing more hot chocolate.

"Sure you do. But she has to want it too." He readjusted his position and pulled the blanket over his head. Only his face was exposed. "Callie is in a spiritual battle."

"I don't fight those, Dale." I nodded to the holstered Ruger that was sitting on the sofa. "I tend to fight the more physical kind. It's what I'm equipped for."

"Of course. But this isn't that kind of fight. Not this time. Now you're battling for her heart. You're battling her resentment."

"Resentment toward me," I said.

He slowly shook his head. "I'm not so sure anymore. I think her anger is toward God. You just happen to be the scapegoat in all of this."

I drank more chocolate. It didn't burn as much this time. "That's not what you've been saying for the past two years," I said. "Not you, or her psychologist, or even Mary."

"There's no question that she's angry with you," he said. "But her spiritual battle is with God. If it was solely with you, she never would have called."

I lowered my mug. "She called me Daddy, Dale. She hasn't done that in years. Not since I was teaching her to ride a bicycle."

"What does that tell you?"

"That she's dependent. She's still a child."

"In a sense, yes. But she's also a young woman. She called you to tell you that she's run away. Yet she's using terminology that a dependent child would use." He pulled the blanket off his head. The man's face was red—almost glowing. "Far from wanting you *not* to find her, she very much *wants* you to come after her. She wants to be saved."

"That's what I'm trying to do, Dale."

"This isn't like any battle you've fought. You can't win this one with a gun. You'll need help."

"Wilkins is doing all he can, and Mary is in Chicago. I can't sit around and wait for the cavalry to arrive," I said.

"The cavalry is already here. Ask God, Colton. He's an expert in finding lost sheep."

CHAPTER TWELVE

My time with the preacher was what I had come to expect. Instead of concrete help, I got platitudes. Instead of applicable insight, I got ephemeral advice.

As soon as Millikin left, I picked up the phone and called Dr. Sebastian, Callie's therapist.

Not long after Anna's death, Callie began her slide. At first, it manifested itself as a change in her disposition. Then her grades began to plummet. Then a new group of friends began to emerge, and finally, she attempted to harm herself by taking an overdose of her grandmother's medication. Her life had been spared, and Dr. Sebastian had intervened as part of a long-term solution.

He was a pleasant and jovial man who resembled the actor Sebastian Cabot. He also identified himself as a Christian, which pleased the Shapiros and their minister. Callie liked the man instantly, and I had to admit, so did I. I was fortunate to find him in when I called. I told him everything I knew.

"Had she given you any indication she was planning on leaving?" he asked.

"None." I paused to rethink my answer. "None that I noticed."

"And she said she didn't want you to find her?"

"Yes."

"Of course, that means she does."

"Yes."

"And you are."

"Yes."

"You've already notified the police?"

"I told Detective Wilkins everything I've told you."

"But since she's classified as a runaway instead of an abduction, they're not pursuing it as strongly."

"Correct."

There was a pause so long that I was about to ask if he was still on the line.

"What do you know about vampirism?" he asked.

"Not much, I'm afraid. I've seen Bela Lugosi's movies," I said, half in jest. "And I know it's a fad with kids today. But beyond that—"

"It's considerably more than a fad," he said. "It's a dangerous belief system that's spreading."

"Are you speaking from a professional perspective or a religious one?"

"Both. The thing is, I've seen the kinds of trouble kids get into, and it almost always involves a spiritual component. Take this vampire movement, for example. Almost all of the kids that get involved in it are looking for a connection. They want to be near someone who understands them."

"Sure, but we all want that," I said. "It's why we join groups like fraternities, clubs, associations…even marriage."

"Yes, but this is a bit different. In those instances, people who are functioning within normal parameters—and I'm talking about the confines that society has set for all of us—seek to become more normal. Common interests drive them to find others who share those interests. And since society has placed a high value on the interest they share, it becomes viewed as a socially redeemable thing to do."

"So people join the Rotary Club—"

"Because it's an organization whose motto is Service Above Self. In other words, it's an organization with values that society appreciates. People who join Rotary will find others of like mind who are not only compatriots, but who can also help in finding an acceptable place in society."

"Vampirism is different because it's not accepted by society."

"Correct."

"And the danger?"

"That is the danger—the fact that they're not accepted by society."

"Sorry, Doc," I said, "but I'm not following you now."

"Most counterculture groups tend to attract people who have already been designated as misfits by one standard or another. Sometimes that standard is money. For example, someone who comes from a family that's less well-off but who is working or living among people who are wealthy can find himself rejected by that group. On the other hand, someone who is financially secure but who lives and works among people who aren't can find an opposite but no less equal rejection." He cleared his throat. "Of course there are other bases for rejection. Our belief systems, our style of dress, our social circle, virtually anything that makes us stand out can become a source of rejection by anyone who doesn't share the same thing."

"I'm still not following, Doc," I said.

"When people define themselves as unacceptable and then find others who are defined in the same terms—regardless of the reason for the rejection—they become acceptable."

"Sure," I said, wishing he'd get to the point.

"The result is that they become acceptable to each other. They bond. And as they bond, they come to realize that the tie that binds is their rejection by the rest of society."

"So in a sense," I said, "they become antisociety."

"Yes. You've got to remember, Colton, these people are looking for something. It's the same thing we're all looking for—acceptance."

"Love," I said.

"Not always. Many have rejected the love of good homes, of caring parents, and of devoted friends. Instead, they tend to want to be accepted by those whose views they respect."

"So you're telling me that their parents and friends may represent the society that they feel has rejected them."

"Yes. So they find an alternative society. One in which the only standard of acceptance is to follow."

"The best way to get along is to go along," I said.

"I would say that's a very concise way of putting it. Of course there's always someone who's willing to lead. Usually someone very charismatic."

"Like Hitler was willing to lead Germany," I said.

"That would be one example," Sebastian said. "Hitler convinced an entire nation to follow him by making everyone feel accepted."

"So long as they hated the Jews," I said.

"Correct. Hatred of the Jew became the way to acceptance. A way to feel part of something that was bigger than self."

"The Third Reich," I said.

"Yes."

"Manson comes to mind too," I said.

"On a smaller scale, yes. He too was charismatic and convinced a group of misfits to follow him."

"Misfits because they didn't fit in with the rest of society."

"Yes."

"If Callie has fallen into a cult of people who consider themselves to be vampires, she is susceptible to becoming like them. Correct?"

"I would say that if Callie has fallen into the type of group that you seem to think she's with, I'd be very surprised if she *didn't* become like them. Remember Colton, Callie is lost. She's seeking to fill the void that was created by her mother's death. And if she looks long enough, she'll find something or someone who will fill the hole in her heart."

"Are you speaking as a professional, or as a Christian?" I asked.

"Does it matter?"

CHAPTER THIRTEEN

After my conversation with Sebastian, my sense of urgency began to fester. Callie was at risk. Spiritual risk. And that meant I needed to find her before she slipped irretrievably away to the influence of Tony Mason and his boss—and whatever bizarre "alternative society" they were offering her.

I downed a quick dinner of frozen pizza before slipping back into my shoulder rig and jacket.

The plan was to tail Binky and find out where he was heading. It was almost four thirty, twenty-five and a half hours since I had discovered Callie was missing. But as Wilkins had pointed out, Callie wasn't abducted. All evidence pointed to the fact that she was a runaway, and that would automatically place her on a lower priority with the authorities.

IPD was very good at what they did. And I knew that Wilkins would give it an extra push. But like all police departments, they were overloaded. Too few good officers were overwhelmed by too many depraved and sometimes violent sociopaths. With odds like that, one little runaway just didn't add up to a whole lot of budgetary expenditure.

I climbed into the car and pulled away from the curb as the sun began its final approach toward the horizon. By the time I reached Binky's house, night had fallen.

I drove around the block and positioned myself three doors down, where I could watch the house from curbside. Or at least I tried to. For the hundredth time since I bought the car, the engine continued to run on, and I made yet another mental note to have it checked out. Since buying the thing, it had suffered multiple scars from buckshot and one episode of a blown-out rear window, which I had managed to repair. It was not only a mechanical defect but a visual one as well.

When the car finally gave up the ghost and let loose with a long, slow cough, I settled in for the wait.

A glance around the neighborhood revealed that most people seemed to be at home. Houses were aglow, and the aroma of dinner filled the air. All of this further drove my despair. I missed Callie. I missed Anna. I was tired of being alone.

I turned the ignition key and listened to the radio as I divided my attention between Binky's house and the clock on my dash. Ten minutes later, I saw my subject come out of his house.

The bloated Capone look-alike climbed into a black Lincoln Continental. He was dressed in a charcoal gray suit with a red silk handkerchief in the jacket pocket. I half expected to see a fedora and spats, but the best he could come up with was Big Al's lumbering gait.

I ducked in my seat as he drove past and then slid upward to watch in the rearview mirror as he turned right and went around the block. I started my car, made a U-turn, and went after him.

We drove to Shelby Street and turned north. I stayed fifty yards behind him and allowed other vehicles to get between us to further protect my cover. Within ten minutes, we had zigzagged to Madison, where we began heading north again toward downtown Indianapolis. The unusually clear night yielded an unhindered view of the city's skyline.

We continued driving until we reached a small Italian restaurant on Illinois Street, just north of the city. The restaurant had been at the same location for more than fifty years and was still run by the founding family.

Mizzeli's served some of the best linguini in the city and had managed to keep the home-cooked feel that many in the local community had come to expect. Given his Capone-like persona, I was not surprised to discover that Binky enjoyed good Italian food.

I continued to follow as his car slowed and parked in a small lot across the street from the restaurant. A few seconds later, he rolled out of the car and lumbered across the street toward Mizzeli's. To keep from being spotted, I drove around the block before parking several yards down from Binky's Lincoln. I had a good view of the inside of the dining area, and I watched as the gangster and part-time pool-hall entrepreneur sat alone at a table near the center of the room. It was slightly after five thirty.

After placing his order, Binky opened a newspaper the waitress had brought him. My stomach growled as I recalled my own dinner—a frozen pizza that resembled cardboard and ketchup more than an Italian specialty.

I watched the fat man read the paper for what I thought was an interminable amount of time. When I moved my watch out of the shadows and into the small ring of light from the overhead street lamp, I saw that only a few minutes had passed. It was five minutes to six. *If there's going to be a meeting,* I thought, *it would be helpful if it were to happen now.*

No sooner had the thought run through my head than I noticed a tall, dark-haired man wearing a ponytail, jeans, and a leather jacket entering the restaurant through the front door. His back was to me, and I couldn't see his face. But years of law enforcement had given me a sixth sense. I didn't like the way the man carried himself.

As he approached Binky's table, the man's hand came out of his jacket with a large-caliber revolver. Binky looked up from his paper just in time to see the bullet that would kill him.

I jumped out of my car as the gunshot echoed. Screams came from the restaurant.

I began dodging traffic as I ran toward the front door with my gun in my hand. Angry drivers honked and flashed their lights, as I weaved my way between the cars.

By the time I hit the restaurant and burst into the dining room, I knew that Binky was dead and that I would not find the shooter. Whoever he was, he had quickly escaped by way of the back door— into a waiting car.

The hit was professional—one shot to the forehead. The .45 caliber pistol, with its serial number missing and its handgrip wrapped in tape, was lying on the floor in a pool of brain and blood.

CHAPTER FOURTEEN

I sat at the counter, drinking a glass of water, and watched as detectives measured off the room and took photographs for later review. The crime lab was also there, going over the gun, the table, the doorknob, and anything else the killer may have touched. Several officers were interviewing the customers and employees.

"You the one that called us?" a detective asked.

"Yeah."

"What's your name?"

I told him my name, and he wrote it down in a notebook.

The detective was short, about five-eight, and middle-aged with a face that was lined beyond its years. He was wearing brown pants, an open-necked yellow shirt, and a brown zipper jacket. A Glock was tucked into a holster anchored on his belt.

"Did you get a good look at the shooter?" he asked.

I told him what I saw.

"This looks like a hit," I said.

The detective took a step back and looked me over. "Does it now?"

I sighed. "I was a cop. I know a hit when I see one. This is one."

"Where were you a cop?"

"Chicago PD. Then FBI."

"You were a FeeBee?"

"Yeah."

"How come you're not now?"

"The bureau and I had a difference of opinion."

He gave me a wry smile. The kind that's supposed to let you know that he knows everything about you but that there isn't enough in your life to make it interesting.

"And what were you doing here?" he asked, turning his attention back to his notes.

"I was tailing the victim."

He raised his head from the notebook. "You were tailing the victim?"

"Yeah. I'm a private detective. My daughter has run away, and this guy was a possible lead."

He turned to look at Binky's lifeless body. It had gone slack and slumped out of the chair, landing on the floor faceup. His mouth was open, and his eyes were eternally fixed in the vacant stare of the dead.

"How?" the detective asked.

I couldn't tell him about the burglary, yet he was investigating a homicide in which I was a principle. So I lied. Again.

"I heard from a source that he had a meeting at five o'clock with someone who I felt might lead me to my daughter."

"And who would that be?"

"A guy named Tony Mason."

The detective wrote the name down. "And why is this Tony Mason a suspect in your daughter's disappearance?"

"I heard they were running in the same crowd. A crowd I didn't know about. When I heard there may be a connection, I wanted to talk with him."

"How does your daughter know this Mason?"

"He went to her school for a while, but he dropped in and out before getting expelled."

The detective wrote everything down.

"I need your piece," he said.

"I didn't shoot anyone."

"Right. I still need your piece."

I handed him the Ruger.

He passed the gun, butt-first, to a uniformed officer. "Have the lab run this. Check for ballistics, priors…that sort of thing."

She took the gun and left. The detective turned to me again.

"When will I get it back?" I asked.

"Tomorrow. Maybe the day after. Or maybe not. Depends on what we find and how soon we find it."

My throat was dry, so I drank more water. I could see that the restaurant's employees were shaken. Murder is an abstract thing for most people. They hear about it on the nightly news, maybe even read about it in the local paper, but they never ever expect to see it happen in front of them. Time may heal all wounds, but it doesn't erase their memory. I knew that these people would never be the same.

"Did you report your daughter's disappearance?"

"Yes. As soon as I discovered it."

"Uh-huh. And who did you report it to?"

"Harley Wilkins."

The man lowered his notebook and pen. "That so?"

"Yeah."

"Okay, hold on a minute."

He idled over to two other detectives, and the three of them huddled together, glancing my way on occasion. After a minute or two, one of the detectives went outside, and the first detective came back to where I was sitting.

"How do you know that your daughter ran away?"

I told him about the call and the troubles we'd been having. I told him about Anna, and how her death had disrupted our lives. By the time I was through, I didn't think he would want to ask me any more questions. But he did.

"You ever meet the victim?"

"Yes." I didn't see any point in lying again. Binky's neighbors could easily have seen me enter his house.

"When?"

"Today."

"What did you talk about?"

"My daughter. I asked him if he knew where I could find Tony Mason."

The detective shook his head. "Huh-uh. You already said that your sources"—his voice dropped on *sources*—"told you he'd be here tonight, meeting with Mason."

I said nothing. My tangled web of deceit was going to land me in jail. That is, if the truth didn't do it first.

"The question," he said, "is how did you know that the victim here, knew this Mason?"

"I have sources," I said.

He looked at me for a long time. I looked back.

"Uh-huh," he said. "Well, you see, here's the problem. Your sources are now my sources. This Mason could be a suspect in a homicide." He moved closer, crowding my space. "I want him."

"You haven't been listening," I said.

"Yeah? How's that?" he asked, putting both hands on his hips, one of them still holding his notebook, the other his pen.

"My sources don't know how to find Tony."

"And why am I supposed to believe that?"

I pointed to the body on the floor. "Because that's who they told me to ask."

CHAPTER FIFTEEN

I didn't sleep well that night and was awakened at six by a phone call from Harley Wilkins. He said he wanted to meet with me. The call was not entirely unexpected.

I showered, shaved, and ate a breakfast of bacon and eggs before leaving for IPD headquarters with a travel mug full of black coffee. It was seven thirty. Forty-one hours had elapsed since I discovered Callie's disappearance, and one man was already dead.

After signing in with the front-desk personnel and depositing my Taurus .38 snub nose with them, I met with Harley Wilkins in the detectives' squad room. I sat in the same chair I had sat in two days before.

"Sounds like you had an exciting evening," he said, leaning back in his chair and resting his arms on top of his head.

"I could have done without it," I said, setting my mug on top of his desk.

"Want to tell me about it?"

Although Harley was gracious enough to make it sound like a request, it wasn't. As a good detective in his own right, he would be on top of any business his fellow officers brought to him. The officer who had stepped outside the restaurant after I mentioned Harley's name had probably called the captain of detectives at home to verify my story. Harley's request was a nice way of making me feel less threatened.

I told him about the evening at the restaurant, everything I had seen, and why I had decided to tail Binky.

When I was through, his lack of surprise tended to support my belief that he had already been told.

"Colton, have you noticed that people who get too close to you tend to end up dead?" he asked, still sitting with his hands on top of his head.

"You might want to move back a bit," I answered.

"You think Callie has run off with this Mason?"

"I don't know. He's the strongest link I have to the man in the photo."

"Stillwell seems to think this thing was a professional hit."

"Stillwell? He the guy who interviewed me last night?"

"Yeah."

"I agree. One tap to the head, right between the eyes, and in full view of witnesses. From what I could see, the gun was clean and left at the scene. The hitter fled through the back."

"We have the gun, but like you said, it's clean. Untraceable."

"Gee," I said, "I don't want to sound condescending or anything, but—"

"We still have to check it out. You know the procedure."

"Sure." I leaned forward in my seat. "Speaking of guns, I believe you have one of mine."

"You'll get it back."

"When?"

"When we're through."

I eased back into the seat.

"Is the picture you gave me a photo of Mason?" Wilkins asked.

I shook my head. "No. I already ran that past a few people."

"Was one of those people Binky?"

I nodded. "Binky's bouncer too. He said he's seen the guy in the photo come into the pool hall a lot, and the guy is often seen with Mason."

Wilkins's eyes narrowed. "You know where Mason lives?"

"Yes."

"Did you visit him there?"

"I knocked, but he wasn't home," I lied again.

"How can I be sure of that?"

I caught something in Wilkins' expression I hadn't seen before.

"Because I told you so," I said.

He removed his hands from the top of his head, leaned forward in his chair, and rested his arms on top of his desk. He looked at me through narrowed eyes the way cops do when they're searching your inner self for the lies your outer self is desperately trying to conceal.

"That isn't good enough," he said. "I'm going to need more than that."

I reached for the mug and took a long swallow. The coffee had grown cold.

"Then try this," I said, setting the mug on his desk. "Callie's still missing, and Mason hasn't turned up dead."

He sighed. "Wrong, my friend. Mason is very much dead."

CHAPTER SIXTEEN

I've never liked the morgue. The place is cold, sterile, and has always made me feel like a hundred maggots were dancing under my skin. Even heat in the building wouldn't have done any good. With a dozen bodies waiting to be claimed, all of them with tags on their toes and all of them a ghastly blue, the place would give Dracula the willies.

Wilkins and I met with an attendant named Benny Dean. He was a tall, gangly kid with an Adam's apple that bounced up and down like a basketball. He had agreed to meet us when Wilkins called prior to leaving headquarters. I guessed him to be in his late twenties.

"This isn't CSI, you know," he said.

"Sure," I said. There was no point in telling the kid that I'd been in morgues before.

Benny turned to Wilkins. "Sign here." He handed Wilkins a pen.

Wilkins signed a form on a clipboard and gave the pen and board back to Benny.

"He going to be okay?" the attendant asked, nodding toward me. "If he passes out and hits his head, I could be in a lot of trouble."

Wilkins looked at me. "You going to pass out on us?"

I crossed my heart.

"If he does," Wilkins said, "I'll personally pay for any damage to the floor."

The kid cast a wary eye in my direction.

"Okay, but just be sure he don't fall out. I don't want no trouble."

"Scout's honor," I said.

The kid motioned for us to follow him.

Wilkins whispered, "Scout's honor?"

I shrugged.

He shook his head, and the two of us followed Benny into the holding room for recent arrivals. After checking a spreadsheet on the computer, he went to a refrigerator drawer and jerked it open. A sheet-covered body was stretched out on the slab.

"I'll be in the next room if you need anything," Benny said, casting an eye in my direction before leaving the room.

Wilkins pulled back the sheet.

The man on the slab had died young. He looked to be in his early twenties. He was short, with long black hair that was braided and which seemed to spring from blond roots. He had a thin mustache and goatee, and needle tracks dotted both arms. Like all the other bodies, he was a ghastly blue. Unlike the rest, he had a round hole just above the left temple.

"Took a nine to the head," Wilkins said.

I leaned forward to get a closer look at the wound. "No burns."

"Doesn't mean it wasn't done up close," Wilkins said. "Just not close enough to leave powder residue."

I glanced at the other side of the man's head. There was a larger hole just under his cheekbone. "The exit wound is lower than the entry wound."

"Meaning that the shooter was either taller than our victim, or—"

"Or the victim was sitting down."

Wilkins nodded. "How tall are you?"

"Six feet."

"Mason is five-six."

"I didn't kill him, Harley."

"He was killed with a nine."

"You have my nine."

"We didn't get it until late last night. This man was killed sometime before that."

"I'm looking for Mason as a link to Callie. That's all."

"You'd kill for your daughter."

"Yes, I would. But killing Mason would also kill my best chance of finding her. Killing him would only satisfy my need for justice."

"Revenge," Wilkins said. "There's a difference." He re-covered the body and slid the table back into the freezer. He closed the locker's door.

"I was at the restaurant waiting for Mason to show," I said. "The man that did show had black hair and was at least six feet tall."

Wilkins leaned against the wall of freezer drawers. "We already know that. Remember? We had witnesses—besides you. And despite the fact that witnesses never seemed to agree, they actually did in this case."

"Then why the grilling?"

"Because this man was killed before Binky."

"You running ballistics?"

"As we speak."

"Didn't waste any time."

"Like you said the other day, the longer this thing goes on, the less likely we are to find Callie."

"You're not interested in finding Callie," I said. "You want to find the killer of this dude, and I'm the best shot you've got."

"For the moment, you're the only shot I've got."

I ran a hand through my hair. "Come on, Harley. Do you actually think I killed this guy?"

Harley frowned, then sighed. "No. But I've got to check it out."

"Then check it out. But don't try to pin something on me that I didn't do." I turned to leave the room. "I'm going," I said, pausing to turn and face Wilkins again. "I'm going to find Callie. And when I do, you might have a body or two to pin on me. But at least wait until then."

I opened the door.

"Colton, you're not going anywhere," Wilkins said.

My anger had reached its summit.

"You can't stop me, Harley."

"I don't have to." He dangled a ring of car keys off his index finger. "I drove. Remember?"

CHAPTER SEVENTEEN

By the time we reached IPD headquarters, I had cooled down. Wilkins was just doing his job, and I understood that. Even if I didn't appreciate it.

"We'll look into this Mason guy. If we find anything that could help in finding Callie, we'll work it," he said.

"And tell me?"

"And tell you."

After I left his squad car, I reclaimed my .38 from the front desk and drove to the pool hall. When I arrived, I found the bouncer sitting behind the cage again, reading a six-month-old copy of a supermarket tabloid.

"Where is everyone?" I asked, approaching the cage.

The hall was nearly empty—only a couple of patrons and no hookers. Not even a drug deal.

"Gets busy around noon," he said, keeping his eyes on all the news that's fit to print.

"Binky's dead."

"I know. The police called last night." He lowered the paper. "How'd you know?"

"I saw it go down," I said.

The bouncer left the newspaper on the counter and came from behind his cage. "This way." He gestured toward the back stairwell.

I followed him up the stairs to a narrow hallway that ran perpendicular to the pool room below. As we moved down the hall, I counted four rooms, each fitted with a mattress, before we came to a fifth room at the end of the hallway. This room served as an office and was finished in dark paneling. It was furnished with a metal desk, a chair that stood in front of the desk, a file cabinet, a water cooler, a rack of cues, stacks of newspapers, a small refrigerator, and a TV that sat on the desk and that had tin foil wrapped around the rabbit ears. A rerun of *Matlock* was playing.

I sat in the chair as the bouncer sat behind the desk and turned off the television.

"Close the door," he said.

I closed the door.

"You saw Binky go down?"

"Last night. A single shot to the head."

"Where?"

"Mizzeli's. A little place on—"

"I know the place," he said. "The Bink practically lived there."

"Any idea who might want him dead?"

The bouncer was a big man—tall and thick. The kind of man who had been built for the type of work he did. He leaned back in the chair and crossed one leg over the other. He massaged one knee while he talked.

"I can think of a couple," he said.

"Got some names?"

"Why? What's your interest in Binky?"

I repeated what I had told him about Callie. I also told him about the connection Binky might have to her disappearance.

"That guy you were looking for," the bouncer said, "the guy in the photo. Did you ever find him?"

"No. But I did find Mason."

"The address I gave you was good?"

"Yes, but I didn't find him there. I found him on a slab at the morgue. This morning."

The bouncer stopped massaging his knee. "Was he murdered?"

I told him that he was but that a different gun had been used. "Binky was hit with a .45," I said. "Very professional. Mason was killed with a nine." I waited for a reaction, but none came.

"Do you think they're connected?" he asked.

I told him about the note I found in Mason's apartment. I told him the man I had seen kill Binky wasn't the same man I saw on the slab. "Don't you?"

"Now that you put it that way, yeah, I do. Do you think there's one shooter?"

I shrugged. "Maybe. Binky had his share of enemies. Any idea who might want him dead?"

"Mason for one. Binky fired him a while back."

I already knew that. But I wanted to see if the reason the bouncer would give matched the explanation I got from Binky.

"Why?" I asked.

"Mason is one sick dude." The bouncer shook his head in disgust. "He used to run women for the boss." He clasped both hands around his knee. "Like you noticed the other night, this place is built for hustlers. And not just the kind that hustle pool."

"Sure."

"The boss was always a bit on the paranoid side. You know? Always afraid that sooner or later he was going to get busted."

"Seems like a reasonable fear," I said, recalling the open drug deals I saw in the parking lot and the hookers who were moving in and out of the building.

The bouncer waved a hand. "He paid enough."

"He bought cops?"

The man shook his head. "No. He bought politicians. It's easier. You know what they say. Money is the mother's milk in politics."

"Sure. So how does Mason come into all of this?"

"Mason had a way with girls. Young ones. The guy would talk them up and make them think he was a stand-up kind of guy. You know, like he truly cared. Then when their guard was down, he'd turn them."

"Into prostitution," I said.

The bouncer swiveled slightly in his chair. "Right. The problem was that Mason was bringing so many women into the place, Binky couldn't keep up. He wasn't into that part of the business like Mason was. For Binky, it was always a moral dilemma. He didn't like turning the girls, but it was extra money."

"Man of principle," I said.

The bouncer grinned. "Yeah, sure."

"Go on," I said.

"Mason started taking the women to some hotel on the west side. The original deal was that he'd split the profits fifty-fifty with the boss in exchange for the protection the boss could provide. All the boss wanted was a piece of the action."

"Mason could strike out on his own, use a different location to keep visible traffic to a minimum, and hide under the graft Binky was shelling out."

"Yeah. That's pretty much the way it worked."

"Except something went wrong," I said, recalling that Jason had told me Mason had failed to show for work.

"Yeah. Something always does, doesn't it?"

"Binky and Mason had a falling out?"

"That'd be one way of putting it."

He unclasped his hands and stood from the desk. "Want a beer?"

"No."

He opened the refrigerator, pulled a can of beer from it, and kicked the door closed. After sitting again at the desk, he opened one of the drawers and took out a partial bag of cheese curls that was held closed with a paper clamp. He unclamped the bag and pulled out a handful.

"Turns out that Mason was sampling the goods," he said. "And he wasn't gentle about it." He shoved the curls into his mouth.

"That's where the *sick* part comes in?"

"Yeah," he said as he ate. "He was violent. Some of the girls started showing up in the emergency room with broken noses, broken ribs. Word got back to Binky that if it didn't stop, there would have to be more money in the till or else justice would have to be served." He ate another handful of cheese curls. "Mason was drawing heat onto the boss, so the boss had to cut and run."

"Right. But without Binky's protection, Mason wouldn't last long."

"And that made the punk mad. Very mad. I had to throw him out of here a couple times."

"And the guy in the picture?" I said.

He downed some beer. "Sorry, but I don't know him. He came in with Mason a few times and shot some pool. He was here once when Mason talked to the boss, but that's it." He plunged his hand into the bag…but then paused. "Except, the guy was weird."

"How?"

He shrugged as he pulled his hand from the bag and stuffed more curls into his mouth. "I don't know, for sure," he said, crunching the snack while he talked. "Just…weird. Like he wasn't completely here. You know what I mean? Like his mind was somewhere else." He shoveled yet another handful of curls into his mouth.

"But you don't know his name," I said again.

"No."

"You mentioned there could be others who might want Binky dead."

He nodded thoughtfully. "Sure. The Bink had enemies. It's hard to be in this business for long and not have those. But there's this guy named Wells. Anderson Wells."

Wendy's father.

"What about him?" I asked.

"The guy was livid. Came in here once, looking for his daughter." He paused to fold the bag of cheese curls and replace the paper clamp. He tossed the bag onto the desk and wiped his hands free of the cheese dust. "The guy marched in and went right upstairs. By the time I got here, Binky had a gun on him. But the guy just didn't care. Started making all these threats. Even tried to pull Binky out of the chair."

"What happened?" I asked. *Livid* wasn't a word I could attach to Anderson Wells. And he'd never mentioned an encounter with Binky.

He shrugged. "I got here and pulled him off the boss." He shook his head as he recalled the incident. "He was strong for an old guy. Real strong. The boss didn't want to shoot him, he just wanted to hold him off until I could get up the stairs."

"Sure. Shooting the angry father of a girl you're running as a prostitute tends to make for the wrong kind of PR."

"Yeah, that's right. And that's one of the reasons that Binky had to get rid of Mason."

"I don't understand," I said.

"The guy's daughter was hooking for Mason. Binky didn't want the heat, so that's when he decided the whole deal was off."

"And that Mason would have to go his own way."

"Right. And that's exactly what happened."

"Not exactly," I said.

He cocked his head.

"They both went to the morgue."

CHAPTER EIGHTEEN

All was not well on the south side of Indianapolis. A man I had met only two days before, and whose daughter was also missing, had threatened a man whose murder I had witnessed. And the man he wanted for introducing his daughter into prostitution was also killed. I had a genuine mystery on my hands.

I drove back to the Wells' home, and knocked on the door. Mrs. Wells answered. She was in tears.

"Is something wrong?" I asked.

She remained behind the closed screen door with eyes that were puffy and red. She worked a hanky between both hands.

"Anderson's been arrested," she said. "I don't know what I'm going to do."

"When?"

"A few minutes ago. The police said I should call a lawyer and that I could visit him later." She began to stretch the hanky with a renewed enthusiasm. I opened the door and entered the house uninvited.

"Why don't you have a seat," I said, steering her toward a chair next to the door.

After getting her seated, I went into the kitchen and brought back a glass of water. I handed it to her, and she drank.

"How many officers were there?" I asked.

"There were three," she said, her voice breaking. "One of them was a detective, I think. He was wearing a business suit. The other two were wearing their police uniforms." Her expression was pained. She was pulling the hanky in two different directions at once.

"What are the charges?"

"They said he was being arrested for murder. For killing the man that took Wendy away."

I sighed. "Do you have a lawyer?"

She shook her head. "We don't even know one. We don't even have a will."

I asked if I could use her phone, and she directed me to the kitchen. I called Benjamin Upcraft.

I had met the attorney soon after opening for business as a private investigator. In time, I had begun doing some preliminary work for him as a means of supplementing my irregular income. Although he had some of the pomposity that seems to come with a law degree, he also had the heart that often doesn't. I told him about the situation.

"Where's he at now?" he asked.

"In lockup, I assume," I said. "He was just arrested."

"What do you think?"

"Don't know. But from what I've heard this morning, he could be good for it."

"Always like a challenge," Upcraft said. "Any attorney can defend the innocent. No effort in that."

"Sure."

"Tell his wife I'll take the case. Tell her that I'm free right now and will head down to IPD lockup. She can meet me there if she'd like."

"I'll tell her," I said, thanking him for agreeing to defend her husband.

After the call ended, I went back into the living room and sat in the chair next to hers. I told her that I had secured an attorney for her husband.

"Has your husband expressed any notions of revenge to you?" I asked.

She nodded.

"You still haven't heard from Wendy?"

She continued to work the hanky. "No."

"Was Anderson home last night?" I asked.

She was hesitant.

"Anything you say to me stays with me," I said. "I just want to find my daughter."

She continued to work the cloth. "No. He wasn't."

CHAPTER NINETEEN

I drove Barbara Wells to IPD headquarters. Upcraft met us in the lobby and introduced himself to her. His rich baritone voice and confident manner seemed to put the distraught woman at ease.

"Have you met with Anderson yet?" I asked, steering the lawyer out of the woman's earshot.

"Not yet. You know this situation better than I do, so I thought we'd both talk to him. Then let his wife come in later."

I glanced at her. The hanky was gone, but she had found a replacement. She was working the handle of her handbag.

"You think she'll sit still for that?" I asked.

"I'm her lawyer," Upcraft said. "Persuading people is what I do."

I waited as the attorney did what he did best and persuaded Anderson's wife to wait in the lobby while the two of us met with her husband. She reluctantly agreed.

We met with the alleged killer in a concrete-block room that was furnished with a steel table and four chairs. I sat next to Upcraft. Anderson sat opposite us.

"I'm going to ask you this question one time," Upcraft said. "Before you answer, I want you to know that I don't care if you did it or not. I'm your lawyer. That means I'm on your side regardless. Understand?"

In the orange jumpsuit furnished by the city, Anderson Wells looked less imposing than he had in his dining room when we first met. Like all the inmates I had ever seen, he had the dehumanized look that goes with being a number, guilty or not.

"I did it," he said.

"Did what?" Upcraft asked, avoiding any ambiguity.

"I killed Tony Mason."

I glanced at Upcraft.

The attorney said, "You didn't kill Janus Bigelow?"

"Who?" Anderson asked.

"Binky," I said. "His real name is Janus Bigelow."

He shook his head. "I have nothing against him. He didn't pull my daughter away."

"You threatened him," I said.

He sighed and hung his head for a moment, before raising it to look at us again.

"Yes, I did. But just so I could find Mason."

"How did you locate him?" I asked.

"I found him at the pool hall and followed him home." His eyes began to tear. "He ruined Wendy's life. He caused Barbara and me so much pain." He shook his head. "The man deserved to die."

We were all silent for a while until Upcraft said, "Fill me in. And I want the details. I need to know everything if I'm going to defend you."

Anderson sighed and said, "You're my lawyer, right?"

"That is correct."

He folded his hands on top of the table and hung his head. "After my run-in with Binky, I figured the best approach was to watch the pool hall. That's when I decided to start hanging out across the street and keep an eye out for him." His hands trembled. "I did it whenever I could, and one night I got lucky."

"Then what happened?" Upcraft asked.

"Last night, after dinner, I drove to my parking spot and waited it out. That's when I saw him coming out."

"Was he alone?" I asked.

He shook his head. "No, he wasn't. He was with a tall, muscular guy. It was dark, and I couldn't see the other man's face that well. The only one I wanted was Mason."

"Go on," Upcraft said.

"I watched as the two of them talked for a while. Then Mason left in his car, and I followed him."

"Where?" I asked.

"I followed him to his apartment. He parked, and I waited a few doors down until he got out and began to go up the steps. I was going to follow him inside…try to find out where Wendy is. But as I got out of my car, I noticed that he stopped at the top of the stairs. He acted like something was wrong with his door or his door lock—I couldn't tell. Then he jogged down the stairs like he was really mad."

I said nothing about breaking in to the apartment.

"Then," Anderson said, "when he got into his car, I figured there wouldn't be any time like the present. I was afraid I'd lose him, and I wanted to find Wendy."

"Shooting him wouldn't help you find your daughter," Upcraft said.

Anderson nodded. His hands remained folded on top of the table. "I know. So I walked up to the car as he was getting in and put the gun in his back. I told him to get in and drive. I climbed into the backseat and slid down between some suitcases."

"Suitcases?"

Anderson nodded.

"Why?" I asked. "Was he planning on going somewhere?"

"He said he was leaving for Las Vegas."

"Did you ask him why?"

He shook his head. "I just told him to drive."

"Where'd you go?" I asked.

"We just drove. I told him to start heading south. We drove for about forty-five minutes and found a little place to pull off the road."

Upcraft looked at me. "Franklin is about thirty minutes south of Indy, so he must have been just south of there."

"Then what?" I asked.

"I made him get out of the car. Told him I was Wendy's dad and that he had caused a lot of pain for me and my wife. I made him get on his knees."

Anderson paused, and his face grew red. "I feel sick," he said, laying his head down on the table.

Upcraft stood and knocked on the door. A guard opened it.

"Can we have a pitcher of water?" the attorney asked.

The guard glanced at Anderson before closing the door. He returned shortly with a plastic pitcher of water and three Styrofoam cups.

Upcraft poured some water into one of the cups and handed it to Anderson.

Anderson took the water and drank. Another minute or two passed before he could continue.

"You made him get on his knees…" I said.

"Yes." He visibly struggled with his emotions.

We waited again while he composed himself.

"I told him that I wanted to know where Wendy was. He said he didn't know. He said she had left to work with someone else."

"So the relationship between them was business?" I asked. "Nothing personal?"

"I don't know, Mr. Parker," Wells said. "I always thought there was something personal in it. She seemed enamored with him. But then, when she disappeared, I lost track of her."

"Were you aware that Mason was prostituting young girls?" I asked as delicately as I could.

"Yes. I was hoping against hope that Wendy hadn't allowed herself to get involved in something like that. But I always knew she was capable." He let out a long, deep breath. "She was always susceptible to manipulation. So easily led."

"Did Mason say who she might have gone with?"

Wells shook his head.

"Any thoughts?" I asked.

He shook his head again as tears welled in his eyes. Upcraft put his hand on Anderson's.

"He said he didn't have anything to do with it," he said.

"With what?"

"Wendy. He said he was following orders from Malak."

"Who?" Upcraft asked.

"Malak. He said that he answered to this guy. That Malak was the Supreme and controlled all things."

I glanced at Upcraft as I recalled the websites I had seen on Mason's computer.

"Did he say anything else?" I asked.

Anderson grimaced. "He said that whatever Wendy got, she had asked for." His voice broke. "That's when I shot him." He dropped his head into his hands, and began to sob. "Lord, forgive me. I killed a man."

CHAPTER TWENTY

I left the interrogation room and went directly to the detective squad room. Upcraft remained with Anderson and Barbara.

Wilkins raised his head as I entered. His shirt was opened at the neck, and his tie was only partially knotted. "Is this personal or professional?" he asked.

"Both."

"Callie?"

"Yes. And Anderson Wells."

"Yeah. About that—it seems like he's good for the shooting. At least the one that involved the nine millimeter. You want your gun back, I presume?"

"Yes."

He picked up the phone and told someone on the other end to bring up my gun.

"Anything on Callie?" I asked.

Wilkins shook his head. "I've been keeping a watch on all the teen hangouts we know about, and I've been keeping an eye on the bus terminal, Union Station, and the airport. If she buys a ticket in her name, we'll find her."

He didn't say it, but I also knew he was keeping his eye on the local hospitals and the morgue. It's what I would have done if the situation had been reversed.

"Did you talk to Anderson Wells?" I asked.

"I'm a little more involved than I would be normally because you're connected."

"He came up with a name," I said. *"Malak.* Ring a bell?"

Wilkins turned in his chair, crossing his legs. "No. No bells with me. But I've heard the term. It means angel or messenger."

"More like Satan's emissary," I said. "Who's working the case?"

"Which case? Yours or Anderson's?"

"Anderson's."

"Goldman."

"Can you ask him if he's heard of a Malak?"

Wilkins turned to look around the squad room. Not seeing Goldman, he picked up the phone and called dispatch. "I'll have them raise him," he said.

When the dispatcher came on the line, Wilkins told them to contact Goldman and have him call the office on a landline. Within a few minutes, Wilkins had his detective on the phone.

"Aaron, do you know anything about a Malak? The name came up with your Mason suspect." There was a pause. "Uh-huh," he said into the receiver while glancing at me. "No kidding. Anything else?" After another pause, Wilkins ended the call with a "thanks."

"And?" I asked.

"Goldman said that *Malak* has come up, but he can't link the name to anyone in particular. He also said that his postmortem check into Mason isn't turning up a whole lot. So far, we know that he was into vampires and that his taste in music ran toward what Goldman called, 'the macabre.' We know that he was expelled from school and that he was running some women. Goldman also said that someone had broken into Mason's apartment. And that whoever it was wasn't too concerned about having his crime discovered. Mason's door was kicked off the hinges."

"In other words, you don't know much," I said.

Wilkins rested his hands on top of his head and began to gently rock in his chair. It squeaked in a rhythmic beat. "Goldman thinks Mason may have been competing with Binky's operation."

"Wells said that Mason indicated that Malak was the Supreme. That sounds like the operation is probably run by Malak."

He shrugged. "Maybe. Who's to say? None of us even know who this Malak is yet. But we do know that Binky was running women through the pool hall. Mason got in on the ground floor, under cover of Binky's protection, but somewhere along the line, the two got into a dispute."

"It sounds like Goldman and I have been talking to some of the same people," I said.

"That's when Binky canned him. And that," Wilkins said, "is what started the ball rolling."

"Guys like Binky have enemies," I said. "He could have been killed by one of them."

"Maybe. Of course, the odds are that Mason wasn't running the women alone. From what we know so far, he was busy. Yet the money doesn't show in any of his accounts and certainly not in his lifestyle."

"So he was a worker bee."

"Seems like it."

"If so, then this Malak is probably running the show. It would certainly seem to fit with what Mason told Wells before he killed him."

"The Supreme...the Supreme *what?*" Wilkins mused out loud.

I shrugged.

"You know," he said, "we're pretty good at what we do, and we usually know who's running what and who's doing what. But if this Malak is running an organization that's powerful enough to start knocking off guys like Binky, how come we don't know about it?"

"I don't know," I said. "But it seems like finding Callie is going to hinge on finding Malak."

CHAPTER TWENTY-ONE

Thirty minutes after leaving IPD headquarters, I found myself in the Lucky Dice again. Although the place wasn't open yet, it was full of women who were busy stocking cases of liquor and who looked as though putting away the stock wasn't their normal line of work. Like the manager, these girls were doing double duty.

"We ain't open," a whiskey-voice said.

I turned to see an older man who was dressed in a tight fitting T-shirt and jeans. He was standing to one side of a small workstation and looked as though he had been involved in muscle work for the better part of his life. He was staring at me through eyes that were void of warmth and shrouded beneath heavy lids.

"I'm here to see the manager," I said. "It's about a friend of hers."

"She has lots of friends," he said.

"Tony."

He gave me a weary look. Not the look of someone who has seen it all, but the look of someone who is tired. Who has long since lost interest in the job he's hired to do.

"Wait here," he said, leaving for the back office.

I waited as the girls who were stocking supplies began to disperse and go to other parts of the room. Some of them were pulling chairs off of tables, some of them were lighting the stage, and some were leaving entirely—presumably to dress the part of a dancer.

None of them gave me a second look.

"Back here," the bouncer said, motioning me to the office I had visited before.

I walked past the stage, past the bar, and into the office. Pam was sitting at her desk again, but this time she wasn't wearing jeans and a blouse. She was wearing a robe that was pulled closed. I assumed her costume was underneath.

"Thanks, Mike," she said.

"Sure thing, doll." He closed the door.

"You again?" she said. "What do you want this time?" She crossed her legs and reached for a pack of cigarettes on her desk.

"I found him," I said.

She lit a cigarette and tossed the lighter onto the desk as she blew smoke upward. Her elbow was resting on the arm of the chair as she held the cigarette between the first two fingers of her right hand. Her robe had fallen open, revealing that I had been correct in my assumption about what was underneath.

"That didn't take long," she said.

"He's dead."

She held her pose for a moment before reacting to the news by stubbing out her cigarette.

"When?" she asked.

"Day before yesterday," I said.

"How?"

"An angry father shot him. The police have the guy in custody."

She pulled her robe closed and crossed her arms tightly. Her eyes reddened as she began to recede.

"I'm sorry to have to be the one to tell you this," I said.

Her eyes flushed with tears.

"The police seem to think that Tony was cutting into another man's business," I said. "That man is dead too."

She wiped at the tears with the back of her hand.

"Tony was running women," I said. "And he wasn't doing it alone. He was involved with others. Who are they?"

The tears began to trickle, and despite her best efforts, she couldn't keep up.

"Why?" she asked. "What does it matter if they have the man who did it?"

"Because Tony was the best chance I had at finding my daughter. Now that chance is gone."

The bar had just opened. The sound of thumping music began to waft through the walls.

"He...I don't know all of his friends. I know that one of them was called *Anwar.*"

"Do you have a last name?"

She began to speak but couldn't. She put one hand to her mouth and shook her head.

"Do you know where I can find this guy?"

The trickle turned into a steady flow.

"I know that he tends bar," she said, her voice wavering. "Some place called The Spot."

"Who is Malak?" I asked.

"Who?"

"You don't know him?"

She shook her head.

"Tony was into some unusual stuff," I said.

"Unusual stuff?" she snorted. "You have a smooth way of putting it." She reached for another cigarette. "He was into vampires and stuff like that when he was in high school. He used to like to watch slasher movies and horror flicks." She wiped the tears from her eyes before she lit the cigarette.

"Is that who you are?"

She exhaled the smoke into the air above her head.

"No. I liked Tony. I didn't like everything he was into." She held the cigarette with one hand as she wiped tears away with the heel of her palm. She drew on the cigarette until the embers began to glow.

There was a knock on the door. "You okay?" the bouncer asked.

She cleared her throat and told him she was fine. He reminded her that she was due on stage in five minutes.

"Are you going to be okay?" I asked after he left.

"Does it matter?" she said.

"It does to me," I said. "If there's anything I can do…"

"There isn't," she said. "Tony's dead. And nothing can change that."

"No," I said, "but my daughter is still missing, and you can help me change that."

She took another long drag before crushing the cigarette out. The ash tray was full of partially smoked Camels.

"If she's with Tony's crowd, she's changed. She's not the girl you knew."

"She's my daughter," I said. "I'm bringing her home."

Pam stood and removed the robe as she wiped at her eyes again. "If she was with Tony, the best chance you're going to have of finding her is to find Anwar. But even if you do, you ain't bringing the same girl home." She opened the office door. The sound of the music became louder. "She's too far away. And every day that passes takes her even further."

CHAPTER TWENTY-TWO

The Spot was located in Broad Ripple, Indianapolis' answer to Greenwich Village.

The bar was upscale, and housed in a building that was large enough to accommodate a dance floor. When I arrived, the lot was full, and I was engulfed in thumping music as soon as I entered the room. The beat was strong and overrode any chance at having a normal conversation. Multicolored lights were strung from one end of the room to the other and cast an unearthly glow on the bobbing and gyrating customers dancing in the center of the room. A DJ was sitting at a console off to one side opposite a long bar tended by several men. A quick glance around the room revealed that nearly everyone was under twenty-five, upwardly mobile, and fashionably dressed—even if they weren't dressed well. I saw a spattering of bouncers moving about the room. They were dressed in T-shirts, and nearly all of them had shaved heads.

I must have stood out more than I thought. It didn't take long before one of the bouncers approached me. He looked to be about twenty-three or twenty-four at most and stood four inches taller than me. I guessed he outweighed me by thirty pounds.

"Can I help you?" he shouted.

"I'm looking for Anwar," I said. "I was told that he tends bar here."

The man nodded, and turned to scan the bar. After seeing Anwar, the bouncer turned to me and yelled, "Over there. The tall Middle Eastern dude with the stud in his ear."

I yelled my thanks and walked to the bar.

Four men, all young and all charismatic, were using their drink-pouring antics to entertain a large group of young women who had gathered at the bar. The women watched with rapt attention as the men enthralled them by tossing bottles over their shoulders, pouring shots, making mixed drinks while sliding the glasses along the bar, and juggling other drink-mixing paraphernalia. I watched as one young woman, dressed in low-slung jeans and a revealing long-sleeved shirt, leaned across the bar to talk to the man I was trying to meet. He seemed to revel in her attention and had yet to notice me.

Anwar was a tall man with close-cut hair, dark eyes, and a dazzling smile. A diamond-encrusted silver stud was embedded in one ear, and he wore a white silk shirt with long flowing sleeves, and dark slacks. A black onyx ring decorated the index finger of his right hand.

I worked my way through the throng in time to see Anwar leave the bar with the young woman. They moved toward the back of the room, weaving their way through the twisting crowd of dancers, as they inched their way toward an unmarked door.

"What'll you have?"

I turned to see a smiling bartender. He was younger than the shoes I was wearing.

"Nothing," I said.

I began to move around and through the crowd of young women, trying to keep my eye on the couple that had left the bar. I couldn't see them, so I stood on my toes and tried again.

Nothing.

I followed the same path they had taken and eventually reached the unmarked door. It opened to reveal a narrow staircase.

I went up and closed the door behind me.

At the top of the landing, I found a short hallway that had a door at each end and one straight across from where I stood. I heard voices coming from the middle room.

I opened the door.

Anwar was sitting on a sofa with the young girl. The two of them were dividing a small mound of white powder on a glass coffee table in front of them. A few twenty-dollar bills were lying on the table. I closed the door.

"Well, well, Anwar," I said. "You still ripping these kids off?"

Anwar and the girl had the same look of merriment they had when they left the floor. Neither of them registered surprise.

"Honey," I said to the girl, "don't let him steal from you. If you want the good stuff, go somewhere else. He's been cutting that junk so thin for so long, you could give it to your grandmother."

The girl looked at Anwar. His expression changed from glee to anger.

"Who are you?" he asked.

"A guy who knows cheap dope when he sees it. Cheap for you, that is." I looked at the girl, who now seemed confused. "You're getting ripped off, sweetie. That's nothing more than a quarter gram of coke, cut with four grams of sugar. You'd get a better buzz with a Snickers bar."

Anwar stood. "Get out of here," he yelled. "Get out of here, now!"

"Sorry," I said, "but I can't do that. I've just witnessed a customer getting ripped off, and I'm pretty sure that qualifies as a crime."

The girl swallowed hard and stood.

"Are you a cop?" she asked.

"He ain't no cop," Anwar said before I could answer. "A cop wouldn't come in here alone. He'd have backup—and a gun. And a badge. Where's your badge?"

I opened my jacket and revealed the Ruger. "One out of three isn't bad," I said.

The girl's face was flushed as she came around the coffee table and walked past me, leaving the room with a slam of the door.

"Who are you?" Anwar asked again.

"You're probably not going to believe this," I said, "but I'm your worst nightmare."

I smiled, relieved that I had finally gotten to use the line.

Anwar turned to pick up a phone on a nearby end table. I moved toward him and jerked the phone from his hand before pulling it from the wall. I shoved him to the sofa and tossed the phone onto the floor.

"You're a friend of Tony Mason," I said. "And I want to know who you two are working for."

His face was red, and his breathing was labored. He was angry. But he was also scared. His eyes were wide, and he withdrew deeper into the sofa. "There are people downstairs," he said.

"That doesn't help you much."

"What do you want?"

"I just told you, Anwar," I said. "I don't believe you're paying attention."

He shifted on the sofa as his eyes darted about the room.

"You got more stuff here?" I asked.

He didn't say anything, so I kicked the coffee table over and spilled the cocaine onto the aging carpet.

"Hey!"

"I've got all night, Anwar," I said. "I'll find the rest of your stash and flush it out of existence if you don't tell me what I want to know."

"I haven't seen Tony for a couple of weeks."

"And here I thought you two were buds." I closed the distance between us as he withdrew deeper into the sofa. "Who are you working for?"

"What're you talking about, man?"

"Tony was running women," I said, "and now he's dead."

"Dead?"

"In the morgue with a hole in his head. And you could be next."

His eyes widened.

"Who are you working for?" I repeated.

"I'm not running any girls, man. I don't get into that."

I ground some of the powder underneath my shoe.

"Could have fooled me. Who's Malak?"

His face grew dark.

"Anwar, who's Malak?"

"Where did you hear about him?"

I sighed and began to tear down the room. I started by opening the desk drawers and dumping them out onto the floor.

"No stuff in here," I said, moving on to the file cabinet. I opened it and dumped several drawers full of files onto the floor before tipping the cabinet over. "Nothing here either."

Anwar jumped off the sofa and bolted for the door. I caught him by the shirt and spun him back onto the sofa. His eyes were wide with fear.

"My daughter is missing," I said, "and I think Mason knew where she was. Mason was a friend of yours, and he knew Malak. That means you know Malak."

"No."

I was losing patience—and control. I had begun to cross the floor to the sofa when the door opened and one of the bouncers stood silhouetted against the light from downstairs.

"You've got to go, pal," he said.

I ignored him and grabbed Anwar by his shirt, pulling him off the sofa. The bouncer moved toward me.

I dropped the bartender back onto the sofa and swung at the bouncer, hitting him on the right side of his head with a left hook. He staggered, and I hit him on the left side with a right hook before driving a straight left into his chest. He staggered backward out the door and onto the top step of the stairwell. I hit him again, and he fell backward, rolling down the steps all the way to the dance floor. It was like watching Mr. Clean get cleaned.

I went back into the room and pulled Anwar off the sofa again, dragging him to the stairwell.

"Wait," he said. "Wait."

I paused.

"Malak is in Las Vegas."

"How do I find him?" I said.

"I don't know. I really don't. I helped Tony find girls. He was running them like you said. But I don't know this Malak. That was Tony's thing. Not mine."

"What was Tony's thing?" I asked.

"The girls, man. He was working with this Malak by running the women. That's all I know. Really."

"What's Malak's full name?"

His eyes darted back from left to right, partly out of fear, and partly because he was trying to think under pressure.

"Devlin, I think," he said. "Yeah, Leroy Devlin."

"You're done here," I said. "I'm closing this place down."

"You ain't a cop, man."

"I'll pass it on to them."

"You can't close this place down. People want this place."

Judging from the reverie that flowed from downstairs, I knew he was right. Laws can be made and enforced. But people must want the laws they choose to obey if they are to be effective. Closing The Spot would just move the problem from one location to another.

"You can't do nothing, man," he said.

He was wrong, and it cost him a trip down the stairs.

CHAPTER TWENTY-THREE

I left The Spot with nothing more than a warning from the bouncers not to return. A call to the police, after all, would expose their illicit operation, and they weren't eager to invite trouble.

I drove back to IPD headquarters and found Wilkins readying himself to leave. When I entered, he settled back behind his desk with a sigh. I sat in the chair next to his.

"Malak's real name is Leroy Devlin," I said. "He lives in Las Vegas."

"Las Vegas?" He frowned. "Isn't that where Anderson said Mason was heading?"

"Yep."

"How did you find this out?"

"I know this little spot," I said. "All kinds of stuff there."

Wilkins knew I wouldn't reveal my source. I couldn't. Telling him about them, would be as bad as them telling him about me. The bouncers and I had a mutually beneficial arrangement that was best served if we kept our mouths shut. After all, I wanted to find Callie, and I couldn't do that if I was in jail for assault.

Wilkins glanced at the wall clock and did a quick mental calculation before picking up the phone.

"They're three hours behind us," he said. "I'm going to call the Vegas PD. Someone should still be there."

I waited while Wilkins dialed. Within a minute, he had someone on the line. After identifying himself, he was directed to a detective at Vegas' Central Division.

"You have anything on a guy named Leroy Devlin?" Wilkins asked. "Goes by the aka *Malak,* and I don't have any identifiers."

By *identifiers,* Wilkins meant a date of birth, driver's license number, or Social Security number. Without that information, it could be harder to find the *right* Leroy Devlin—if there were more than one. We got lucky. There wasn't.

"Yeah?" Wilkins said, followed by a long pause. "And who was the investigating officer?" He pulled a notepad from a caddy on his desk and began to write. "He still with the department?" He wrote again. "Where is Devlin now?" There was another pause, followed by, "You're kidding." Another pause. "Thanks, this helps," he said, ending the call.

"And?" I asked.

"Leroy Devlin has been arrested on several occasions. When he was a teenager, he was arrested for animal cruelty." Wilkins lowered his voice. "Seems like he had a thing for cats. Then he was arrested for assault on a fellow student, and later, for assault on a teacher. He even got into a fight with an off-duty Vegas police officer and was arrested for that."

"Has he served any time?"

Wilkins made an O formation with his thumb and forefinger. "In all cases, he was either placed on probation or the charges were dropped."

"Dropped?"

Wilkins shrugged.

"Can they talk with him?"

"Nope. They don't know where he is. It seems he just disappeared."

"If I can find that this guy is with Callie—"

"Then we can arrest him for child endangerment, contributing to the delinquency of a minor…or whatever. But we don't know that he's involved with her, we don't know that he even knows her, and we don't know where she is."

"My only real lead is lying in the morgue. That means the only lead I have left is in Vegas."

Wilkins agreed. "I can ask Vegas PD to look for her," he said. "Put out an APB."

I shook my head. "It'll take more than that," I said.

"That's the best I've got, Colton. The rest is in their ballpark."

"Then that's where I'll go."

"Where?"

"To their ballpark," I said. "I'm going to Sin City."

CHAPTER TWENTY-FOUR

I left IPD headquarters with more than I had when I arrived. I had known that Wendy was hooking for Tony Mason, who also knew Leroy Devlin, aka *Malak*.

But now I knew that Devlin had an arrest record and that the Vegas PD had lost track of him. I also now knew that Mason had planned on heading for Vegas. That is, before Anderson derailed his plans. And I also had my gun back. I appreciated the weight of it under my left arm.

But I would have traded all of my gains for the one thing I still didn't have: information on Callie's whereabouts.

Was she with Devlin? Had she been with Mason? Was she with Wendy? Was she okay?

I drove home and checked for messages as soon as I entered the house. I had two, one from Mary and one from the Shapiros. I hadn't received a call from Pat, so I knew Callie hadn't called. But that didn't lessen my disappointment on discovering I had been right.

I played the messages.

Mary wanted to let me know the trial was taking longer than expected and that she would be in and out all day. She asked me to leave a message and update her.

Before calling Mary, I called the Shapiros and told them what I had, except for the part about prostitution. I didn't want them to carry any more of a burden than they already were.

The next call was to a travel agent. I told her that I needed the first flight out of Indianapolis bound for Vegas. She booked me on a red-eye for later that evening. She also booked me for an extended stay at the Eureka, a low-budget hotel just off The Strip.

I glanced at the clock. I had four hours until my flight.

After the call to the agent, I called Mary. She still wasn't in her room, so I left a lengthy message telling her all I knew. I gave her my flight number and the phone number for the Eureka. After ending the call, I went to the hall closet and pulled a suitcase down from the shelf. I had begun throwing a few clothes and other articles into it when the phone rang. It was Millikin.

"Any news?" he asked as soon as I answered.

I sighed. I didn't have the time or the patience for a go-round with the preacher.

"I had a couple of leads," I said.

"Had?"

"They're dead."

There was a long silence. "Dead?"

"I saw one get killed, and I viewed the body of the other on the morgue slab."

"Oh."

"And now I'm heading to Las Vegas to find the only lead I have left."

"Vegas?"

"Sin City, Dale."

"I know Vegas, Colton."

I didn't want the minister to go with me, and I was about to lay it out for him when he said, "I can't go. This thing has just about got me down."

"Sorry to hear that," I said, relieved. "But I'll make out okay."

"Have you ever been to Vegas, Colton? It's a big town."

"I'll find my way," I said. "Wilkins has called ahead. I'm supposed to look up a cop when I get there. Wilkins told me that Central Division's headquarters is on The Strip."

"He's right," he said.

"You a gambler, Dale?" I asked, trying to balance the phone between my shoulder and ear as I slid out of my shoulder holster.

"No. But I know Vegas."

I tossed the gun and rig onto the sofa and went into the hallway to get a box from the closet.

"Is it true what they say?" I asked. "That what happens in Vegas stays in Vegas?"

I went back to the living room and put the gun and holster into the box. The fit was tight enough to keep the gun from moving around and arousing suspicion.

"Nothing is kept from the eyes of God, Colton. Even in Las Vegas."

"Of course. He wouldn't be God otherwise, would He?"

I went into the kitchen and found some paper grocery bags. They would make excellent wrapping.

"Vegas is where He found me."

I cursed to myself.

One of the things that I disliked most about Millikin was the way he could hook me. Like any good fisherman, he had the inherent knack of tossing out just enough bait to reel me in.

"What do you mean, Dale?" I glanced at the clock. I had three hours and fifty minutes until flight time.

"I used to be a dealer, Colton."

"No way," I said, truly shocked. "I'm having a hard time picturing you standing at a poker table, Padre."

"Blackjack," he said.

"Wow. I'm learning more about you every day."

"And I led the life of a single bachelor," he said. "Until I found God."

"And how did you do that?"

I found a pair of scissors in the kitchen drawer and began to cut the bags into several large sections, suitable for wrapping the box that contained my gun.

"I hit bottom. I'm not proud of that, Colton. But I'd be less than honest if I didn't say that once I was blind, but now I see."

"Drugs?"

"Yes."

"Women?"

"Yes."

"How long ago was that?"

"Fifteen years."

I had the pieces of the bags cut into the size and shape I needed.

"Why are you telling me all of this, Dale?"

"I can make a call. I have a friend there. He can help you navigate the city."

"I can do it alone," I said.

"No, Colton, you can't. If Callie's there, she's in trouble. You need to know where to go. To the places the tourists never see. Understand?"

I was beginning to.

"What's his name?" I asked.

"Marty Cruise."

I had a new respect for the minister.

"I'll call him," he said. "Give me your flight number, and I'll have him meet you."

I gave the information to Millikin.

"Be careful," he said. "And keep me posted."

The call ended with three and a half hours until my flight left.

I wrapped the package and wrote the name of the hotel where I would be staying across the front. Since I couldn't take the gun on the plane, and I was loath to try and check it through, I had decided to overnight the package to myself.

I had made a promise. If Callie was hurt, Anderson Wells wasn't going to be the only father in jail.

CHAPTER TWENTY-FIVE

The plane landed at Las Vegas' McCarran International Airport at precisely eleven thirty, local time. Given the three-hour time difference, it was now two thirty in the morning, Indianapolis time. My eyes felt like scratching posts.

I disembarked the plane with a single carry-on and began looking for signs that would direct me to the baggage claim and rental car area. I was tired and wanted to get to the hotel as quickly as possible. But as I cleared the gate, I saw a tall man dressed in black jeans and a black denim jacket standing just to my left. He was wearing a blue denim shirt, string tie, and a white Stetson. His handlebar mustache completed the image.

He was carrying a sign that read, Colton Parker.

"I'm Colton," I said.

The man lowered the sign, smiled, and extended a hand. "I'm Marty Cruise. Dale asked me to meet you."

I shook his hand. His grip was firm.

Marty reached out and took my carry-on. "Come on," he said. "The tram's this way."

Marty was built like the coil in an electric motor. His wiry frame was lean and sinewy, and the explosiveness in his sudden movements indicated a reserve of energy that went beyond his physical appearance.

As soon as he mentioned the way to the tram, he was already ten yards ahead of me. I raced to catch up.

"I need to pick up my luggage," I said.

"That's where we're going," he said.

I followed him up an escalator and through a lobby full of beeping slot machines. Most of the stools in front of them were occupied—even at eleven thirty—with wide-eyed people feeding change into the machines with one hand as fast as they could push the electronic handle with the other.

"*There's* something you don't see every day," I said.

"Yeah? What's that?"

"People eager to give their money away."

My new friend grinned. "You will see a lot of it out here."

We dashed through the lobby and down another escalator. We were soon in a long hallway between two trams. Prerecorded voices announced the impending arrival of each train and the terminal it would serve. We paused to wait for our transport.

"Did you talk to Dale before you left?" Marty asked.

"Yes. He told me about you."

Marty nodded. "Dale's a good man."

I couldn't disagree. Even though the minister seemed to have a God-given ability to find my hot button, I knew his actions were always well-intentioned.

We were silent for the next minute or so, and several attempts on my part to retrieve my carry-on were dismissed by a wave of the hand. When our transport arrived, Marty stepped to one side and directed me to board the train before him. Once we were on the transport, the doors hissed with an electronic sigh, and we were off to baggage claim. We both held tightly to the chrome-plated passenger support rails.

Within a minute, we arrived at the appropriate terminal and stepped off the tram before heading toward the baggage claim area. By the time we arrived, my bag was making its rounds on the carousel.

"Got it," I said, pulling my suitcase off the rotating belt. "Now, if you could just show me where I could rent a car—"

"No need," he said. "We can take mine."

He burst forward again, and I sprinted to catch up.

"Listen," I said. "I appreciate your help. I really do. But I'd feel better if I rented a car."

He stopped and looked at me through eyes that were squinty and lined. "Aren't you tired?"

"Of course."

"Then why not wait until tomorrow? The place will still be here."

"Saves me a trip. I'd like to hit the road running tomorrow."

He slid one hand into the pocket of his jeans and paused to think. "Okay, tell you what. Why don't I just have the car brought, and you can hit the road running a bit faster."

"You don't have my credit card."

He pulled the hand from his jeans and held it up like a cop stopping traffic. "No need. The car is on me."

I began to protest, and the man held up his hand again.

"I try to help where I can," he said.

"And I appreciate it. But I can't accept it."

"Why not?"

"Well," I said, "I'm kind of hard on cars." I was recalling my Beretta, sitting in the long-term lot of Indianapolis International Airport, full of pockmarks from buckshot.

"Do you expect trouble?" he asked.

I was a bit confused. "Didn't Dale talk to you?" I asked.

"Yes sir."

"Did he tell you why I'm here?"

"Yes sir."

"Did he tell you anything else about me?"

Marty took a deep breath. "Yes. He said your daughter has run away, maybe with someone who's in Vegas, and that you intend to find this man and rescue her." He shifted the carry-on to the other hand. "He also said you can be stubborn, aggressive, and confrontational."

I gave him my best *well, duh* look.

"I owe Dale a great deal, Mr. Parker. If helping you find your daughter will restore your family, then it's worth the price of a car."

I was stunned. And ashamed.

"I'm sorry, Marty," I said. "I'd be honored to wreck your car."

"Okay then. That's settled," he said, resuming his run-walk. "Follow me."

I followed the Sam Elliott look-alike out of the terminal and toward the far end of the parking lot. We stopped at a white Cadillac.

"Go on and get in," he said, gesturing toward the right front seat as he took my bag from me. "I'll tuck these away, and then we'll get you to the hotel."

I did as I was told and sunk into the plush leather of the Caddy's front seat. I felt the car sag a bit as Marty slammed the trunk lid shut before sliding behind the wheel.

"Eureka, right?" he asked.

"Right."

He shifted into reverse and backed out of the stall.

"What do you do?" I asked as he moved the transmission into drive and drove toward the exit.

"You mean now?"

"Sure," I said. "Or before. Whatever."

"Well sir, right now, I ranch. But there was a time when I had a different kind of ranch." He turned to look at me. "Know what I mean?"

I nodded.

"But then I ran into Dale Millikin."

"And he saved you?" I asked.

The man turned to look at me again. "No sir," he said. "Jesus Christ saved me. Dale just pointed the way."

I didn't say anything else until we stopped at the exit booth and Marty handed his parking stub to the attendant.

"I'll get it," I said, reaching for my wallet.

"No sir." He put a hand on my wrist. "I'll take care of this."

After paying the clerk, we were on our way toward the business district of the city.

"How long have you known Dale?" I asked.

He glanced over his left shoulder, flicked on the turn signal, and moved into the flow of traffic. After we had successfully merged, he said, "Long time. I knew Dale when he was dealing. How 'bout you?"

"A little while," I said. "He was my wife's pastor."

"Was?"

"She died," I said.

He expressed his condolences, and for the next few minutes, we rode in silence until the traffic began to noticeably slow.

"This is The Strip," Marty said, breaking the silence.

Although the clock had already ventured into the early morning hours, the area buzzed like bees throwing a party at the hive. Some of the people were driving; most of them were not. But all of them seemed mesmerized by the flashing lights, the sound of dinging bells, and the allure of a quick way to wealth.

I motioned toward several small groupings of people who were standing on the sidewalks and flipping small pocket cards against the palm of their hands. "What are they doing?" I asked.

"They're trying to attract the attention of the tourists. They work for the brothels."

"Prostitution is legal here, isn't it?" I asked.

He shook his head. "No sir. Not in Vegas. But it is in other parts of the state." He turned to look at me. "That doesn't mean it doesn't go on."

"Maybe not," I said, "but it certainly seems to be celebrated here."

CHAPTER TWENTY-SIX

Despite his earlier assertion that I could get my rental car in the morning, Marty and I agreed to meet in the hotel's breakfast bar at seven. By the time he left and I entered the hotel through its revolving doors, I was moving on my last leg.

I approached a young desk clerk and told him my name.

"Yes sir," he said. "We have you in room 501 for…" He frowned as he looked at the computer.

"Five nights," I said. If I couldn't find Callie within that amount of time, either she wasn't in Vegas or I would need to extend my stay.

"Five nights it is," the clerk said, typing something into his computer.

"I'm expecting a package tomorrow," I said as I signed the register.

"Yes sir. We'll hold it for you."

I had been told my gun would arrive by three o'clock the next afternoon. Although I wasn't licensed to carry a gun in Nevada, that wouldn't stop me from being killed by one if I suddenly found myself unarmed in a one-sided conflict.

"But you do have some messages," he said, sliding me three notes that had been stapled closed. "And here's your room key. Would you like a wake-up call?"

I told him to call me at six, grabbed my key and the messages, and lifted my bags.

"Elevators are to the left," he said, pointing the way.

Within two minutes I was in my room with my bags on the floor, going over the messages.

Before leaving, I had told Wilkins, Mary, the Shapiros, and my renter where I would be staying. If Callie called, came home, or was found, I wanted to know.

As I opened the first of the messages, my hand trembled with fatigue.

> When in Vegas, contact Sgt. Todd Roper, Central Division. He knows you're in town and is willing to help.

Wilkins had promised to reach out to someone at the LVPD. It looked like Roper was the man. The next message was from Mary.

> Trial is going on longer than anticipated. I will call you as soon as I'm free.
>
> If you find Callie before I can call, let me know. Miss you!

The third message was from Millikin.

> I asked Marty to meet you at airport. Call me when you arrive regardless of time. I'll fill you in.

I glanced at the clock. It was one thirty in the morning, and my body ached. Yet I felt compelled to call the minister. He answered on the second ring.

"You awake already?" I asked, surprised he had been able to answer so quickly.

"This cold or flu or whatever has got me down. Can't sleep." He coughed.

"You wanted to fill me in," I said, getting down to business. I only had a few hours of sleep coming, and I didn't want to use them talking on the phone.

"You met Marty?" Millikin asked.

"Yes."

"He's a longtime friend." He sniffled.

"Sure."

"When I was a dealer, it wasn't in a casino. It was in Marty's brothel."

The pastor never failed to surprise me. This new revelation piqued my curiosity. I had that *fish dangling on the end of a hook* feeling again.

"You worked in a brothel?"

"Yes. Marty owned the Paradise Ranch. He had nearly a dozen girls working for him off and on and ran a small casino in an adjacent building. It was all housed under the one name."

My eyes were beginning to invert on themselves. "Dale, get to the point."

"Marty became a Christian a few months after I did."

"And?"

The preacher coughed. I glanced at the clock.

"After he became a Christian, he closed the brothel."

"Shouldn't he?"

"Now," Millikin said, ignoring my comment, "he spends his money helping troubled young girls get their life together. He runs the Last Hope Ranch. It's part cattle ranch, part halfway house. He funds it with the money he makes from selling the cattle."

"Is that why you hooked me up with him, Dale? Do you think Callie is working in a brothel?"

The anger in my voice was apparent, even to me. But it was misdirected at the ailing minister.

The thought that Callie might have been enticed into prostitution had occurred to me, of course. She was, after all, not thinking clearly and could be susceptible to the leading of someone she might admire. Or for whom she might have feelings. And she'd need money. Either way, the end result would be the same. The thought of someone enslaving my child both hurt and angered me.

"She's hurting, Colton. She's lost her way. Anything is possible."

"Sure." I sighed as I dropped my head into one hand while holding the phone to my ear with the other.

"If she's in that world, Marty can help. He has connections. He knows people."

"We're meeting for breakfast in the morning."

"Marty has no family, Colton. He's focused entirely on his ministry. If Callie is involved in…" Millikin let the word die on his tongue. Whether it was in deference to me or because he couldn't bring himself to say it, I appreciated his tact. "Whatever she's involved in, Marty is your best chance of finding her."

"Thanks, Dale," I said. "We're going to start looking tomorrow."

"One more thing," he said.

"Yeah?" I ran a heavy hand through my hair.

"Marty is a man's man. He's incredibly strong. If you get in a jam, you'll have the kind of backup you'll need."

"Always good to have backup," I said, making a mental note to pick up my special package when it arrived.

CHAPTER TWENTY-SEVEN

The Koffee Konnection was located in the southeast corner of the Eureka and was furnished in a 1970s motif, not because of a love for retro design but because no one had bothered to revamp the place since Jimmy Carter was president.

When I walked into the restaurant at precisely seven, I saw Marty seated at a booth, drinking coffee and reading a section of the newspaper that he had folded lengthwise. When I slid into the booth opposite him, he looked up from his reading and raised his cup in a welcoming gesture. "Morning," he said, in his baritone voice.

Dressed again in cowboy style, he wore the same white hat and string tie, strung this time over a white, Western-cut shirt, along with denim jeans and boots. A gold watch was wrapped around a thick wrist that seemed much more solidly built than it had at the airport the night before.

"Coffee?" a waitress asked as soon as I was seated.

I nodded, and she poured a cup.

"You two ready to order?"

"Go ahead," Marty said to me.

"Two eggs, scrambled, and two strips of bacon."

She wrote the order down.

"That it?" Marty asked.

"That's it."

He shook his head. "Two eggs, over easy," he said to the waitress, "four strips of bacon, some of them home fries you got, two pieces of toast, and a large glass of juice."

"Orange?" she asked.

"Tomato."

She told us her name, said to let her know if there was anything else we wanted, and moved away.

"You don't eat much, do you?" he asked.

"Not too hungry right now," I said.

He sipped at the coffee while his range-hardened eyes focused on me over the rim of his cup. "Yeah, I reckon you're probably not," he said, setting the cup down and pushing the newspaper aside. "Listen, I think I know where we might want to start."

"I'm all ears, Marty," I said. "I don't know this town from Jersey."

He pulled a napkin from the holder and began drawing on it with a pen he pulled from his shirt pocket. "It's all laid out like a grid. This ain't like them river towns that curl around every which way and such. Vegas is real easy to get around in."

"Except The Strip," I said.

"Well, even it ain't that hard. It's just crowded is all."

He drew a tic-tac-toe design on the napkin. "This here part would be The Strip," he said, making an X on the paper. "And this here is where folks live." He made a couple more Xs. "And this part here," he said, drawing a circle that was nearer The Strip than the residential area, "is where we're likely to find your daughter."

"What's that?"

"That there is the red-light district. It's where most of the bad stuff goes on." He slipped a hand into the pocket of his jeans and tossed me a set of car keys.

"What's this?" I asked.

"These are the keys that go to your car. I rented you a Toyota Camry. It's gold colored, sitting in the top floor of the hotel's garage."

I didn't know what to say. When I tried, he held up a hand.

"Don't worry none about it. If we get ourselves separated from each other, you'll have a car."

I sighed and rubbed my eyes.

"You ain't sleepin' much either?" he asked.

"No."

"Well, I reckon that's understandable too. But don't worry none. We're going to find your daughter. If she's in Vegas, she's as good as found."

"Finding her is not what's worrying me," I said. "It's the shape she's in when I do find her that has me concerned."

"Yes sir," he said, easing back into his seat. "Now I can't promise you that she'll be the same little girl she was when she lit out."

I could feel the tension in my body. I sighed again. It was the only thing that seemed to help.

"But whatever she's like when we find her, we can work with it."

"Work with it?"

"Yes sir. Everything and everyone is redeemable, no matter what."

"Here we go," the waitress said, setting our orders on the table. "I'll be right back and warm up your coffee," she said before leaving again.

"If God can save people like Dale and me, He can do wonders for anyone else."

"Sure," I said.

"Yes sir. God will find that little sheep. It's what He does."

CHAPTER TWENTY-EIGHT

After finishing breakfast and leaving the hotel, Marty and I drove to the Las Vegas Police Department's Central Division Headquarters. The drive should have taken less than ten minutes, but The Strip was loaded with tourists and other passersby, so the trip took almost twenty. I watched as we passed electronic signs that advertised the shows of Wayne Newton and Lance Burton.

We parked in a small lot that rimmed the front half of the modern-looking facility, and within minutes we were meeting with the detective sergeant that Wilkins had spoken about earlier.

Todd Roper seemed to be everything a cop ought to be. Professional, concerned, and engaged, he stood well over six feet, was built like the mountains that rimmed the city, and was dressed in traditional detective garb. A dark suit, white shirt, and subdued tie. His hair was cut in military fashion.

"I spoke with Captain Wilkins," he said. "He told me about your predicament."

Roper settled into the chair behind his desk while Marty sat on the edge of an unoccupied desk with his arms folded across his chest and his hat pulled over his eyes. I stood.

"I have reason to believe she's here," I said.

"If she's as young as Wilkins indicated, she probably came here with someone or to meet someone. You find that someone and you'll find her."

"Sure," I said.

"Vegas gets its share of runaways," Roper continued, "just like any other big city. But most of them aren't fifteen years old. And most of them come here thinking this is a fast track to stardom." He rocked in his chair. "Do you have a picture?"

I gave him one of the copies I had made for the trip.

"She seems like a nice kid. This is no place for her."

I agreed but didn't say so.

"I can put this out if you want. See that our officers keep an eye out."

"I want," I said.

He tossed the picture on the desk. "People come here to have fun."

"Not me," I said. "I came here to find my daughter."

"That's my point. Wilkins told me that two men who were on the periphery of your search are already dead."

Marty raised his head.

"One of them was peripheral," I said. "The other was central."

"Would that be Mason?" Roper asked.

"Yes."

"Wilkins said that Mason was a pimp."

"Yes."

"Is that why you brought Marty along?"

"Yes."

He glanced at the cowboy before finishing his point. "Wilkins said Mason was killed by an irate father."

I said nothing.

"You're irate."

"Wouldn't you be?"

He continued to gently rock in his chair. "Yes, I suppose I would. But you need to know that we run this city. Not the pimps and not you."

"Sure," I said.

"If you cause trouble, raise a ruckus, or become a nuisance, we're going to have a problem."

"I wouldn't want that."

He ceased rocking as he unclasped his hands and leaned forward. "This town gets its revenue from tourism. People come here to have fun. To do things they can't do at home. And we won't let anything interfere with that."

"Most," I said.

He gave me a quizzical look.

"*Most* people come here to have fun. I came here to find my daughter. And I won't let anything interfere with that."

"As long as we understand each other," Roper said.

"We do."

"Okay then. About your man—his name is Leroy Devlin. He's thirty years old, six feet two, one hundred ninety pounds. He's been arrested on several occasions…Wilkins filled you in on those details, I believe."

"Yes."

"He seems to have dropped off the radar screen lately. No driver's license, no credit cards—nothing."

"Any background?"

"His mother and father are deceased, and he has one sister."

"She in town?"

He told us the address.

"It seems," he said, "that little Leroy and his sibling were raised by parents who were missionaries before the dad became the pastor of a local church. The sister took to religion, but Leroy didn't."

I glanced at Marty. He had lowered his head again.

"At the present time, we don't want him," Roper continued. "If we did, we wouldn't know where to begin."

"His sister?" I asked.

"Good luck."

"Meaning?"

"Meaning that she hasn't seen him in years and doesn't care to.

Leroy assaulted her once. Her parents wouldn't press charges. Talked her into forgetting the whole thing."

"How do you forget something like that?" I asked.

Roper shrugged. "The guy's parents thought that given enough time, God would reform him. Or he'd see the light and do it himself."

"Looks like they were wrong," I said.

CHAPTER TWENTY-NINE

Marty steered the big Caddy onto Las Vegas Boulevard and headed north as we passed a nearly full-sized replica of the Eiffel Tower.

"Where we going?" I asked.

"Remember that little circle I drew on the map?"

"Map? You mean your napkin?"

"What's a napkin to some folks is a map to others."

"I remember."

"That's where we're headin'."

"The red-light district," I said, acknowledging that I had been paying attention.

"That's right. We're goin' to talk to Carlene. She's the one who's in the know on this stuff. If your daughter's...well, you know, if she's...doin' it, Carlene will probably know about it."

"How do you know Carlene?"

"She's the queen bee in this town. The madam's madam."

Madam, in conjunction with my daughter, didn't sit well. But facts are facts. And finding Callie was going to require me to face the facts regardless of how unpleasant they may be.

"Will she know about the girls who aren't working in an organized way?" I asked.

"Streetwalkers?" he asked as he maneuvered his way along The Strip.

It was a term I had been trying to avoid. I nodded.

"Nobody knows everything. But I'd say our best chance at finding your little girl is to start with Carlene."

"*Callie,*" I said. "My little girl's name is *Callie.*"

We continued to inch our way along Las Vegas Boulevard, pausing long enough to allow other cars to merge, exit, or otherwise confound what was already a highly confused artery. To my left, a gold pyramid that Marty identified as the Luxor shimmered in the morning sunlight.

We didn't talk for the next few minutes as we continued to creep northward, watching as the casinos and their flashy facades melted into the more decadent and more garish wedding chapels, bars, and other adult establishments. By the time we reached Tremont, I was becoming increasingly depressed.

"Anna would die if she knew this," I said. "She'd die all over again."

"Anna your wife?"

"Yes."

We turned right onto Tremont. Just to my left was the portion of the street I had seen in nearly every movie or television show that had been filmed in Sin City. But now, the street was roofed over, turning what had once been a public thoroughfare into a downtown mall without walls.

As we cleared the turn, the city's underbelly became visible. Large numbers of people, some in clusters and some not, panhandled their way to the next drink or the next fix. Some of them were young. Some weren't. But all of them bore the look of hopelessness that belied the luster and allure of the casinos less than a mile away.

"Behind us is the sin," Marty said as we turned away from The Strip. "And just ahead are the consequences."

We continued to drive for another block or two and came to an out-of-place house that stood next to a row of storefront buildings. Most of them, and the houses beyond, were in severe disrepair. Or vacant. The house we stopped at, however, was nicely painted and sat on a lot that overflowed with decorative shrubbery. A fence encircled the yard, and a padlock secured the gate.

Marty parked the Cadillac alongside the curb.

"Here we are," he said, turning off the car. "You better stay here though. Let me go up there first. She doesn't know you, and you look too much like the law."

"Years of being the law take their toll," I said. "Before long, you're looking in the mirror and Jack Webb is looking back."

Marty eased his frame out of the Caddy, topped his head with the big hat, and ambled up to the gate. When he reached it, he took off the hat and waved it high overhead before putting it back on. Less than a minute later, a thick-necked man with a T-shirt stretched tightly over his muscular frame came out of the house and unlocked the gate. After Marty entered the yard, the two began talking. A couple of minutes later, Marty was motioning for me to join him.

"Colton, this here is Michael," Marty said as soon as I joined them. "He works with Carlene."

I shook Michael's massive hand. After meeting Marty, Roper, and Michael, I was getting the impression that at six feet and two hundred pounds, I was apparently the smallest man in Vegas.

"We won't be but just a minute or two," Marty said to Michael.

"Okay with me."

Michael closed the gate and locked it in place as I followed Marty up the steps and into the house.

As soon as we cleared the foyer, we were greeted by an attractive woman whom I guessed to be in her late forties. Dressed in a form-fitting pair of light gray slacks and a white blouse, she looked more the part of June Cleaver than Heidi Fleiss. When she smiled, I could easily have mistaken her for a host on the Home Shopping Network if I hadn't known what she was selling.

"Marty, it's been too long," she said in a throaty voice. She put her arms around the tall cowboy and lingered in the embrace long enough for me to be embarrassed. "And who's this?"

"Carlene, this is the man I told you about. His name is Colton Parker."

"Colton," she said, dragging out my name the way people do who are greeting a long-lost friend. "How are you?" She extended a hand.

"I could be better," I said, taking her hand.

Just as the facades of The Strip had vanished after we turned the corner, Carlene's smile changed into a look of genuine empathy.

"Yes, I imagine so. Marty telephoned me last night and told me the story."

"Everything I knew, anyway," the cowboy said. "Colton will need to tell you the rest."

She reached out and took my right hand into both of hers. "Why don't you come into the parlor, Colton, and tell me how I can help."

CHAPTER THIRTY

I laid out the entire story for Carlene, beginning with Anna's death. The whole time I talked, she held tightly to my hand and maintained an expression of genuine concern. As I continued to talk, I began to understand how she remained in business. The physical interaction isn't what men were seeking. It was the relational. I couldn't judge her on the basis of the former, but I could certainly evaluate her on the basis of the latter. The woman made me feel like she cared. She listened.

"Colton, I know that this probably won't mean much coming from someone like me, but I am truly sickened by what I've heard."

"Can you help us?" Marty asked.

She released my hand. "Maybe. How old did you say Callie is?"

"Fifteen."

"And how long has her mother been gone?"

"Just under two years," I said.

She stood from the sofa. It was a period piece, probably Victorian, and matched the interior decor of the house.

"She and her mother were close?"

"Very," I said.

"But you and she aren't."

"No."

She began to pace.

"This is a predatory business, Colton. There are as many women who are waiting to fill the void for her as there are men." She paused long enough to smile and put a hand on the cowboy's shoulder. "Except for Marty. He always treated me right."

Marty patted her hand.

"Most likely," she said, "if your daughter came out here alone, she will end up working the streets. It's how all of us get our start if we don't have a connection." She began to pace again.

"A manager," Marty said, choosing a more tactful term.

"But if she came out here with someone, as you seem to believe, that person almost certainly has a connection." She paused her pacing and faced me. "Neither way is a good life. But if you have to choose, take the connection."

"Sure," I said. "As long as I have to choose."

"There are several families in Vegas," she said, "and most of them have several houses."

"Families?" I asked.

"It's a term that's used to refer to groupings of girls. It's a way to corner the market in a town where prostitution isn't legal."

"Kind of like a joint-marketing venture," Marty said.

"That way if one house gets busted, all is not lost," Carlene said. "And if one group of girls wants to specialize in one type of…activity, the house can attract a regular crowd. That's nice on one hand because the girls know exactly what's going to happen, and the customer becomes a regular."

"It's bad on the other hand," Marty said, "because the police catch on."

"Because the same men keep coming around, and that attracts attention," I said.

"Right," Marty said.

"Ease in getting noticed can help the bottom line," Carlene said, "but it also means it's harder to remain underground."

"A double-edged sword," I said.

"Yes," Carlene said.

"So the question is," Marty said, "which family is Callie in?"

"Or not," Carlene said, casting a cautionary glance at the cowboy. "There are still some houses that remain unaffiliated. And there are also some that rove."

"In what?" I asked.

"Anything," Carlene said. "Motor homes, trailers…some of them are simply outcall services."

"The roving houses are the trend," Marty said. "That way, if anyone gets caught, the girl takes the hit. If she rats out the house, or the manager, she could wind up dead. And of course, there's no way to find them since there is no physical location."

"I'm a dying breed," said Carlene.

"Where do I go from here?" I asked.

Carlene sighed and looked at Marty. "I'll take a run through the families," she said. "I'll see if I can find Callie."

"Then you might need this," I said, pulling a photo of Callie from my jacket. "And if you see her, call me at this number." I wrote my name, cell number, and the number of my hotel on the back of the photo.

I handed it to Carlene and thanked her for her help.

"No, Colton, don't thank me. I don't know if I can be of help. And if Callie is on the streets or roving, your job is going to be a lot harder. I don't have a lot of clout in those areas."

"Maybe," I said. "But with your help, I can eliminate one of the three possibilities."

Marty shook his head. "No," he said. "You've eliminated one of the three possibilities as far as it relates to prostitution."

"A young girl can get into a lot of things out here," Carlene said. "We don't call it Sin City for nothing."

CHAPTER THIRTY-ONE

The next stop was a small house on the near west side of the city, less than two miles from The Strip. The neighborhood was considerably nicer than the one we had just left and considerably more populated.

Row on row of houses lined the streets, with each of them looking essentially the same. Nice and well maintained in a Stepford sort of way.

We drove to the address for Leroy Devlin's sister that Detective Sergeant Roper had given us and pulled into a nicely paved yet very narrow driveway. The garage door was open, and a late-model minivan was parked inside. We left the car and walked to the front door by way of a narrow sidewalk. When we knocked, an attractive woman in her midtwenties answered the door.

"My name is Colton Parker. I'm a private detective, and I'm looking for Alyssa Devlin."

I didn't display my ID because it wasn't valid in Nevada. I was hoping the girl wouldn't ask to see it.

She didn't. Instead, she looked at Marty.

"Who're you?"

"He's my partner," I said. "His name is Randolph Scott."

Marty dropped his head into his hand.

"What's this about?" she asked.

"You Alyssa?" I asked.

Her eyes gave her away. "What do you want?" she asked.

"To talk."

"I'm working," she said.

"So are we. This'll just take a minute."

"What do you and Mr. Scott want to talk about?"

"Leroy," I said.

Her face fell as she glanced back into the house and then opened the door.

"He's nuts," she said.

"When did you see him last?" I asked.

We were sitting in the living room, drinking lemonade. Alyssa was on a recliner, I was sitting on the edge of a love seat, and Marty was on a sofa with hat in hand. She told us she didn't live at the house. She was the nanny.

"It's been a while," she said.

"Any idea where he might be?" I asked.

She drank some lemonade. "He could be at Jerry's. Max's."

"Friends?" I asked.

"Jerry Thom and Max Minor," she said. "They're just as nuts as he is."

I gave Marty a questioning look. He shook his head.

"Where can I find these guys?"

The girl sighed. "Max works at the Esparanda—"

"It's a hotel and casino," Marty said.

"Yeah. And Jerry is a bouncer at Club Harem."

I glanced at Marty.

"North end of town," he said. "I know the places, but I don't know the men."

"We'll introduce ourselves." Turning back to Alyssa, I said, "Anything we need to know about him?"

"He likes girls. The younger the better. Started molesting me when I was fourteen years old." She frowned and shook her head. "He nearly killed me when I told our parents." She pulled back a lock of blonde hair to reveal a grotesque scar that ran along the right side of her neck, just behind her right ear.

"What did your parents do about it?"

She shrugged. "They told him to leave."

"No charges were ever filed?" I asked.

She shook her head.

"This Jerry and Max, have they been friends with your brother for long?"

"Yeah. Jerry and Leroy go way back. He's the one that got him started."

"He's into drugs?" Marty asked.

"Probably. But that came after."

"After what?" I asked.

She gave Marty and me a confused look. "You mean you guys don't know?"

I looked at Marty, who shrugged.

"I guess not," I said.

"He's very heavy into the occult. He's a Satanist."

"I think I already knew that," I said.

"Then you know he'll be hard to stop. There's nothing he won't do for his god."

CHAPTER
THIRTY-TWO

After leaving the house, I suggested that Marty and I split up, each taking one of the two names that Alyssa had given us. He declined.

"You don't know these good ol' boys, Colton. They'll stick a shiv in your back while you're talkin' to 'em, and no one will ever know what happened to you." He shook his head as he wheeled the big Caddy back onto Las Vegas Boulevard. "No sir. It'd be best if I went along on this one."

After maneuvering back onto The Strip, we began to creep northward again, winding our way through a street that was overflowing with traffic—both auto and pedestrian.

We continued to work our way north of town, past the Fremont intersection where we had turned to find Carlene's place, to an area where Las Vegas Boulevard veered toward the northeast.

"Where we going?" I asked.

"To the Club Harem. It's near the air base." He glanced sideway at me. "A lot of those kind of places are near military bases."

We drove in silence for a while as the traffic began to thin and we began to pick up speed.

After a while of watching the road pass by, I said, "I'm going to need to find this guy soon. Before any damage is done." I was concerned about the long-term physical ramifications to Callie, especially if she had fallen into prostitution.

"We'll find her if she's here," Marty said again. "And like I said earlier, we can work with whatever we find."

I looked at my driver. He was comforting to have around. A true stalwart. The kind you can depend on in a pinch. And yet he didn't know me. What he was doing, he was doing for Millikin and for Callie.

"Dale said you've spent the last few years going after the kind of girls that you used to…"

"Sell?" he asked.

"Yeah. Something like that."

"Yes sir. That's exactly what I'm doin'. I'm puttin' back into the well the very things that I used to draw from it." He rested his left arm on the door frame and began to steer the car with one hand. "It's like this," he said. "I've got a lot to make up for. And when Christ saved me, I was in a position to help these kids and pay back for what I'd done. So I told the Lord that if He wanted me to stay right here in the slums of the city, workin' to set these girls free the way He did for me, then that was what I'd do."

"Most of these kids end up out here," I said, "because there wasn't anything for them at home. Either their parents didn't care, or maybe a stepfather or a boyfriend of their mother was molesting them. What do they have to go home to when they leave here?"

"They're running away, to be sure," he said. "Most of the time, anyway. But we counsel them. We try to—"

"We?"

"My girls." He took his eyes off the road just long enough to gauge my reaction. "My girls, Colton. The ones that used to work for me. Now they help me work for the Lord."

"Oh," I said.

"So we counsel them. Try to help them see that they aren't bad. They've just done bad things. We begin by attacking their problem—not them—on a spiritual level. After all, you heard that young lady say that Leroy is very heavy into the occult."

"Yes."

"And that's where the problem lies."

"Not all runaways are involved in the occult. As I said, some are just trying to escape bad home conditions."

"All of them are trying to escape something," he said. "School, home…whatever. The point is that they won't find what they're looking for without Christ."

"I hate to sound like a spoiler," I said, "but there are a lot of happy people who aren't Christians."

He nodded. "Sure. But happiness comes and goes. True joy, though, and true peace, will only come from a relationship with Jesus Christ."

It was like riding with Millikin. Only I was getting the Bonanza version.

"These kids are looking for joy," he said. "But what they find is temporary happiness, whether it's in acceptance, or drugs, or whatever. But that soon fades, and then they have to dig deeper for the water they need."

"All of this is nice, Marty," I said. "And I've heard this from Dale already. But don't you think that the best thing is to get Callie away from wherever she is and get her home first?"

"In a physical sense, yes it is. If your little girl is in imminent danger—and we don't know for sure that she is—then we need to remove her from that. But if we do only that and don't address her spiritual needs, she'll falter again."

We turned down a dusty side road. Large sections of paved land lay on either side of the roadway. A military jet whined overhead.

"This Leroy is into the occult."

"Yes." I was weary of the discussion.

"A lot of Satanists don't even believe in Satan."

"Then what's the point?" I said.

"The point is that they're so focused on being contrary to God, they'll put their faith in anything that stands against Him. Even if their faith is in someone they don't believe even exists." He glanced at me. His eyes were alive. "But that's exactly what he wants them to believe, Colton. Satan doesn't care if people believe in him or not. His fight is with God. Going after God's creation is just one way of hitting the Almighty where it hurts the most. And any means will do. He uses subterfuge, rebellion, half-truths, and innuendo. It doesn't really matter. It's all lies, and lies work for him."

I was about to answer the cowboy when I saw a large concrete building standing just ahead. A large sign identified it as Club Harem.

"There it is," I said, glad to have the opportunity to take the conversation down a different road.

Marty squinted against the sun as he looked at the club. Crow's feet lined his face, giving him that quintessential cowboy look that every actor from John Wayne to Clint Eastwood has tried to perfect.

"Yes sir," he said. "This'd be just one more of the devil's playgrounds."

"Well, after all, it is Sin City, isn't it?"

"Yes sir," he said, steering into the lot. "Yes sir, it is."

CHAPTER THIRTY-THREE

The Club Harem appeared to be much bigger on the inside than it was on the outside. That was an illusion, of course, but so was everything else they offered.

The place was dark, and no one was seated at the door when we entered. A huge bar ran along the back wall, a few tables were scattered about the main floor, and a large area in the center of the room appeared to have been set aside for dancing. A handmade sign listed the cover charge and indicated that fighting would not be tolerated. Marty knocked on top of one of the tables.

"Anyone here?" he bellowed.

"You want something?" a woman asked. She was standing in the doorway of the office, located to the left of the bar, and was dressed in jeans, a T-shirt, and tennis shoes. Her face was lined yet youthful. She wore a heavy coating of makeup, and her strawberry blonde hair was pinned on top of her head.

"We're lookin' for Jerry Thom," I said.

"Who are you?"

"I'm Alan Ladd and this is Jack Palance."

Marty groaned.

"I don't know you two," she said.

"How about *Shane?*" I asked.

She gave me a quizzical look.

"City Slickers?"

She frowned. "Like I said, I don't know you two."

"And you're better off for it," I said.

"Is he here, ma'am?" Marty asked, breaking the repartee.

"I'm here."

Marty and I turned to see a tall, sinewy-looking man, about thirty, with shoulder-length black hair and gaunt eyes rimmed with eye-liner. He was wearing a black T-shirt, black jeans, and tennis shoes. A metallic bracelet dangled around his wrist.

"What do you want?" he asked.

"I want to talk," I said.

"Yeah? Well, then, I'd start by dropping the wise guy routine. Ear-line may not have seen *Shane,* but I did."

The man smelled of cannabis.

"I'm Colton Parker," I said. "And this is Marty Cruise."

The man pulled a chair from a nearby table and sat, placing one boot-covered foot on top of the table. He lit a joint, offering Marty and me a hit. We shook our heads.

"You know Leroy?" I asked.

The man frowned. "Leroy...Leroy," he said to himself before slowly shaking his head. "No, I can't say I do."

The woman we had met earlier was still standing in the doorway, listening intently.

"Earline, you think you could make some coffee or something?" Jerry asked.

He inhaled deeply on the cigarette.

"How about Malak?" I asked.

The man exhaled and held the marijuana between his thumb and forefinger. His eyes narrowed as smoke escaped his nostrils. "No, can't say I do. Why?"

"I was told you do."

He grinned and inhaled again.

"You were told wrong," he said.

I studied the guy. His long hair, eye-liner, and macabre look told me he was a fit with Tony Mason. Mason was a fit with Malak.

"We were told you're a friend of his."

"I have a lot of friends."

"Good for you," I said. "I just want the one named Malak."

"Hey, man," he said, raising his voice. "That ain't my problem. I told you I don't know where he is, so take off." He flipped the butt of the joint at me, and it bounced off my chest.

I slapped his foot off the table, grabbed his shirt, and pulled him from the chair. As soon as he cleared the table, I heard the click of a switchblade. He leveled the knife at my abdomen.

Marty stepped forward and grabbed Jerry's wrist with one hand while bending his elbow with the other. The cowboy forced the bouncer's arm backward, and the knife fell to the floor.

"Now," I said, still holding Jerry by the shirt as Marty continued to pretzel his arm, "I want to find Malak. I want to find him now, or my friend, here, is going to break that arm."

Jerry was hard-core. Although his eyes and facial expression revealed the pain he felt, he wouldn't give in to it. Wouldn't acknowledge his discomfort with audible sounds.

"You can go—"

Marty forced the arm over the man's shoulder. His hand was at a ninety-degree angle off his wrist.

"I'm only going to ask once more," I said. "Where can I find Malak?"

The man grimaced. Anyone else would have already cried out. "If he's in town, you might try some of the shops."

"Shops?"

"New Age stuff," the man said. "Malak's into the occult."

This fit with the information we had been given by Alyssa.

"We've already heard that," I said. "But we were told that you were the one that introduced him to it."

Despite the pain, a brief yet recognizable flash of confusion shined from the man's eyes. "I didn't introduce him to anything, man. That dude was sick to start with."

"How?"

"Everything, man. He'd stomp on a cat as fast as he would a bug. I've seen him do stuff that'd just haunt you. You know, the kind of stuff that just stays with you."

Marty and I exchanged glances.

"What about the Esparanda?" I asked.

The man grimaced, again. "Yeah. Maybe. He and a guy named Max are tight."

"And you?"

"We get along, but I ain't into his kind of stuff no more."

I glanced around the bar.

"Could have fooled me," I said.

"I ain't into young chicks. That's his thing, not mine."

Marty held the man's arm firmly.

"What do you mean?" I asked.

"He runs them. Gets them mainlining, and then they do anything he wants for the next fix. It's how he makes his dough. He sells the girls."

"He's running a roving house," Marty said.

"No, man. That ain't what I mean. I mean he's *selling* them."

The cowboy and I exchanged confused looks.

"*Selling* them. He sells them to other dudes. They put them to work in houses all over the place."

Marty paled. Beads of sweat broke out on his face, and he let go of the man's arm.

"Lockboxes," the cowboy said. "He's feeding lockboxes."

Jerry was massaging his arm. "Yeah, man. That's it. Lockboxes. And that's when I said, 'No way, dude. I ain't doing this.'" The man raised his T-shirt. "And that's when I got this."

A thin but visible scar ran across the man's stomach.

I kicked the knife across the floor.

"You ever been to Indianapolis?" I asked.

"I ain't been anywhere but here in years," he said. "I got all I want right here."

I watched as the man continued to massage his arm.

"Let's get out of here," I said to Marty. "This place is making me sick."

"Ma'am," Marty said to Earline, "can I get some of that coffee to go?"

CHAPTER THIRTY-FOUR

Marty and I had reached Las Vegas Boulevard and were on our way back to The Strip before he talked.

"You know what a lockbox is?"

"No. I worked vice in Chicago for a brief time, but I never ran into anything that was all that well organized."

"A lockbox makes street walkin' look like a stroll through the park on a nice sunny Sunday afternoon."

"Where are these places?" I asked.

"All over. They're big in Thailand, but the States have them, the—"

"Thailand?" I was flabbergasted.

Marty glanced briefly at me as he steered the car with one hand while drinking the coffee he had gotten from Earline with the other. "Lockboxes are international."

"What are they?" I asked.

"When a girl is too hot to handle—for example, if she's too high profile or too young—she can be fed into a system that has houses all over the world. They could be in Las Vegas, Mexico, New York, or—"

"Thailand," I said.

He nodded. "Yes sir, or Thailand." He drank some of the coffee. The speedometer showed increasing speed as Marty hightailed it for downtown Las Vegas. "These places cater to men who are well-to-do, high paying, and sometimes highly visible. Clients whose images or careers could be ruined by being seen in the normal establishments. Sometimes these guys' tastes run a bit wild of the norm."

None of this was what I wanted to hear.

"These girls are led into these places by trust. It's one of the strongest bonds there is, Colton. These girls trust the man who recruits them. They think he loves them. They think he cares when no one else did. These recruiters fill the void I was talking about earlier. They give these girls what they want the most. What we *all* want the most. Love."

"Or at least their version of it," I said, trying not to lose control, trying to remain objective.

"Of course. But these kids don't know the difference. How many of us do at their age?" He sipped more coffee. "So when the relationship is established, these girls go to the houses that were intended for them all along. Some go to roving houses, some go to places like Carlene's, and some go to lockboxes. And that's where the bond of trust is usually broken."

We turned southward as we began to work our way back to the city.

"The girls in the lockboxes are often shackled in their rooms, and the clients have no limits placed on them. If one of the girls gets too roughed up or dies…" He shrugged. "They can be replaced. There are always more in the pipeline."

I became nauseous.

"The good thing," Marty said, "and the thing that's working in our favor, is that Callie is too new. She hasn't had the time it normally takes for a girl to be flavored for a lockbox."

"Flavored?"

"Yeah. It's a term that means she's *ready.* Not just any girl can go to a lockbox. Even though they're shackled or confined against their will in some other way, they must have their will broken. They must be willin' to do what the client wants."

"And that comes with the loss of hope."

He nodded. "Yes sir, that's exactly right. No hope, no resistance."

"And the best way to lose hope," I said, "is to feel no love." I was beginning to get the picture.

"That's it, Colton. A girl who has felt no love at home and then learns that the love she thought she had is a lie—that's a girl who has lost hope."

"I love Callie," I said to myself.

"Of course you do. And that's what we have going for us. She didn't run away because she doesn't believe that you love her," Marty said. "After all, didn't she call and ask you not to look for her?"

"Yes."

"Then that means she knew that you would. And that means she knows she's loved."

None of what he was saying helped much. My nausea grew. Callie had run away. And right now, that was as much truth as I needed.

Marty dropped me off at the Eureka. According to Jerry Thom, Max Minor wouldn't be at the casino until after dark, so we agreed to meet later before going to the Esparanda and quizzing our prey.

"Did a package arrive for me?" I asked, checking with the desk clerk.

After taking my name, he left for a room in the rear of the front desk area. He returned shortly with the package I had mailed to myself before leaving Indianapolis. I tipped the kid and went straight up to my room. When I entered, I saw the red message light on my phone blinking furiously.

I picked up the receiver and pushed the Message button. Within seconds, I heard Wilkins' voice.

> Colton, I have some news that I thought you might want to know. I'm afraid it's not very good. Wendy Wells' body was found this morning. Her throat was cut, and she had been assaulted. From the looks of it, there was more than one assailant. Maybe as many as ten. This little girl died hard.

I hung up the phone, and the nausea hit again. This time, it won.

CHAPTER
THIRTY-FIVE

I awoke thirty minutes before I was due to meet Marty and splashed cold water on my face. The taste of bile remained.

I called the Shapiros and filled them in on what I had. I didn't tell them about roving houses or lockboxes. In this case, less was enough.

After the call ended, I slipped into the shoulder rig and chambered a round in the Ruger before jamming it back into the holster. The metallic *clack* of the gun's slide echoed in the otherwise silent room.

When I stepped off the elevator and into the lobby, I found Marty standing at the front of the lobby, leaning with his back to the wall. His arms were crossed and his head was down, forcing the hat over his eyes. When I approached him, he raised his head and peered at me from under the large brim.

"You eat?" he asked.

"Slept."

"One out of two ain't bad," he said as he followed me through the open doorway.

The air was cool, and I appreciated its revitalizing effects. I also appreciated the weight of the Ruger under my arm. It was something familiar in unfamiliar surroundings.

"The Esparanda is two blocks that way," Marty said, nodding

toward the south end of The Strip, "and then two blocks that way." He gestured in like fashion toward the east.

"Let's walk," I said. "I need the exercise."

We began moving south along the east side of The Strip, and I watched as tourists passed, seemingly oblivious to the underbelly of the city. Not that they cared. The allure that had attracted them was the same lie that had attracted generations of others before Vegas even existed. Something for nothing.

For most, the something was money and the security, happiness, or love they felt it could buy.

For others, the something was more spiritual. They sought a connection with anything other than what they had at home. Maybe another man or woman. Maybe a celebrity. Or the aura of a city that boasted of itself in decadent terms. As though that alone was proof that hedonism could openly coexist with any form of morality, so long as the hedonistic activity remained buried in The Strip—and in the heart of the people who walked it.

What happens in Vegas stays in Vegas. But the consequences of those happenings don't remain within the confines of the city. The loss and the pain follow many home. And then the hurt ones would touch others. Others who hadn't chosen to step out of bounds and into the abyss of a life lived without boundaries. Those who were innocent would be hurt by those who professed to love them.

"If I find this guy, and he has hurt Callie, I'm going to kill him," I said.

Marty's expression remained unchanged. "You think that will get your daughter back?"

"I don't know. But it will break his spell over her. It will free her."

He shook his head. "No, Colton. It won't. If that were the answer, God would have crushed evil a long time ago."

"Why hasn't He? Why does He let it go on? If He's God, He must be willing to let evil continue to exist. If He's God, He could end it."

We continued walking past the flashing lights, past the beckoning call of the slot machines and the roulette tables. And past the row on row of street hucksters who vied for the attention of lonely men by slipping them literature bearing the nearly naked bodies of young women for rent.

"Yes, Colton, God could end evil right now. But that would mean He would have to end you too. And me."

"I've never sold a young girl into slavery. I've never—"

"Maybe not," Marty said. "But you have lied. You have expressed unrighteous anger toward your brother."

"Killing Malak, if he's harmed Callie, is not unrighteous anger."

"It's still murder. And murder is wrong."

"It's justice."

"No, Colton. You would just be passing judgment and dispensing punishment." He stopped walking. "See, God loves us enough to allow us to make our own choices. Yes, He could destroy evil. But then we'd live in a world that's ruled by fear instead of love. God wants us to come to Him because we love Him, not because He leaves us no other choice."

"He allows this to go on." I gestured around The Strip.

"Colton," Marty said, smiling. "Evil isn't just in Vegas. It's everywhere. It's everywhere because it resides in our hearts, not just within the city limits. And none of this is God's will because He has a desire for it. It's in God's will because He wants us to be able to choose Him out of love, not fear. And sometimes our choices will have ugly consequences."

"Sure," I said. "And Malak will come to understand that."

Marty sighed. "Will you, Colton? Will you figure that out?"

CHAPTER THIRTY-SIX

The Esparanda was off The Strip in more ways than one. The crowds inside the casino weren't as large as those that filled the others, nor were they as sophisticated. For the most part, the people inside the Esparanda were younger, louder, and drunker. More hip but less in tune.

Marty stopped just inside the open doorway and began to scan the room.

"You don't know this guy, do you?" I asked.

He shook his head. "No. But I know his type."

I began scanning too, but Marty spotted him first.

"This way," he said, taking off toward the rear of the room.

Along the back wall, near the office and the slot machines, a group of young women sat clustered around a man with a dark complexion, dark hair, and dark eyes. He was lanky, with one long leg crossed over the other, and was wearing a black silk shirt over black leather pants. He had an earring in one ear and a long silver chain around his neck that featured a pentagram. His eyes were highlighted with eyeliner, and his teeth had been filed to resemble fangs.

"Let me handle this one, Colton," Marty said.

"You *do* know him, don't you?"

He shook his head. "No sir. But I know a couple of the young women with him."

Marty and I sauntered toward the group. The man was drinking beer from a long-necked bottle and was whispering something into the ear of one of the women who was sitting with him. She giggled and stood to leave when he spotted us.

"You Max?" Marty asked.

The smile began to erode from the man's face as he looked first at Marty and then at me.

"Who wants to know, Tex?"

Some of the girls giggled.

"I don't believe you answered my question," Marty said.

Despite the noise of the nearby slots, Marty's voice seemed to resonate within the small, cornered area of the casino.

The man stood. "I don't believe I have to, Tex."

Marty put a firm hand on the man's chest and pushed backward. He landed on the couch from which he had just stood.

None of the girls giggled this time.

"We're looking for a guy named Malak. And we've been told you are a friend of his."

The man's brow furrowed, and his face flushed. He had just been humiliated in front of his harem by a middle-aged guy in a Stetson and string tie. He stood again.

I moved to the right of Marty and let my jacket fall open. The butt of the holstered Ruger caught Max's eye.

"I ain't seen Malak for a long time," he said.

"Sure you ain't," I said.

The girls looked first to Max, then to Marty and me, and back to Max.

"I don't know if I believe him, Colton," Marty said. "He just don't have the look of someone who's reliable. Know what I mean?"

"I agree. Your perception of the nuances of human nature is impeccable."

"Take Amy over there, for instance," Marty said, nodding toward a young woman to the left of Max. "I've pulled her out of more than one predicament. And it was always with guys like this feller right here," he said. "Ain't that right, Amy?"

The young woman was dressed in a black leather halter, black leather pants, and spiked heels. Both of her ears, her nose, and her lower lip were all pierced and decorated with matching silver rings.

She turned her attention away from Marty.

"How 'bout you, Jenny?" Marty asked. "Remember the time your manager drove you to a party? Remember how it got out of hand?"

Similarly dressed, Jenny said, "Yes."

"And now here the two of you are, hanging with the same kind of guy but expecting things to be different."

"Watch your mouth, old man." Max was red faced now and back on his feet, moving toward Marty.

Marty shoved him onto the couch again.

Some of the women giggled this time.

"And now you can see how guys like this are all mouth. Paper tigers, preyin' on young women like you. They can't make you do anything unless you give 'em the power to take you to places you don't want to go."

Max's face was violet, and he was clenching his teeth. The muscles in his neck were twitching.

"Guys like this lie. They have to. How else could they ever attract women like you?"

Marty was attracting a crowd. I glanced at the cameras overhead.

"You can choose a different path," he said, turning in the direction of Amy and Jenny. "But you seem to be believin' a lie instead of the truth. It's not too late to turn around."

His voice was becoming almost shrill. Over my shoulder, I could see casino security approaching us.

"Look at him, ladies," Marty said. "Look how small and helpless he really is. How vulnerable he is."

I reached into my jacket and pulled a photo of Callie from my pocket. I tossed it on the table. "If any of you have seen her, let me know. My name is Colton Parker and I'm staying at the Eureka. She's my daughter."

Security was on us.

I turned to Max. "Tell Malak I'm coming," I said.

"Maybe," one of the guards said, placing a hand on both Marty and me. "But for now, you're leaving."

CHAPTER THIRTY-SEVEN

For a Bible-thumper, Marty was a lot of fun.

"I haven't been thrown out of a place like that for a long time," I said. "If it weren't for the seriousness of the situation, that would have been enjoyable."

We were walking along Flamingo Road, heading back toward The Strip. The night air remained cool and pleasant. I left my jacket on only to cover my gun.

"I lost control, Colton," Marty said. "I shouldn't have let my anger get the better of me. It isn't a good witness."

I smiled. "I don't think that Max or his harem is too interested in your witness, one way or the other. You talked to them on a level they understand. Whether it'll make any difference or not is up to them."

He shook his head and thrust his hands into the pockets of his jeans.

"Amy and Jenny are sisters," he said. "They come from Arlington Heights, a little town just north of Chicago. A couple of months ago, I got them away from one house, only to see them end up with someone like that."

He spit "that."

"You can't save them all," I said.

"No, I know I can't. But I sure wanted to get those two straightened out. Their father is dead, and their mother told me they've been a handful ever since he died."

"You talked with their mother?"

"Yes sir. I ran across them when one of my girls told me that they didn't belong. That she saw something in them that was redeemable, if they would just take hold of a helping hand. I tried to be father and protector."

As we continued to make our way toward The Strip, Marty sighed and looked briefly along the skyline before continuing.

"Amy was the first to go off-line," he said. "She ran away from home at nineteen and coerced her sister to do the same."

"Amy's the oldest?"

"No. Jenny was twenty-one at the time. And bein' as how they were legal adults, there was very little that anyone could do. None of us, not their mother, not me, not the police, could make them go home. But one night, Jenny's manager drove her to a party, and the party got out of control. Before long, Jenny was in way over her head, and her manager didn't intervene." He looked at me. "She almost died."

"And yet she's back," I said.

"Yes sir, she is. Kick in the head, ain't it?"

"All of that effort gone to waste," I said.

He shook his head. "No. None of it was wasted effort. Now the girls know that someone cares. They know the crop they reap is the one they've sown. They know where to go for help. And they know that nothing good can come from living a lie."

"You don't think they knew that before?"

We rounded the corner and began heading north toward my hotel.

He shrugged. "Maybe. Maybe not. Either way, they know it now. And now they're without excuse. And that's a bit of salvation in itself. Knowing how things stand, knowing the light from the dark. Knowledge like that can define their world. It's like a compass. Without it, they have no chance. With it, they can still get lost, but it won't be because they didn't know the way."

"The choice is theirs," I said.

"Yes sir. The choice is theirs."

CHAPTER THIRTY-EIGHT

Marty dropped me off at the hotel. By the time I got to my room, it was nearing eleven o'clock. I had a message on my phone.

"Colton, call me back."

It was Mary.

I removed my jacket and tossed it over a chair before sitting on the edge of the bed and calling Mary. She answered on the first ring.

"You must have been sitting on the phone," I said.

"I'm getting tired of this hotel room. I'm getting tired of this trial."

"How much longer?" I asked.

"A day. Maybe two. How're things going there?"

I told her everything I knew.

"You need me there, Colton. When I get out of here, I'll fly to Vegas. I have some AL coming."

AL, annual leave, was the bureau's term for vacation time. Mary had always been one of the hardest-working agents I had known. She rarely took time off, so using her annual leave was a clear indication of her commitment to me and to Callie.

"I'll be glad to see you," I said.

"You mean Clint Eastwood isn't filling the bill?"

"Actually, in a way, yes. He knows Vegas like the back of his hand. He's got a local madam looking for Callie."

"Well, maybe you don't need me after all."

"Yes, I do need you," I said. "I need you and Callie needs you."

Absence makes the heart grow fonder. In this case, it made the heart yearn.

"You might want to go back to the local police," Mary said. "Callie's fifteen. You may have a case of child endangerment, or—"

"Or we could drive all of our help underground."

There was a pause.

"I don't follow," she said.

I stood and slid the phone between my right ear and shoulder as I slipped my left arm out of the sling of my shoulder holster.

"We have madams, hookers, and bouncers keeping an eye out for Callie." I changed the phone to the other ear while I slid my right arm out of the holster's other sling. "Unless I have more to go on, I'm not going to endanger the help we have." I wrapped the straps around the holster and tossed the gun and rig onto the bed before sitting back down.

"Maybe," she said. "On the other hand, getting the police motivated and behind you will find Callie a lot faster."

"True. But right now, they're neither motivated nor behind me. If I have something on this guy they can use or something comes up that will get them involved, I'll tell them. Until then, I'm going to keep working the crowd, so to speak. Besides, this guy has gone underground. No driver's license, no credit cards. Nothing. Nothing that's in his name."

There was another pause.

"Any plans for tomorrow?" she asked.

I laid backward on the bed, allowing my feet to dangle over the side. "Marty and I are going to start looking through more of the houses."

"Houses?"

"Houses," I said.

A pause.

"Oh, houses."

"A friend of Marty's is keeping an eye out for us on the stationary ones. But we're going to start looking through the mobile ones. The mobile homes, trailers, and outcall services."

"You think Callie's involved in that?"

I sighed. "I don't know. I hope not. But right now, it's a lead I have to check out."

"Didn't you say this Malak is involved in the occult?"

"And that's next on our list."

"You could split up, you know."

"I don't know this town like Marty," I said. "I think I can cover more ground with him than without him."

"Sounds like you have all the help you need," she said. "If you don't need me…"

"Need you, yes. Want you…definitely."

CHAPTER THIRTY-NINE

I met Marty in the Koffee Konnection at six the next morning. As before, he was seated at a booth with a cup of coffee in one hand and a section of the newspaper folded lengthwise in the other. He raised his cup in a salute when I slid into the booth.

"We going to hit the roving houses today?" I asked.

Before Marty could answer, the waitress approached our table and poured me a cup of coffee without asking. After pouring, she paused. I took the cue.

"I'll have an egg, scrambled, and two slices of bacon."

She looked at Marty.

"Four eggs, two sausage patties, home-fried potatoes, and four pieces of wheat toast. Extra butter too, ma'am."

She moved away without writing anything down.

"Nope," he said, sliding the paper across the table. "Read this."

Marty had been reading some advertisements.

"Where?" I asked, scouring the paper.

He reached a big hand across the table and tapped the lower right-hand corner of the page with his index finger.

There was an ad for a New Age shop. It advertised books, crystals, and "everything for the discerning shopper."

"That's where we go next," Marty said.

"You don't think she's in one of the houses?"

He shook his head.

"Then why have we been spending all of our time chasing mad-ams and hookers and—"

"Ease up there, pardner," he said, looking about the restaurant. "No need to tell everyone your business."

A quick scan of the room revealed several glances coming our way.

"Especially," he said, "when it's *that* business." He smiled.

"Sorry," I said. "I'm a bit stressed."

He drank some of the coffee and eased back in the booth with his right arm over the back of the seat.

"Understandable."

"But it seems like we've spent a lot of time looking at prostitution, just to up and change direction so suddenly."

"Yes sir, it does. But we're not changing direction. We're just add-ing a direction."

I wasn't following.

Marty was about to speak again when the waitress brought our orders. She set them down in front of us, gave us a look that said if we wanted anything else we should speak now or forever hold our peace, and moved on.

Marty bowed to say grace and then reached for the salt. "We have never known for sure that Malak is involved in prostitution. But it seemed like the reasonable place to begin, because fifteen-year-old runaway girls have very few options for support. And Malak isn't known by the other girls in town." He paused to salt his eggs. "So we can assume he's running his girls through roving houses or forward-ing them on to a lockbox somewhere." He forked a bit of eggs.

"But we don't know that, right? We don't know what he's into other than young girls. In particular, my young girl."

Marty swallowed and moved the potatoes into a neat pile before scooping them onto his fork. "We know more than you might think. We know, for example, that he's into the occult. Remember?"

"Sure."

"And as you say, he's very heavy into young girls."

I drank some of my coffee.

"And we know he's violent," Marty said. "And we know that two of his friends have said they haven't seen him in a long time. And one of those friends hinted that Malak may be feeding these girls into a lockbox."

I pushed the cup of coffee and the plate of breakfast aside.

Marty continued to eat as if it was his last meal. "I'm thinkin' we should check out some of them New Age shops and see if he's been by any of those."

Marty knew Vegas well, and for that reason alone, Millikin was wise to hook us up. But the cowboy was also a shrewd judge of character.

"You should have been a cop," I said.

He had just raised his cup to his mouth but suspended it midhoist. He gave me a wry grin. "Not me, pardner. I spent too many of my years runnin' from 'em."

CHAPTER FORTY

The Nevada sun was playing tricks again. Although it had presented itself on time in the morning, it was now ducking behind a vast cluster of dark clouds. The temperature was still unseasonably cool, and that made the jacket I wore seem necessary for more than a cover for my gun.

The crowds had already begun to jell on the city's streets, and many people looked as if they had been up all night. I knew how they felt. Even though I had been in bed, I hadn't slept.

Marty and I climbed into his Caddy and drove for the northwest part of town. We took The Strip north to Charleston Boulevard and turned east. Marty was driving with one hand on the steering wheel and his left arm resting on the door frame. I was buckled in and scanning the streets for any signs of Callie.

"When I was running my girls," Marty said, "a lot of them were into drugs, booze, stuff like that. It goes with the territory."

"Sure," I said. I kept my eyes open.

"And a lot of them were into the occult. New Age stuff, mostly, but some of them were into some darker stuff too."

He eased into the left lane as we passed the Clark County Library. "Those girls—the ones that were darker—they just didn't care about anyone. They'd mess with the other girls, start fights, agitate the customers…just bad for business."

"And?"

"And I learned to recognize where they'd hang out. I learned to know who I wanted working for me and who I didn't."

We turned left onto a narrow residential side street.

"Sometimes one or two would slip by, but it didn't take long to learn who was good and who wasn't. When I learned the lingo, I learned how to stay out of trouble."

"Where we going?" I asked.

"Athena's Fountain of Wisdom."

"I'm going to go out on a limb here," I said, "and guess that this is probably not an institution of higher learning."

"You'd be safe on that limb," Marty said, pulling to the curb and turning off the engine.

"This it?" I asked.

"Yep."

The Fountain of Wisdom looked more like a two-story house in need of repair than a place in which to gain enlightenment. The building needed a new roof, a new sidewalk, new fence, new windows, and new shrubbery. A small electronic sign was jammed in an open window and flashed, Fountain of Wisdom. Another sign, tacked over the door, read, Welcome—All Open Minds.

"How many of these places are there?" I asked.

"Like this? Or all of them?"

"This place special?"

He shook his head. "No, not really. It's just that this one is more well-known. Been around a lot longer. Some of the others are in the backs of houses, in garages…a few in storefronts. The darker stuff is underground."

"You think Malak may have been here?" I asked.

Marty shook his head. "No, this is probably too sedate. Did you see the pentagram hanging around Max's neck the other night?"

I had. And I had seen the same symbol at Mason's apartment.

"I know Athena," Marty said. "She was one of my girls till she got into this."

We climbed out of the car and walked up the uneven sidewalk to the front door. When we entered the shop, a bell tinkled overhead. The smell of incense was overwhelming.

"An angel just got its wings," I said.

"Not in here he didn't," Marty said.

The big cowboy moved to a glass display case that stood on the right side of the room. The case had a cash register sitting on top and what seemed to be a thousand different items on the shelves inside. A slew of crystals, beads, incense burners, and other paraphernalia filled the case. I saw a box of less expensive-looking crystals sitting on top of the case, next to the register. I picked up a green one.

"This stuff looks like kryptonite," I said. "I wonder if Superman ever—"

"It's not kryptonite," a woman said, coming from a room in the rear of the store. "But I can assure you it's just as deadly when misused."

She was middle-aged and hard looking, and she wore a smock that featured stars and moons. She took the crystal from my hand and set it back into the box.

"What's the matter, Marty?" she asked. "Not enough girls to save, so now you're saving miscreants like this?"

"How you doin', Terry?" Marty asked.

"Terry's dead. Athena lives." She didn't smile.

I let out a low, long whistle.

"You don't believe in the power of the crystal?" she asked, directing her question to me.

I glanced at Marty who gave me a "be careful" look.

"I don't believe in anything anymore, Athena," I said. "I've been around too long. Seen too much."

She smiled. "Ah, a skeptic." She looked at Marty. "I love a challenge."

"We need your help, Athena," Marty said.

"Do you now?"

"Yes," he said.

She moved from behind the counter and began to pace about

the shop, stopping here and there to straighten a display or replace an item that had been set in the wrong place.

Marty sighed.

"Who is it this time, Marty? One of your girls goes off the deep end, and some mean old New Ager is to blame?"

Marty was about to speak, but I cut him off.

"My daughter is missing. She's run away from home."

The woman abruptly turned to face me. "And how am I supposed to help you, Superman?"

"You may know the man she's with," Marty said.

"And why would I know that?" Her question was directed at Marty, but her eyes were fixed on me.

I didn't know how to answer her. I was out of my depth. I knew where to find missing teens. I even knew the trouble they could get into. But I didn't know Las Vegas. I knew sin, but I wasn't familiar with its capital city.

"Because the man she's with is into the occult," Marty said.

"So?"

"So you know this town," Marty said. "You knew it before I introduced you to it."

She nodded. She smiled. She was being coy.

"You did introduce me to it, didn't you? And then you found religion, and everyone is supposed to follow you in that too. Right?"

Marty said nothing.

My patience was waning.

"I have a daughter who's run away with someone who means her harm."

"And she ran away with him?" Athena asked. "Why would she run away with a man who means her harm?"

I moved in on the woman. "Malak. I'm looking for Malak."

The woman's eyes diverted.

"Where is he?" I asked, closing the distance between us.

She looked at me again and then past me toward Marty. "You helping him?"

"Yes."

She studied Marty for a second or two and then turned her attention back to me. "Malak is on the fringe. He isn't into the occult; he's into Satanism."

"There's a difference?" I asked.

The woman's face hardened. "Yes." She moved back toward the counter and reached toward a small rack of literature. She tossed a booklet to me. "Read this. It will tell you about us."

The book was an introduction to New Age beliefs. I tossed it back. "I don't care what you believe," I said. "And I don't care what Malak thinks about you or what you think about him. All I want to know is where my daughter is."

The woman seemed to soften. The barrier between Marty and her didn't seem to separate her and me.

"I haven't seen him in a long time. The last I heard, he was leaving town. Things were getting too hot for him."

"Why?"

"He had a run-in with a cop. The official version was road rage, but we all knew it went a lot deeper than that." She pulled a stool up and sat down behind the counter, wrapping her flowing gown behind her.

"The cop and he had a personal beef?"

"Yeah. *Very* personal."

"How?"

"Leroy had started moving in on the cop's daughter. She wasn't legal at the time, but by the time her dad discovered what was going on, she was. That didn't stop her old man from trying to get the guy on statutory. Know what I mean?"

"Sure," I said.

"But for some reason, the charges were never brought. The whole thing just kind of died down. No one heard any more about it until Leroy was involved in a scene on 15."

I must have looked confused. Before I could ask, Marty said, "Interstate 15."

The woman ignored Marty.

"What kind of scene?" I asked.

"No one knows for sure, but it involved Leroy and the girl's dad."

"Leroy was arrested?" I asked.

The woman nodded. "Yeah, but charges were dropped."

"Because it was the same cop involved?"

She smiled. "Partly. Most people think the charges were dropped because the cop was the girl's dad and the whole thing smelled too much like a setup."

"Sounds like it was."

The woman looked at Marty and smiled. "That's what I said."

"What happened after that?" I asked.

"Leroy disappeared. Left the girl with a broken heart and the cop with a loss in his column."

"Was foul play ever suspected?"

"You mean did anyone ever think that the cop took old Leroy for a ride?"

"Right."

She dismissed the notion with a wave of the hand. "No. We all knew that Leroy left on his own. And we all knew he'd come back one day."

"Who's we?" I asked.

She waved an arm around the store.

"All of us," she said. "I may be a religious person, but I'm also a business woman. I sell the things that other religions need."

"Why is Malak coming back?" I asked.

"Because his power grows. He has been attracting followers. Some from the Internet, some through...other means," she said cryptically. "And these followers are devoted. They've been very active since he's been away. That's a safe bet that Malak is returning." She glanced at Marty. "In force."

CHAPTER FORTY-ONE

Roper was in and was busy doing paperwork. He seemed grateful for the interruption.

"You're kidding, right?"

"That's what she told us," I said. "Malak is coming back…in force."

He turned his seat to face his monitor and typed some information into his computer before picking up his phone and dialing a four-digit number. "We're putting everything on computer now," he said to Marty and me, "but it takes time. Chances are, the file on Devlin hasn't been scanned yet. The case is closed, so it will have low priority."

Someone on the other end answered, and the detective asked her to send the file over. He gave her the case number and hung up.

"I don't remember too much about all of that," Roper said, "because I wasn't in Central when all of that went down."

"Who was the officer that mixed it up with Devlin?" I asked.

Roper shrugged. "Search me. Like I said, I wasn't here."

I was sitting in a chair in front of Roper's desk. Marty was sitting on the edge of a metal table to one side of the detective's office with hat in hand.

"I don't like the sound of what she said," Marty said.

"What's that?" Roper asked.

"That Malak is growing stronger and that his followers are waiting for his return."

Roper grinned. "Sounds like a cult. Sounds like some crazies…"

Marty wasn't amused.

"Terry isn't a nut, detective," he said. "When I was in the business, she was as shrewd as they come. Very savvy. She knew exactly who to deal with and which palms to grease."

The grin vanished from Roper's face. "Yeah, I've heard you imply that kind of thing before. If you got something to say, then say it. If you think some of my cops are on the take, tell me. Otherwise, I'd suggest you keep your mouth shut."

Marty was about to say something but thought better of it and closed his mouth.

Roper, though, was still agitated and was about to speak when a young woman came into his office with a medium-sized file.

"This is the file you wanted," she said, handing the folder to Roper.

He thanked her, and she left without acknowledging Marty or me.

Roper opened the file and leaned back in his chair to read. I remained silent. Marty helped himself to a cup of the detective's coffee.

After a few minutes, Roper said, "Looks like your soothsayer might be right. At least as far as the department is concerned."

"The whole thing was a setup?" I asked.

Roper was still leaning back in his chair with one leg crossed over the other and the open file on his lap.

"The officer involved was livid when he discovered his teenage daughter was dating Devlin. The file shows that he accosted Devlin on two occasions and that a scuffle ensued on at least one of them." He flipped the page. "Then, and this is where it gets bad for the officer, Devlin lodged a complaint. When the department investigated, it found no evidence that the officer had assaulted anyone, but it did find witnesses who said the officer had threatened Devlin."

"That explains the reason why the case of road rage never came to trial," I said.

Roper said, "Yep. After the whole incident was over, nothing more came of it, and the officer left not long after."

"Left?" I asked.

"The department," Roper said. "He quit."

"Any reason given?"

Roper shook his head. "Not according to this. Just turned in his badge."

"That's unusual," I said. "Good cops just don't quit."

"He did," Roper said.

I looked at Marty. He was drinking coffee.

"Who was the officer that investigated the road-rage incident?" I asked.

Roper said, "Jennifer Kleinman."

"She still with the department?" I asked.

"Yeah," Roper said. "I know her."

"Straight?"

"As they come," he said.

"Any chance we could talk to her?"

Roper shrugged. "I can try. If she's on duty, I can ask dispatch to have her meet you somewhere."

I looked at Marty. He shrugged.

"Okay," I said. "Do it."

Roper picked up the phone again and dialed. He waited until someone came on the line and then asked if Kleinman was working. He paused, covering the mouthpiece with his hand.

"She's on patrol. Where do you want her to meet you?"

I looked at Marty.

"The Koffee Konnection sounds as good as any," he said.

I turned back to Roper. "The Koffee Konnection. It's in the Eureka."

Roper told the dispatch to have Kleinman meet us at the coffee shop.

"Okay," he said to us, after ending the call. "She'll be there."

Marty finished the last of the coffee and turned to leave the room. I allowed him to go ahead of me, and as soon as he was out of earshot, I said, "One more thing. Can you check into someone for me? Maybe call me later and let me know what you've got?"

Roper looked over my shoulder toward the departing cowboy. "Sure," he said. "What's the name?"

CHAPTER FORTY-TWO

Officer Jennifer Kleinman arrived at the restaurant ahead of Marty and me. It was midmorning, so the place was nearly empty.

"Thanks for meeting us," I said after introducing Marty and myself.

"Dispatch said you wanted to talk to me about an old case?"

"Yes." I motioned toward one of the booths. Marty and I sat on one side, and officer Kleinman sat on the other.

"You investigated a road-rage incident about two years ago on I-15," I said. "It involved—"

"You talking about the one with some nut-job devil worshipper?"

"That'd be the one."

"You guys lawyers or something?"

I looked at Marty, who seemed amused.

"Him?" I asked. "Have you been watching reruns of *McCloud?*"

"And what's wrong with *McCloud?*" Marty asked. "It was a good show."

Jennifer asked, "What's *McCloud?*"

Marty said, "It was a show that—"

I held up a hand. "It doesn't matter. But to answer your question, no. We're not attorneys."

She seemed skeptical. "Then what do you want?"

"My daughter has run away from home. I have reason to believe that she might be with Leroy Devlin."

She rolled her eyes. "Your daughter has a strange taste in men."

"She doesn't have a taste in men. She's fifteen."

Before the officer could respond, a waitress appeared.

"Howdy," she said. "Are you ready to order?"

None of us had looked at a menu, but Marty and Jennifer seemed to know what they wanted. Despite the midmorning hour, they both ordered lunch. I had coffee.

"Sorry about the wisecrack," the officer said after the waitress left.

I dismissed it.

"I'm looking for Devlin, and everyone we talk with hasn't seen him in a long time."

"Last I heard, he left town," she said.

"He did. He came to Indianapolis."

"Is that where you're from?"

"Yes."

She shook her head. "I pity Indy."

The waitress came back with my coffee and two iced teas for Marty and Jennifer. After she left, Marty opened a packet of sugar for his tea and extended the caddy full of sweetener to the officer. She declined.

"I think Devlin is back in town," I said.

She snorted.

"We know that the officer that had a run-in with Devlin was pursuing him on a personal level," Marty said.

"And we don't care," I added.

"Good. Teddy was one of the best cops this city ever had."

"Why did he quit?" Marty asked.

She shrugged. "I don't know. Pressure, I guess. He was getting a lot of heat from the brass over the fact that he let a personal situation turn into a crusade that ended up involving the department."

"I was a cop too," I said. "And I know how much pressure the higher-ups can bring. But good cops are cops who like what they do. Those guys don't just up and quit."

"Yeah. That's what I know. It just doesn't make any sense." She shook her head. "I guess he just couldn't take the heat anymore."

The waitress brought the food that Marty and Jennifer had ordered. After setting the plates in their place, she dropped the checks on the table and left.

"Did you know him well?" I asked.

She reached for the ketchup and began pouring it on her onion rings.

"Well enough. I knew he had a reputation for being a stand-up guy. And that he was a good cop. We backed up each other on occasion, but that was as far as it went. We never socialized or anything." She ate an onion ring.

"Did you witness any of the pressure?"

Marty was having a rib-eye sandwich. He bit into it and reached for a French fry at the same time.

Jennifer shook her head. "No, I didn't see anything. But I could see Teddy just…melting away."

"What do you mean?"

She shrugged again as she chewed around an onion ring. "I don't know, specifically. Just little stuff, you know? He would come in late. Miss calls. Sometimes he'd get a little too aggressive with suspects. Or spout off to some of us." She picked up another onion ring. "He just wasn't the Teddy we had known before."

"Did he tell anyone he was getting pressure from upstairs?"

She shook her head. "If he did, he didn't tell me." She ate the ring.

"So you're assuming he resigned because of pressure," I said. "But you don't know for sure."

She picked up her hamburger. "We all assumed. It was scuttlebutt." She bit into the burger.

"That doesn't mean it didn't come down like that," Marty said. "Scuttlebutt often has its basis in fact."

I drank some coffee. "Have you stayed in touch?" I asked.

She shook her head. "No. Like I said, we didn't socialize."

"Any idea where he's at? What he's doing?"

"Is he going to hear this from me?"

"No."

She patted her mouth with a napkin.

"He's working floor security at the Dover."

I looked at Marty.

"It's a small casino off The Strip, way north of town."

I reached for the checks. "Do you think it'd be worth our time to talk to him?" I asked her.

She smiled. "He's been waiting to meet someone like you for a long time."

CHAPTER FORTY-THREE

After I paid for lunch, Marty and I drove north of town to the Dover.

The casino was located in one of the many strip malls that lined Las Vegas' streets and was neighbored by a newsstand and a small grocery store. For the most part, the customers were older and more sedate than the people who were flocking to Las Vegas Boulevard. These people weren't here for bustle and show. They were here to gamble.

We entered the casino and saw a bar that ran along the left wall and a small coffee shop and gift store that lined the other. An impressive grouping of slots and gaming tables filled the central core.

"See anyone who looks like security?" I asked.

Marty was already glancing around. "Yeah, but no one in uniform."

"Why is it that you can't get thrown out of a gambling joint when you want to?"

"We didn't have any problem at the Esparanda," Marty said.

"I believe that was because you were accosting a man and his harem."

Marty lowered his head. "I was wrong to do that, Colton. I lost control of myself."

"Felt good though, didn't it?"

"Yes. But it don't make it right."

I was about to tell the cowboy how I would probably have handled it a lot worse than he did, but I paused when a young, scantily clad waitress approached us. She was carrying an empty cocktail tray that provided her with more coverage than the uniform she was wearing.

She asked us if we wanted anything.

"We'd like to talk to Teddy," I said, not knowing for sure if the man was working.

The woman smiled. "Sure." She turned toward the rear of the building and pointed to a man in a dark suit standing near the office. "That's him," she said.

We thanked her, and worked our way back to where Teddy was standing. As alert as any cop, he stiffened when we approached and kept a wary eye on our hands.

"Can I help you?" he asked.

"We're hoping so," I said. "My name is Colton Parker, and this is Marty Cruise. We'd like to talk to you about Leroy Devlin."

Teddy's eyes went from me to Marty and back again. "Who sent you?" he asked.

"No one sent us," I said. "We—"

"I'm not running anymore. You want to jack with me? Bring it on."

I looked at Marty. It was the first time I had seen the man dumbfounded.

"We don't want you to run," I said. "In fact, we've spent most of the morning trying to find you."

Like any good cop, ex or otherwise, he was suspicious. "Why would you want to find me?"

"Because I'm trying to find my daughter, and finding Devlin seems to be the best way to do that."

"And we thought you might be the best way to find Devlin," Marty said.

"We hope," I added, with the most endearing smile I could muster.

The man was tall, solid as an oak, and had a thin layer of salt-and-pepper hair. His cold blue eyes began to warm with the new revelation.

"Devlin messing with your daughter?" he asked.

"I think she's with him," I said.

The ex-cop looked at Marty and back to me. "Come on upstairs."

He led us to a stairwell camouflaged behind a nondescript door as he pulled a radio off his belt. He told someone on the other end to take over while he was on break.

The narrow steps led us to an equally narrow hallway. He took us to the third door on the right and into a small office.

The room was a great deal less garish than the casino below. Smaller than the men's room in one of the larger establishments on The Strip, the office was painted in a tasteful yellow with off-white curtains framing the small window that overlooked the floor. The office was furnished with two desks and two chairs. A water cooler stood in one corner.

"Have a seat," Teddy said, sitting behind one of the desks.

I took a seat in front of Teddy's desk. Marty sat behind the other desk.

"Your daughter ran away?" the guard asked.

"From Indianapolis. I have reason to suspect she's under Devlin's influence." I told him most of what I knew.

He sat with one leg crossed over the other. He drummed his fingers on the arms of the chair. "How'd you know I had a problem with Devlin?"

"It isn't exactly a secret," I said.

"It is outside the department," he said. "Who'd you talk to?"

"It don't matter," Marty said. "What matters is that we find his little girl."

Teddy knew we'd never give up our source. He also knew our nemesis, and that made us kindred spirits.

"Devlin was seeing Leah. I didn't find out about it until she turned eighteen."

"He started seeing her when she was a minor?"

"Seventeen. But the age difference didn't bother me as much as the dude himself. He'd been known to vice for years."

I looked at Marty. "We didn't hear anything like that."

"You won't," the ex-cop said. "Devlin's never been convicted of a crime. But he's always on the scene."

"On the periphery but never at the center?"

"Yeah. Do you know much about him?"

"Not as much as I'd like to," I said. "But I know guys like him. I used to be a cop."

The man's eyes had warmed before when I revealed that I had the same issue with Devlin that he did. But now his stone facade crumbled completely. A benefit of the brotherhood of the badge.

"When I found out Leah was seeing this guy, I was livid. I went after him right away. Know what I'm saying?"

Marty and I said we did.

"But when I ran into him, he had this…look. Weird. Like he was pure evil in the flesh." He shook his head. "I told him to stay away from my daughter. He said she was legal, and if he wanted to see her, he would." He ceased the drumming and began massaging his fist with one hand. "I decked him."

"Witnesses?" I asked.

He shrugged. "If there were, they never came forward. Besides, I didn't care. We were talking about my daughter. Understand?"

"Perfectly," I said.

"He's a big dude. But he just kind of laid there on the ground, looking up at me." He shook his head. "I thought it was over, but it wasn't. He kept coming after Leah."

"Persistent," I said.

Teddy grinned. "So was I. I came home one day and saw his car pulling out of my driveway. When I did, I just kind of lost it." He looked at me. "Cops aren't supposed to do that."

"Says who?"

He grinned again. "Yeah, well…anyway, I followed him." He folded his hands around his knee. "I wanted to get him alone. Kill him. You know?"

I did, but said nothing.

"We got onto I-15, and he started slowing down. Real slow. Kind of like he was daring me to do something. Like part of the reason he was messing with my daughter was because he knew it got to me." He sighed. "That's when I totally lost it. I ran him off the road and pulled him out of the car. Then things got out of hand."

"You assaulted him?" I asked.

"That'd be putting it mildly. Anyway, before I knew it, I had him cuffed and laying facedown on the hood of my squad car."

"Were you on duty?" Marty asked.

"No, I had just gotten off duty. But I was still in uniform, so witnesses saw this as a police brutality thing." He shook his head in disgust. "The thing never went to trial because he made it into a personal issue, and the whole thing was just dropped."

"It *was* a personal issue," I said. "Understandable. But personal."

Teddy glanced at the large clock on the wall. "You guys got any other questions? I've got to be getting back on the floor."

"Just a couple more," I said.

"Why'd you quit?" Marty asked.

Teddy sighed. "I was forced out."

"*Forced* out?" the cowboy asked.

"Not by the department. It was by Devlin's crowd."

"How did they force a sitting police officer to resign from the department?" I asked.

"They got to me through Leah."

"Did they threaten her?" I asked.

He shook his head. "No, not in so many words. But they had her. You know? She had become so enthralled with Devlin that she would do anything to be with him. When I first found out she was involved with the guy, I told her she had to stay away from him." His eyes became red as they developed that faraway look that accompanies special memories. Especially painful ones. "She told me where to go." His lower lip began to quiver. He cleared his throat. "That's when I went after Devlin. That's when it became a game between him and me, with Leah as the prize."

"What did they do to make you quit?" I asked, rephrasing Marty's question.

"They put money into my bank account. They told me they'd say I was on the take. Then we started getting a rash of calls about people's animals turning up dead. Cats and dogs were being found shot, run over, cut up. The department opened a file and began investigating."

"And?" I asked.

He began drumming on the arms of his chair again. "I got a call telling me that 'they' had done it. The voice wasn't Devlin's."

"And you didn't say anything?" I asked, hearing my own disbelief.

"What could I say? That Devlin was behind it? Who would believe me after I'd been accused of having a personal issue with the man?"

I glanced at Marty.

"Did you consider charges for statutory?" I asked.

He nodded. "Yeah, but Leah said she would deny it ever happened. Without witnesses, I didn't have a chance of making them stick."

"So what happened next?" I asked.

"They said they wanted me off the department. By this time, Leah and Devlin had ended their…whatever it was, so he was no longer a threat. But he had me." He stood. "My time was over twenty anyway. I didn't want to lose my pension by getting jammed up over some accusation of bribery."

"Or worse," I said. "Your daughter was done with this guy, so you had more to lose than gain by going after him."

"That's the way I looked at it," he said, standing and moving toward the door. "I've got to get back on the floor. You guys got any more questions?"

"Where is Leah now?" I asked.

He shrugged. "I don't know. She never calls. I guess she doesn't want anything to do with her old man."

He left the office, leaving Marty and me to ourselves.

"I think I might know where she is," Marty said.

CHAPTER FORTY-FOUR

We drove west of the Dover, toward a rim of mountains that was beginning to see new development.

"Folks out here are trying to get away from all the hoopla," Marty said. "But of course, they can't."

"Hoopla keeps me in business," I said.

The ex-brothel-owner-turned-savior replied, "Me too."

We reached an area at the base of the mountains that was a hodge-podge of newer homes, older homes, and trailers. Marty pulled off the road and onto a gravel lot before parking in front of a small camper.

"This is one of them roving houses I was telling you about," Marty said.

"Appearing this week on the west side of Sin City," I said, more to myself than to the cowboy.

"That's pretty much the way it is." He nodded toward the trailer. "This here was on the north side last week. It rotates on different schedules but usually shows up at the same place each time. That's how I knew it would be here today."

"I thought we were going to work the cult places," I said. "What're we doing here?"

"When Teddy told us about his daughter, the story sounded famil-iar. I've been working with a girl whose story is similar."

"Leah?"

"I don't know. The girl I know is called Lucinda. But she knew a girl who was at odds with her father and whose father tried to rough up a man she was seeing. I never met her friend, but Lucinda talked about her a lot."

"She here?"

"Yep. It's why we're here. I met with her last week. I was just startin' to make some headway when a john showed up. She told me I had to leave."

"Why didn't you just call the cops? Seems to me you had the upper hand."

"If I call the cops on an operation, and *if* they do something about it, the girl will pay. And she'll pay heavily." He turned to look at me. "If that happens, no one will ever trust me again. My sources will dry up, my funding will dry up, and I'll never be able to help anyone again. Ever."

"Sure. Tread softly."

"Whenever I can. On the other hand, I'll do whatever has to be done to help one of these girls. But I try to take the long-term view. This stuff is never going to go away. Not as long as customers are willing to pay."

I saw a curtain pull away from one of the small windows at the rear. I couldn't see a face.

"Customer in there," he said. "He won't come out as long as we're here." He started the car. "Let's take a ride."

We pulled away from the lot and began driving toward the base of the nearby mountains. After reaching a turnaround, we began our steady descent. We arrived back at the trailer fifteen minutes after we left. The curtain was open.

"We're okay," Marty said, pulling into the lot again. "She'll talk to us now."

We got out of the car and were immediately greeted at the door by a young waif who was already developing the hard look of the resigned. She had long, stringy blonde hair, high cheekbones, and teeth that protruded. Her arms were thin and bore the tracks of someone who has traveled too far too soon.

"Hi, Marty," she said without looking at me.

"Hey, sweetums. How are you?" He hugged her.

"I'm okay," she said.

"Lucinda, this is Colton Parker. He's a private detective."

She stiffened, and her reaction didn't go unnoticed by the cowboy.

"Can we come in?" he asked.

Before answering, she looked at me again but with a more penetrating gaze.

"Okay," she said, moving into the trailer and allowing Marty and me to follow her.

The three of us went inside, and I closed the door, sealing off the small bit of sunshine that had managed to pierce the despair.

Two reclining chairs, a small lamp, and two air mattresses sat on a thin, heavily stained orange carpet.

The girl dropped into one of the chairs.

I watched as she eyed Marty with suspicion. His use of the term "private detective" had not been random.

"I ain't going back," she said. "I'm twenty-one. I can do whatever I want."

Marty sat in the other chair while I stood.

"You're not going back?" he asked.

She shook her head and looked at me again.

"I'm not here to take you back," he said.

"You're not?"

Marty shook his head. "No, I'm not. You can do whatever you like now."

Although the girl should have been relieved, she clearly wasn't. "Are you going to quit coming around?"

"No. I'll never stop caring." He smiled. Then he asked about Leah.

Lucinda said no one had seen Leah in weeks. Since Marty seemed convinced that she hadn't gotten out of the business, her invisibility strongly suggested she was either dead or in a lockbox. Either way, our chance of finding her didn't seem good.

Marty sighed and changed his approach. "Colton is looking for his daughter. She's run away."

The girl directed her attention to me. "Where did she run away from?" she asked.

"Indianapolis."

Lucinda frowned and began twirling her hair with one finger. "That's a long way from here."

"Yes."

"We think she might be in town," Marty said.

The girl continued to twirl her hair.

"We think she might be in a roving house," Marty said.

I handed her a picture of Callie.

"This her?" she asked.

"Yes."

"She's young."

"Fifteen," I said.

The girl studied Callie's picture as she continued to twirl her hair. "She with somebody?" she asked.

"Malak," Marty said.

The girl handed the picture back to me.

"Do you know Malak?" I asked.

She shook her head.

"Sweetie," Marty said, "if you know where this girl is, or if you know where we can find Leroy, tell us."

She sighed and looked at me again. "Is she a good girl?"

"Yes," I said.

The girl pursed her lips as she studied Callie's photo. "You need to talk to a guy named Max Minor."

I looked at Marty.

"Do you mean the guy who works at the Esparanda?" he asked.

She seemed surprised. "Yeah. Do you know him?"

"Not as well as we thought," Marty said.

"We've talked to him once," I said. "And I don't think we made much of an impression on him."

The girl gave Marty a puzzled look.

"We got thrown out of the casino," he said. "Lickety-split."

"Do you want me to set it up?" she asked. "I know him. He'd agree to meet if he thought I was coming."

Marty looked at me.

"Sounds like an offer we can't refuse," I said.

"Okay," Marty said to the girl. "Set 'er up."

CHAPTER FORTY-FIVE

Lucinda gave us directions to an apartment on the city's near west side. She said this was where Max lived and partied and that she knew this from firsthand experience.

We left the small camper and climbed into Marty's car as the Nevada sun began to put out the heat for which Vegas was famous.

Neither Marty nor I spoke for a while as the cowboy drove toward The Strip with increasing speed. As soon as we reached it, the throng of jaywalkers began to thicken, slowing our progress. In a few minutes, Marty found the street he wanted and turned west.

"This is the way to Max's place," he said.

I watched in the rearview mirror as The Strip began to recede, and the neighborhood that preceded Max's place came into view ahead.

They were nice homes—all of them. And they seemed to be filled with families who were at peace with each other and had no knowledge of the evil that hemmed them in on every side.

After a few minutes more, we came out of the nicer area and drove into one that resembled every inner city neighborhood I had ever seen. Apartments were housed in concrete block buildings with gang graffiti painted across the walls. Idle young men stood on the sidewalks or sat on the hoods of their cars, talking, drinking, and watching outsiders. Especially outsiders who drove a white, late-model Cadillac.

"We stand out," I said.

"Yes sir."

"That doesn't bother you?"

"No sir."

I began to see the real Marty for the first time. The white hat, the white car, the silver-plated watch and silver-tipped string tie—they all pointed to the Lone Ranger. A righteous man on a righteous mission who wouldn't stoop to the common solution. A man who lived by a creed that was his own.

"You believe that right makes might," I said.

"Yes sir, I do."

"That makes you different," I said, recalling the opposite notion I had seen on the satanic websites.

"Well, I hope not. I'd like to think that as long as the righteous outnumber the unrighteous, we can continue to survive as a society. Of course, none of us are really righteous." He shook his head. "No sir, not a single one of us."

We drove on for a few more blocks before turning to our right as we began heading north at a slower pace. Marty was looking to his left. Several young men, mostly Hispanic, were looking back.

Marty stopped the car.

"Here we go," he said, putting it into reverse and backing up to an entryway we had just driven past.

He shoved the transmission into drive and turned the steering wheel with the heel of one hand as we turned into the complex.

"Which building did she say?" I asked, trying to recall what Lucinda had told us.

"Forty forty-nine," he said. "Apartment G."

No sooner had he spoken than we came upon a pink building that had lime green gang graffiti spray painted across its outer face. The address was on the front, near the door. We pulled into a stall, and Marty turned off the car.

"This might be tough going in there," he said.

"And?"

"And I don't want this thing to get out of hand." He gave me a knowing look. "Callie is your daughter, and I don't want you losing control."

I laughed. "Aren't you the one who had the problem with our friend in there?"

He nodded. "Yes sir, you're right. And I still feel bad about it."

Wanting to get on with it, I reassured him I would remain in control of myself.

"Okay," he said. "But there's one more thing."

I arched my eyebrows.

"These gang members," he nodded to the young men all around us, "won't take kindly to your piece." He looked toward my jacket.

"You want me to go without a gun?"

He said nothing.

"Forget it, Marty."

He sighed. "Okay, but at least take off the jacket and tuck the pistol in your belt. It's hot outside and the jacket gives you away."

I slipped out of the coat and shoulder rig, sliding both of them under the front seat. I undid my seat harness and tucked the gun in the small of my back, covering it with my shirttail.

As we walked toward the entrance of the building, I noticed that the young men who had been watching as we drove in were staring even more intently as we approached the entryway.

We entered the building by way of a small foyer. A row of dilapidated mailboxes lined the wall to my left, and a TV was blaring behind the door of one of the apartments on the first floor. The walls were partially covered with burgundy colored wallpaper, and rodent droppings littered the floor.

"Lucinda said Max lives in apartment G," Marty said, scanning the mailboxes.

"Upstairs," I said. "A through D is down here. Judging from the layout, G would be near the left-rear of the building."

"The second floor is only about ten feet above ground level," Marty said.

I got the hint.

"I'll go outside and stay by the window," I said. "If you can get him inside, signal me and I'll come in. If he bails, I'll stop him."

I left to go outside, and around to Max's apartment. I positioned myself where I could see his window if he tried to escape but close to the building so he wouldn't be able to get a shot at me.

I had to shield my eyes against the sun. It continued its relentless pounding as visible waves of heat emanated from the crumbled asphalt. Heat of another kind came from the narrow-eyed gaze of the gang members.

I tried to keep an eye on the window and on the men who were keeping an eye on me. I also tried to appear as casual as I could while I waited for Marty to signal me to come back in—or for Max to open the window and jump. But the longer I waited, the more agitated I became. And the more agitated I became, the more interested the local gang members seemed to become.

I tried to inconspicuously keep one hand to my brow and shield my eyes from the sun so I could have an unhindered view of the window. I kept the other hanging loosely at my side but within reach of the pistol. Occasionally, I wiped sweat from my brow and glanced around the complex. Some of the gang members remained interested and continued to watch. A few of them huddled together in groups of two or three and talked among themselves. From their body language, I could tell I was the topic of conversation.

Nearly ten minutes passed without a signal. I was getting concerned.

Deciding that Max would have jumped by now if he were going to, and concerned that I might be on the verge of igniting gang warfare, I left my post and went into the building.

Glad to be out of the penetrating sun, I allowed my eyes to adjust to the darkness as I climbed the steps to Max's apartment. When I reached the second floor, I saw that the door to apartment G was partially open.

"Marty?"

I was answered by the echo of my own call. I pulled the Ruger from my waistband.

"Marty?" I called again.

Nothing.

I held the Ruger in one hand as I pushed open the door with the other.

The apartment was empty—except for Marty Cruise. His body was lying on the blood-stained carpet.

CHAPTER FORTY-SIX

The officers of the Las Vegas Police Department's Central Division have seen everything. After all, they're charged with policing Sin City. But when I called and told them that Marty Cruise had been murdered, they were in disbelief. Until they saw the body.

"I can't believe this," Roper said. "Marty's walked these streets for years. He had the respect of everyone. And the few times he didn't, he was more than capable of taking care of himself."

We were kneeling over Marty's body. He had been laying face-down when I found him, but after the photographers had taken the pictures they needed, Roper and a couple of his detectives rolled the body over. Multiple stab wounds pierced the cowboy's upper torso.

"More than one attacker," I said.

Roper grimaced. "Or he was caught off guard."

I shook my head. "Uh-uh. This guy was always on guard."

Roper stood and ran a hand over his head. I stood with him.

"He was a big guy," he said. "Strong. If it was one man, he had to be a monster to subdue Marty."

I leaned over the still-warm body.

"The wounds are different," I said. "They're similar but not exact." I pointed to two wounds in the central portion of Marty's chest and to two along his side.

"Different depths," Roper said. "That could mean we're dealing with two attackers."

"Or three," I said. "Probably one to subdue him while the other two killed him."

"Or two, and both jumped him at the same time. Or one who was very aggressive and had to fight Marty's defenses at the same time."

Roper knelt again to examine Marty's hands and wrists.

"Look at these bruises. Whoever came after Marty got more than he bargained for." He examined a tan line on Marty's left wrist. "His watch is missing."

"Robbery wasn't a motive," I said. "We were set up."

Roper eased Marty's wrist to the floor and gently rolled him to one side as he retrieved the cowboy's billfold.

"Several twenties and a couple of tens here," he said.

I told him about our conversation with Lucinda and how she had directed Marty and me to meet Max at this apartment.

"Where is this Lucinda?" Roper asked.

I told him.

"You say she seemed to know Marty?" Roper asked.

"Yep. And she seemed to know Leah."

Roper looked confused.

"Teddy's daughter," I said.

One of the lab techs interrupted us. "Detective, you probably need to see this."

Roper stood and gestured for me to follow him.

The tech led us out of the apartment and to the rear of the second floor. A door in an alcove was partially obscured by the slope of the floor. We walked down the few steps to the door. There was blood on the doorknob and frame.

"The murderer must have left through here," the tech said. "We found blood on the other side of this door and on the doorknob of the rear door that leads out of the building."

I cursed.

"I was waiting outside," I said, "in case Minor leapt through the window. It seemed logical at the time."

"Sure," Roper said. "If Marty was in the apartment, it would be reasonable to assume that the only way out for someone like Minor would have been to jump." He turned to the lab tech. "We're going back to the station. Keep me posted on anything you find."

He assured him he would. I was flabbergasted. "That's it?"

"Excuse me?" Roper said, with a confused look.

"There were a slew of gang members standing around," I said. "If the murderer or murderers left through the rear door, someone had to have seen them."

"You're suggesting we interview them?"

"What do you think?"

"I think we know how to do our job."

I was about to lay into him.

"Which means we'll interview those guys, along with a hundred other things we'll do. But that doesn't mean they're going to spill their spit. After all, you were a cop too, right?"

"Yes," I said, running a hand through my hair.

"How many times did you see a gang member rat on anyone?"

CHAPTER FORTY-SEVEN

The drive back to the station was quiet. I knew Roper was right and that we'd get no supportive witness from the gang members we'd seen in the complex. But the growing frustration over not being able to find Callie, combined with the death of a man I had grown to admire—one who had put everything on the line for a total stranger—was moving me closer and closer to the edge. The promise I had made to Marty about maintaining self-control was becoming increasingly difficult to keep.

"Sorry about the crack back there," I said.

Roper shrugged it off. "Marty's death is bringing us into your case now," he said as he steered the car into the lot of Central Division headquarters. "So in a sense, Marty will finish what he started." The detective parked the car. "He'll get to help you find your daughter."

We entered the station and moved to a small interrogation room that looked like every other interrogation room I had ever seen.

Max Minor was seated at the table. Roper had his men pick Minor up at the obvious place to look—the Esparanda. His demeanor wasn't as arrogant as the last time we had met, but he was as self-assured as ever. A smirk animated his otherwise dour expression.

"Hello, Max," Roper said, settling into the chair across from the man.

Max's smirk grew into a full-blown grin as he kept his eyes on me rather than the detective who would work hard to put him away.

"Mind telling us where you were a couple of hours ago?" Roper asked pleasantly.

I sat next to Roper and returned Max's stare.

Max redirected his attention to the detective sergeant. "Why, detective? Am I being charged with something?" His grin remained.

"Not yet, and maybe not at all."

I looked at Max's idle hands. They were folded on the table in front of him. A silver chain dangled loosely from one wrist, and a decorative ring adorned the pinky finger of his right hand. His nails were long, like those of a female hand model, and buffed to a glossy perfection. He still wore the pentagram.

"Listen," Roper said, "we're going to be here a while. You want something to drink?"

Max shrugged. "Sure. Dr Pepper would be fine."

Roper stood and knocked on the door. It opened almost immediately. "Get me a Dr Pepper." He turned to look at me.

"Coke," I said.

"Get me a Dr Pepper, a Coke, and a bottle of water," Roper said to the guard who left as quickly as he had entered.

"Now," Roper said, sitting down again, "we were talking about where you were a couple of hours ago."

"Not exactly," Max said. "You were asking about where I was two hours ago, but I hadn't answered. Technically, we weren't talking about anything."

The kid grinned. Roper smiled. I wanted to lunge across the table and take Max out.

"Of course, Max," the detective said. "I assure you, that was no trick on my part. Nor will there be any. I just want the facts. That's all. If you can alibi yourself, you're free to go."

Max grinned. "You mean I'm free to go as soon as you check it out."

Roper nodded. "Yes, that would be correct."

The knuckles of my balled fists were turning white.

"I was at the Esparanda."

"Okay," Roper said, "now we're getting somewhere. What were you doing there?"

"I was having a drink at the bar."

"Kind of early for that, isn't it?"

"This is the town that never sleeps, detective. I'm a child of the night." He grinned.

"Yes. You are that, aren't you?" Roper's own grin was disrupted by a knock at the door.

As the detective stood to answer it, Max looked at me and raised his middle finger. His grin broadened.

"Okay," Roper said, coming back to the table as the door behind him closed again. "Dr Pepper for you," he gave the drink to Max, "and a Coke for you," he handed the soft drink to me, "and water for me."

He sat.

Max popped the top on his drink as Roper twisted the cap on his. I did neither.

"Now, Max," Roper said, "tell me about your friends. Can any of them vouch for you?"

The kid tried hard to seem mysterious. "In what way, detective?"

"As to where you were. Were any of them with you at the Esparanda?" He raised the bottle of water to his lips and tilted his head back to drink.

"No. I was all alone."

"That's unusual for you, isn't it?" Roper asked, putting the cap back onto the bottle.

"Not really. I often prefer my own company."

"But you've been known to also prefer the company of young ladies. And I do mean young." Roper smiled.

Max returned the detective's smile with a lopsided grin. "On occasion," he said.

"And none of them were with you this afternoon?"

"No."

Roper smiled. "Okay, Max. I believe you. But we do have a bit of a problem."

Max grinned.

"A man was killed today. A man who had a bit of a run-in with you the other day."

"Is that so?"

"Yes. And this man was concerned about young women. Concerned enough that he made it his business to see that they were all right."

"Very admirable of him," Max said.

Roper nodded. "Yes, it was. And this man was told to meet Malak at the apartment in which he was murdered today."

The change of facts in Roper's story caused me to give him a quick glance.

"I was at the Esparanda," Max said.

Roper dismissed his own innuendo with a wave of the hand. "Of course. I'm not implying you had anything to do with it. But I'm wondering if maybe you heard something, or saw something, or…you know, maybe you might know something that could turn us toward the real killer."

"Now detective, honestly, why would I know anyone who would do such a thing?"

Roper shrugged. "I was looking at your medallion. That's a pentagram, isn't it?"

Max rolled his eyes and sighed. "Yes, detective, it's a pentagram."

"And that's the sign of Satan, isn't it?"

"For some people, perhaps. The pentagram has a rich history and can often be worn as a decorative piece. Much like a cross or crucifix. For example, did you know that it speaks to the perfection of man?"

"So you're not a Satanist or anything like that?" Roper asked.

Max grinned. "Not everyone who wears a pentagram is a devil worshipper, detective, any more than everyone who wears a cross is a Christian."

Roper paused to think and unscrewed the cap of the bottle again. "You're quite right, Max. I hadn't thought about it that way."

Both men paused to drink. My heat was building, but it wasn't the kind that would be squelched by a can of Coke.

"So you don't know anything about this Malak character?"

"Who?"

"*Malak*. He's a devil-worshipping twit who's going to prison as soon as I can pin anything on him that will send him there."

Max's grin wasn't reflected in his eyes.

"No?" Roper asked.

"No."

"Okay, because we know that one of our officers was right in taking the geek down, but he ended up doing it the wrong way. But since this Malak isn't a friend of yours, it doesn't matter if we tell you that we're going to redirect his life." Roper leaned forward as though he were about to share the greatest secret of the twenty-first century. "We know he's messing with young women. We also know he's afraid of us. And after all, why shouldn't he be? God is on our side."

Max's face reddened as Roper pressed the point.

"You know how it is, Max. Guys like you wear stuff like that because it's cool. But guys like Malak wear it because they actually believe that devil stuff. Right?" He put the bottle of water down on the table and held an index finger along each side of his head. "A little red dude with horns and a pitchfork is going to take over the world." Roper broke out in laughter as Max stood and hurled his can of Dr Pepper at the detective.

Roper ducked the missile and stood, slapping Max broadside across the face. The blow spun the kid around and he fell to the floor.

Roper sat down again, smiling, as he tilted the water bottle to his lips.

"You wasted a perfectly good can of Dr Pepper, Max," Roper said, after he finished drinking.

The kid eased himself from the floor. His face was flush, but not enough to mask the bold handprint of the detective.

"Have a seat," Roper said, smiling.

Max sat in his chair again. Most of the bravado was gone, but his anger toward me was still reflected in his piercing gaze.

"As I was saying," Roper continued, "Malak is the kind of man…" he snorted. "Sorry, I didn't mean to imply that he's really a man," he smiled as charmingly as possible, "but he's the kind of…creature… who preys on the helpless, the weak, the dispossessed, the type of people who can't think for themselves and who need someone to tell them how to live." He gestured again toward the kid's pentagram. "Take that, for instance. Here I thought you were a follower of Malak's. I thought that since you were wearing the symbol of a defunct and cartoonish character, you were also falling in line with the city's biggest geek. But you set me straight, and I can appreciate that."

Max's face turned purple. His eyes seemed to visibly darken.

"But I guess not everyone is like you, Max. As I was just saying, some people need a leader. They'll follow anyone. Even some loser like Malak." Roper started laughing. "Or even ol' Beelzebub himself."

There was a knock on the door. Roper stood to answer it.

I looked at Max, whose darkened eyes were now fixed on the tabletop.

Roper thanked the guard and stood aside, opening the door.

"Okay, Maxey," he said, "you're free to go."

CHAPTER FORTY-EIGHT

We were sitting in Roper's office. I was drinking the Coke I had taken from the interrogation room. He was sitting with his feet on his desk and his hands folded on top of his head.

"The guy didn't do it," he said. "He wasn't busted up. Marty put up a fight."

"I saw that too. Besides," I said, "his fingernails are too important to risk on someone like Marty."

Roper smiled. "Yeah, I saw that. You still wanted to punch his lights out though, didn't you?"

"For starters," I said.

Roper smiled again. "The cameras at the casino back up his story. He was drinking at the bar and had been there for at least a half hour before the murder. After that, he played a few rounds of poker before hitting the slots. It's all documented."

"So why the third degree? Marty and I were looking for Max. Why did you tell him we were looking for Malak?"

"We know that Minor used to live in the apartment you visited today. He probably knows that we know it too. But I wanted to push him on this Malak thing. I wanted to see where his hot buttons were."

"Do you think the girl was being straight with us?"

Roper shrugged. "Don't know. But she did give you an address that is a former residence of his."

"But she must have called him somewhere else."

"Maybe all she had was a cell number. Maybe she set you up after all. All I can say right now is that we just don't know."

"Maybe we need to take a drive and—"

"Already been done. My guys were doing that as soon as you told me about her. We knew the trailer was already gone before you and I made it back to headquarters."

I smiled for the first time in a while. "I like the way you guys work."

"Unfortunately, the bad guys don't. Did you see the way he was staring at you in there?"

"How could I miss it?"

"Yeah, well, I'd be a bit more careful if I were you. You aren't known around here, and you don't have the connections Marty had. Whoever was gunning for him was gunning for you too."

"I'm not worried about someone gunning for me. I've lived most of my life in someone else's gun sights."

Roper changed the subject.

"Did you see the anger in this guy when I began to criticize Malak?"

"See it? I could feel it."

"Yeah, that's what I mean. Leroy has built himself quite a following. Practically a cult."

"So did Hitler," I said. "But one of his staff tried to murder him."

"That's what we need," Roper said. "One turncoat to open up the whole thing."

"So where do you go from here?" I asked.

Roper eased his feet off his desk and sat forward in his chair. His hands rested on top of his blotter.

"First, we're going to try and find this Lucinda and see if she set you up. If so, we want to know who's directing her. Second, we're going to have the lab run DNA samples off of Max's soda can and check for matches with DNA samples we took from the apartment. If we get a match, we can put Max at the scene."

"But you said the cameras showed him at the casino," I said.

"They did. But that doesn't mean he wasn't there before the murder, helping to set this whole thing up."

"Sure," I said, mentally scolding myself for missing the obvious.

"You might as well know that we've begun to get very heavy into the occult around here."

"Since when?"

He looked at his watch. "Since this morning. I began doing some background reading on Satanism and some of the other fringe stuff. You know what they all have in common?"

"They're all mean?"

Roper smiled. "No."

"They all hate Christians?"

He shook his head. "No. In fact, some of them see Christianity as just another form of the same thing. When I began to look into this stuff, I started to find that they don't agree among themselves on most points, and even the Satanists, who seem to stand apart from the others, don't agree on all things. Some of them don't even believe Satan exists."

"Sure," I said, wanting to tell him I already knew some of this stuff.

"The part they all agree on, though, is the role that man plays in his own destiny. You heard Max, didn't you? He said the pentagram represented the perfection of man."

"How can a man be perfect if he's going after young girls?" I asked.

"Hold on," Roper said, holding out his hand and smiling. "I'm just the messenger. All I'm trying to say is that this cult of Malak's—if that's what it is—is on the fringe. But in a way, they're connected with other similar groups. At least as far as the foundation of their belief."

Sure, I thought as I drank from the can. *And that leaves me with a place to go.*

CHAPTER FORTY-NINE

I left Central Division and took a cab to my hotel.
After entering my room and ordering a hamburger, fries, and iced tea, I splashed cold water on my face and dropped the Ruger onto the nightstand before flopping onto the bed and reaching for the phone.

I dialed the Shapiros and filled them in, minus the parts that would cause them greater concern. I also called Pat and asked if any messages had come in from Callie. None had.

My next call was to Dale Millikin.

"You sound better, Padre," I said as soon as he answered the phone.

"It's coming along, but not as fast as I'd like."

I told him that Callie's disappearance had put me in a position where I was in over my head. I felt powerless.

"But that's not why I called," I said. "I'm afraid I've got some bad news."

There was a protracted pause before he asked, "Callie?"

"No, Marty. He's dead."

Another pregnant pause.

"Dead?" Millikin's voice broke.

"He was killed earlier today."

I told him about the incident, why we were at the apartment in the first place, and how Marty had given his life trying to help a perfect stranger.

The minister wept, and I waited as he slowly regained his composure.

"He was a true friend," Millikin said. "And a real man. A sincere Christian. One who chose to live it and not just proclaim it."

I agreed with Millikin that Marty was all of those things.

"Do the police have any leads as to who killed him?"

"They have some leads," I said, "but the lab tests aren't back yet. When they put it all together, they'll have their man." I was sounding more optimistic than the facts warranted.

"I wish I could get out there, Colton," Millikin said. "But I—"

"Actually, I think the Shapiros are more in need of your services than I am at the moment," I said, trying to assuage his sense of uselessness. "What I need is more along the lines of information."

"What kind of information?"

"Information about the occult. You were right, Dale, when you said I was fighting a spiritual battle. I'm not equipped for that type of fight." I told him everything I knew about Malak, Callie, Max, and Marty. I told him about the things I had seen on Tony's computer. I told him about my conversation with Roper and his research into the occult. By the time I finished, the preacher who always seemed to have something to say was oddly silent.

"Well," he finally said, "you've gotten hold of a lion by the tail."

"Nice cliché," I said, trying to ease tensions, "but what do I do with it now?"

"Don't let go. Not yet. And it wasn't a cliché. The Bible says that Satan prowls around like a roaring lion, looking for someone to devour. And lions prefer the weak, Colton. The uninitiated. The ones who either don't recognize the threat or are incapable of fighting it."

"Like me?"

"Like all of us. None of us can go at him alone. We need God's help. So first, I'll let you know that we'll all be praying for you on this end."

"Okay. Then what?"

"Then you need to see things as they really are. That means that Satan is real, and he will seek to destroy, and he is committed to being successful regardless of what it takes. He doesn't play fair, and he doesn't care who knows it. He's a crafty, cunning personality who thinks, plans, and schemes. He wants you dead, and he wants Callie dead. And as you're beginning to find out, his influence can't be overcome by force, or the threat of force, or even the legal system. His power reaches into all communities and to every level of society. He doesn't care which of the other belief systems you choose as long as you don't choose Christ. He doesn't even care whether you believe he exists. And he doesn't care if you see him as a little red guy with horns and a pitchfork."

I recalled Roper's comments.

"All that matters to him is that you succumb."

"I have to admit, Dale…I haven't given Satan a lot of thought. I know evil exists; I've seen it too many times. But I've got to tell you, what I'm seeing here in Vegas is beyond anything I had imagined. I'm beginning to see why it's called Sin City."

"Sin is everywhere, Colton. Evil doesn't just reside in Las Vegas; it resides in the human heart. The Bible tells us that the heart of man is deceitful above all things. God even destroyed the entire earth once because the thoughts and the heart of man were on evil continuously."

"So how do I get Callie out of all this when I find her?"

"You will need to understand that she wasn't dragged away. She was enticed."

"Sure," I said. "I think I've understood that since I heard the phone message."

"Satan can't make any of us do anything we don't want to do. But he can entice us, and he is very effective at doing that. And he knows just the thing that will move each of us, even though that thing is different for everyone. For example, some of us will yield to sexual temptation while others will not. Some of us will fall into a world of drug abuse when others won't." He paused. "The bottom line, Colton, is that sin is pleasurable. If it wasn't, we wouldn't do it. But the pleasure, however intense it may be, lasts for just a short time. Eventually, we have to face God and answer up for the things we've done."

"Was Callie's weak spot the hole in her heart that came from Anna's death?"

"Maybe. But in any event, Satan's influence has reached her. He's working through others to extend his reach into your home and destroy Callie's life."

The thought angered me.

"Remember, Colton, our battle isn't necessarily with the people involved. It's with a much higher power. We do battle with the god of this earth. And he is no slouch."

"So where do I go from here?" I asked.

"Find Callie. But be prepared to wage a battle for her life. Trust God. He won't leave you to fight this alone. He will be with you. He will give you the help you need."

We ended the call with the minister praying for me. Despite the situation and the fact that I had called him, I was uncomfortable with the prayer. But I was also appreciative. With Marty gone, I felt alone. I didn't know Vegas, and I didn't know the enemy I would be fighting. And in both cases, I felt less confident of my chances than I felt in the darkest alleys of Indianapolis when confronting a thug or a well-armed street gang.

I rose from the bed to retrieve the remote when a knock came at the door. I was hungry and wanted to eat. But after my conversation with the minister, I wasn't sure I could.

How could I eat when the devil had earmarked my family for destruction? And how could I fight Satan himself when my best ally had been murdered? I needed help, and I didn't know where to go.

I opened the door and found that Millikin had been right.

"He will give you the help you need."

I smiled—and Mary smiled back.

CHAPTER FIFTY

I called room service and asked that they send my tray to the Koffee Konnection. Mary joined me there and ordered an iced tea. She had eaten at O'Hare while waiting for departure to Las Vegas.

"You're a sight for sore eyes," I said, picking a French fry off the tray.

She smiled.

"How was your flight?"

"Long. The plane that was supposed to take me to Vegas was delayed, so I ended up sitting in Chicago two hours past my original departure time." She sighed.

"Where are you staying?" I asked.

"Here. I've got a room just down the hall from you." She gave me her room number.

"You armed?"

"Of course. I just came from a bureau assignment. Why?"

I told her about the day's happenings, about Marty's murder, and about the sequence of events that led to it. When I was done, she seemed exhausted.

I took her hand in mine. It was a move that would have been awkward just a few days ago.

"What's on tap for tomorrow?" she asked.

"I'm going to find the girl who set us up."

"Are you sure she did?"

"Guilty until proven otherwise," I said.

"What if she isn't there?"

"Then I'll go to the Fountain of Wisdom."

She frowned. "The fountain of what?"

"Wisdom," I said. "It's a New Age shop that Marty and I visited. The woman that runs it is very strange, and from what I could gather, not particularly fond of the cowboy."

Mary opened a packet of Sweet 'N Low and poured the contents into her tea. She stirred as she talked. "Does Millikin know about his friend?"

"I told him just before you arrived," I said. "We had a good talk afterward."

Mary sipped the tea, wrinkled her nose, and opened another packet of Sweet 'N Low.

"These people are following this Malak like he was their messiah," I said. "Whoever this Devlin is, he's got a stranglehold on these people. And they're motivated to do whatever needs to be done."

She poured the confection into her tea, stirred again, and tasted it. No nose wrinkle this time. "People like that are always hard to defeat. They're fighting for an ideology." She took a French fry off my plate and ate it. I offered half my hamburger, but she declined.

"Am I correct in saying that the Vegas PD is going to get more actively involved in Callie's disappearance now that a murder has occurred peripherally?" She asked.

"You are," I said. "But their interest is in solving Marty's murder, not necessarily in finding Callie."

"But finding the man or men who killed Marty will probably lead us to people who know where Callie is." She ate another French fry.

"One would think," I said. "Of course, Marty made his share of enemies too. You can't be on the streets for as long as he was, pulling the sources of income out of the hands of the hustlers like he was, and not have made enemies."

She gave me a look that was clearly a waffling agreement. "Maybe.

But it'd be pretty coincidental to say that Marty's death was some-how unrelated. Especially when this Lucinda seems to have set the whole thing up."

I ate the last of the hamburger as Mary fetched the last fry from my plate.

"Sure," I said. "I'm just trying to keep an open mind."

She smiled. "I always thought you had the most open mind in the bureau, anyway."

"I believe the term you were using then was closer to implying that a breeze was blowing through one ear and out the other."

Her smile broadened. "Open-minded—airheaded—it's all seman-tics."

"You say tomahto, I say tomayto."

"Yeah, but can you spell it?"

I rubbed the day from my eyes.

"Probably not," I said.

She took my hand. "I rest my case."

CHAPTER FIFTY-ONE

We met again in the Koffee Konnection the next morning. I had a breakfast of two eggs, two strips of bacon, and coffee. Mary ate a bowl of fruit.

"I have a car in the garage," I said. "Marty paid for the thing and told me it would be there if he and I got separated."

"I think this qualifies," Mary said.

After breakfast, we climbed into the Camry and drove west to the area where Marty and I had talked with Lucinda. The sun was continuing its steady climb over the eastern horizon, and the day promised to be as hot as the day before.

As we approached the spot where the camper had been parked, we saw that it was gone, just as Roper had told me.

"Why are we here?" Mary asked.

"This is the area where Marty and I talked with Lucinda. I thought it might be helpful to ask around. See if anyone saw anything."

I drove another hundred yards down the road to a two-story house that had an unattached garage. Pulling into the driveway, I saw that the garage was open and an older looking man was inside, building a bookshelf. He had just approached a table saw when he saw us pull up. He removed his eye protection and squinted against the sun as he approached our car.

"You folks lost?" He smiled as he leaned against our car with one hand on the roof and the other in his hip pocket.

"No, we were just wondering…did you happen to see when that camper left?" I asked, gesturing toward the direction from which we had just come.

He glanced toward the area I had indicated. "It left yesterday. Just up and took off." He leaned closer into the car. "Why?"

Mary showed him her credentials. "FBI," she said. "Did you happen to see who hauled it away?"

"FBI? No kidding?"

We smiled.

"Well, yes and no. I don't know who the guy was, but I could describe him."

"What did you see?" I asked.

He nodded toward the area where the trailer had been sitting. "When that fellow drove in and started hooking up, the little lady that was staying there came out of that thing and just started yelling something fierce. Called him all kinds of names." He shook his head. "You could hear her all over the valley," he said. "Then he told her to shut her yap and get back in the trailer."

"What happened then?" Mary asked.

He shrugged. "She got back into the trailer and shut her yap, I guess. I never did hear anything else out of her."

"Was it a car or a truck that hauled the camper out of here?" I asked.

"A truck. A big ol' Dodge."

"What did the guy look like?" Mary asked.

"Tall with dark hair. He was wearing a ponytail and had on a long-sleeve green shirt, with the sleeves rolled up, and he was wearing jeans and boots."

"You noticed quite a bit for a casual observance," I said, pleased that he had seen what he had seen.

He leaned closer to the window of the car.

"I know what's been going on in that thing," he said, nodding again toward the area where the trailer had sat. "And I don't appreciate it. I came out here to get away from that stuff. Most of us out here did. We just live and let live. We try to stay out of other people's business as long as they stay out of ours."

"Sure," I said.

"Which way did they head?" Mary asked.

He nodded toward the mountains. "That way. Up toward them red rocks you see there."

The red-copper mountains that rimmed the greater Las Vegas area rose from the area where we were talking. They shimmered in the early-morning light.

"We're not from around here," I said. "Are people living there?"

He seemed amused. "Of course people live there. There are plenty of new developments in them mountains. And for the same reason there are new developments springing up here. People want to get away from all of that." He nodded in the general direction of The Strip.

"One more question," Mary said. "When did the camper pull out?"

He paused to think before shaking his head. "I remember seeing them leave, but I don't know for sure what time it was when they did." He scratched his head. "I do remember that they left after some cowboy and another guy came around. It wasn't long after those two left that the guy in the pickup came by and hauled everything away."

I looked back at the spot where the trailer had sat. It was far enough to not be able to recognize me but close enough to remember someone as flamboyant as Marty, and certainly close enough to recall someone who was being cursed at while hitching a trailer.

We thanked the man before leaving the area and driving into the foothills of the mountains. The roads weren't well paved, and we were tossed side to side as the car made its way upward. A smattering of housing developments and individual homes dotted the rugged terrain like whitecaps on a tossing sea of red rock.

"Are we looking for the trailer?" Mary asked.

"Yep. Or a pickup. Chances are, the man is her pimp." I looked at the mountain peaks that rose above us. "There isn't too much that far up that's going to be inhabitable or easy to reach if you're dragging a camper."

"If he can make it, so can we," Mary said.

Undeterred, we continued to drive through the area for another hour. Except for the clusters of homes and developing neighborhoods, we saw nothing. Mary pulled the Camry to a small turnaround along the side the road.

"This is a bust," she said.

"Not really. The man who pulled the trailer away fits the description of the man I saw murder Binky, and we know that they came this direction. That means if they aren't here now, they were."

"Duh, yeah," Mary said.

"But that means there was a reason for being up here," I said. "And I think the most reasonable conclusion would be that they have friends up here."

"Or maybe we're jumping to conclusions. Maybe they don't have friends here; maybe they have a *business* here."

"Sure. Either way, they had a reason for coming to these mountains."

We were silent for a minute as each of us tried to develop the reasons that Lucinda and the man would have for coming into the mountains.

"Maybe," Mary said, breaking the silence, "they just wanted to get away from it all."

"Maybe," I said, ignoring the intended glibness in her remark. "But since they're the reason for 'it all,' maybe they're here because they have something to hide."

"This is Sin City," Mary said. "Pretty much everything goes here. If they feel the need to hide something…it's got to be something big."

CHAPTER FIFTY-TWO

We had several leads I wanted to check out, but our next stop was at Central Division Headquarters. Detective Todd Roper was at his desk, drinking coffee and eating an Egg McMuffin. His tie was undone, and he had a stack of paperwork on his desk that would have rivaled anything Wilkins had on his desk back home.

"This is Special Agent Mary Christopher," I said, introducing her to the detective.

He wiped one of his hands with a napkin before standing and shaking hers. After the introductory formalities, he gestured for both of us to have a seat.

"I've got some news," I said.

"So do I," he said. "Why don't you go first?"

I told him about our search for the camper, the conversation with the nearby neighbor, and our visit to the mountains. I told him our suspicions were now beginning to center around the fact that these people couldn't be found because they didn't participate in the normal exchange of society. No credit cards. No telephones. No driver's licenses. I told him I thought we were dealing with cultic separatists. And that meant their leader, Malak, had to wield incredible sway over his followers.

"And that makes him dangerous," I said. "Waco and Branch Davidian kind of dangerous. Maybe even Charles Manson kind of stuff."

He had listened with interest.

"We went to the location for the trailer too," he said, "and we didn't see anything either. We canvassed the neighbors yesterday evening, but the guy you two talked to wasn't home. So I guess we kind of dropped the ball there. But the people that we *were* able to speak with—and there are only a couple others living along that road—agreed that the trailer had been there until yesterday." He paused. "We found the trailer this morning, twenty miles north of town. A girl's body was inside."

I groaned.

"She had been killed with a forty-five."

"According to the man we talked to, the guy who hitched up the trailer matches the description of the guy I saw kill a lead in Indianapolis. A guy name Janus Bigelow. He went by the name *Binky*."

Roper finished the last of his sandwich.

"I know," he said. "I spoke with Wilkins this morning. I told him about the things that occurred in the past twenty-four hours, and he told me what happened the last day or two before you left town."

He lifted the coffee cup to drink.

"You think I did her?"

He paused for effect—just enough to let me know I wasn't totally off his radar, yet enough to also let me know that I wasn't a serious suspect.

"Wilkins said that people who get around you have a tendency to turn up dead. And now I'm starting to see that happen here."

Mary sighed.

"If I did her, why would I be trying to find her?"

He nodded. "Yep. That wouldn't make any sense, would it? Which is why you're sitting here instead of in a cell." He drank more coffee before setting the cup on the desk. His expression and his voice took on a different tone. "We found a holster in Marty's car. A holster that would fit a nine millimeter. Marty had a conviction, which means he couldn't carry a gun." He extended his hand. "Give me your weapon."

"My daughter is missing," I said. "And I—"

"I know," he said. "And now we're involved. And IPD is involved. We'll find her. But you're not going to shoot up this town before we do."

"I'm not wearing this for fun. It's for protection. I'm—"

His eyes narrowed—hardened. "Give me the gun or go to jail."

Mary put a hand on my arm. "Give him the weapon, Colton."

I struggled to keep my anger in check as I pulled the Ruger from my waistband. I handed the pistol to Roper.

"Thank you," he said, ejecting the magazine from the gun and locking the slide in place.

"I'm going to want it back."

"You can have it back. Just as soon as you leave town."

"I'm not leaving without my daughter."

He eased back in his chair. "I know. And that's why you won't get it until you do."

CHAPTER FIFTY-THREE

Mary tried to soothe my rage as we pulled out of the parking lot of Central Division. I was driving.

"Take it easy," she said. "He's trying to help."

"By disarming me?"

She put a hand on my shoulder. "Did you see the pictures on his desk? He's a father too. He knows how he'd feel if he were in your situation. He's just trying to keep you from doing something you'll regret."

"Like getting killed?" I began to work my way through the never-ending throng of people who weren't in town because their children were missing. "If I get whacked because I couldn't defend myself, I'm going to regret that a lot."

"He can't take my weapon away," she said. "It's not like we don't have some firepower."

Having her near was a comfort. Although we hadn't had the chance to talk, we had broken ice. We knew where we stood. We just didn't know the landscape.

"Mary, I don't need you to protect me." I took my eyes off the road long enough to glance at her. "I want you here because I want you here."

She patted my shoulder. "I know."

"And Callie will respond to you. Maybe better than she will respond to me."

Mary shook her head. "I don't think so. When she left, she didn't call me, she called you. You're her father, not me."

"But I'm the one she *left*," I said.

We stopped at a red light and watched as throngs of people, some elderly, some not, shuffled across the street, carrying bags from the various casinos and shops. Many drank from open containers.

"She's angry with her situation, Colton. We've all been assuming that her beef is with you, but I think it's with God. He always ends up getting the heat sooner or later. Especially when things don't go the way we think they ought to."

Just days before, I would have asked Mary if she'd been talking to Millikin. Or I might have derided her comments with a well-placed jab or an inflammatory statement. But now I was more willing to consider the spiritual aspect of my reason for being here. My perspective was changing, and I was willing to change with it if that's what it would take to bring my daughter home.

The light changed, and we took off again, resuming a speed that would have been considered cruising if we were in any other town.

"Regardless of who she's angry with, who she blames, or who she hates, I'm the one who's got to find her before it's too late. Before she gets hurt, killed, or involved in something that will destroy who she is."

"There were times when I wanted to run away too," Mary said. "After Mom died, Dad threw himself into his work, and I just felt alone."

Mary and I had discussed her story before. It was similar to Callie's and served as the foundation for their relationship.

I put my hand on hers.

"I'm glad you're here," I said.

She smiled. "Did you think I'd stay away?"

"No."

"I couldn't, you know. As soon as I heard, I counted the days until that trial was over and I could get on a plane and get out here."

"Neither of us are kids," I said. "We both have lives that are established and running well." I shot her another glance. "Well, at least you do. Mine is chugging along."

She smiled again. I squeezed her hand.

"My feelings didn't come into play until after Anna's death. Until after you came into my life in a way that was outside our working relationship."

"You don't need to tell me this, Colton. I know Anna was your wife, and I know you were faithful to her. Spiritually as well as physically."

I continued to work my way through traffic. "I know you do, but I need to say it." I squeezed her hand again. "I need to hear myself say it."

She smiled broadly. "And for what it's worth," she said, "I had no attraction to you until I began spending more time with Callie. None. Absolutely none."

"Thanks for clearing that up," I said.

She laughed and my heart jumped.

"You were a colleague," she said. "But events changed that situation for both of us." She turned in her seat to face me. "I don't know where this will lead any more than you do. But we can take it a step at a time. If it's meant to be, it's meant to be. If it isn't," she sighed, "then it isn't."

"Is it awkward for you?" I asked. "Being friends and colleagues one day, and being…more than that the next?"

Traffic began to thin as we continued moving northward, picking up speed.

"No, not really. I can compartmentalize things pretty well. I'm not sure that's a good thing, but that's the way it is."

"Sure."

"Which is probably what Callie is doing. Having been in her position, I know how easy it is to put the grieving part of you in one corner and the living part in another. If she's doing what I did, and still do for that matter, then she's still her mother's daughter. Still the girl that Anna took pride in. But she's also this other girl. The one who can feel anger toward God and express it in her rage toward you. She probably doesn't see herself as a bad person even though she may very well be involved in some very bad things."

Mary's brutal honesty, her ability to see things as they were and to speak of them in a nonthreatening manner, was one of the many things about her that I was growing to love.

"Even Hitler liked puppies," I said.

"Callie's not Hitler, Colton," she said. "She's a little girl who's hurting and isn't equipped to deal with the pain. She's angry with you and maybe even Anna. I know because I've lived this part of her life. But she holds God responsible for all of it."

"I'm not comparing her to Hitler, Mary. I'm trying to make a point."

"I know," she said. "Even the worst of us see ourselves as good."

"Right."

We turned right onto Charleston.

"But we use the wrong standard. We compare ourselves to each other and to people like Hitler." She turned to face me. "And Callie's doing the same thing. And as long as she does that, she will never see what's really happening to her. Her view will always be colored. She will define her life based on how it compares to someone else's. And the someone else will always be worse than her. As long as she compares herself to the worst of the worst, she'll always come out on top."

"We all do that," I said. "It's how I get up in the morning."

"Of course. And we're all wrong. When we quit comparing ourselves to each other and begin measuring ourselves against God's standard, our perspectives change. In His light, none of us measure up. Not any of us." She turned to look at the passing despair of the hidden Vegas. The city that the tourists never see. "Until she sees things as they are, she'll have no hope."

"Then I will do what I have to, to get her to see things as they are. I will do what it takes to bring her home."

CHAPTER FIFTY-FOUR

I parked in front of the Fountain of Wisdom and killed the car. Unlike my Beretta, however, this car knew when to quit.

"Nice," I said.

"It is?" Mary asked, looking at the shop.

"I was talking about the car."

We got out of the Camry and walked up the same uneven sidewalk Marty and I had walked just a day before. When we entered the shop, we were greeted by the same tinkling bell and the same overpowering scent of burning incense.

Mary wrinkled her nose and began to move about the room, picking up various pamphlets, trinkets, and other New Age devices. Before long Athena appeared. She was dressed in a long gown that made her look more like Merlin than a modern businesswoman.

"You again?" she said.

"Marty's dead," I said.

She didn't flinch. Instead, she kept an eye on Mary, who was busily reading a pamphlet.

"Did you hear me?" I said. "Marty's dead. He was murdered."

She redirected her attention toward me. Her eyes were devoid of any sign of concern or compassion. Like two dark circles, they seemed endlessly bleak. Endlessly hopeless.

"So?"

"So I want to know where I can find Malak."

She threw back her head and laughed uproariously. There was no mirth. Only mockery.

"Malak lives where he wants and moves at will. You can't find him. You don't even need to. He'll find you."

I turned to Mary. "Do you smell something in here?"

She answered me while continuing to read the pamphlet.

"Uh-huh. Incense. A lot of it too."

"That much stuff is usually burned to cover up the smell of marijuana, isn't it?"

"Yes, I believe it is," Mary said, keeping her attention focused on the booklet.

"So what?" Athena said. "You're not a cop, and you can't do anything about it."

"True," I said, "but I know someone who is, and he can do something about it."

Mary put the pamphlet down and began to stare at the woman.

Her demeanor changed.

"I had this friend of mine check you out, and it isn't a pretty record. You've been arrested several times, and one of them was for drug possession. In fact, between the counts of prostitution, drunk and disorderly, and drug possession—not to mention distribution—I'd say you've been arrested eleven times. Right?"

Her face contorted into a blend of snarl and smirk.

"And in fact, you're still on parole. And you know that drug possession while on parole is a definite no-no. Right?"

"What do you want?" Athena said, her face rigid.

"I thought I made that clear," I said. "I want Malak."

"I don't know where Malak is," she said flatly.

"But you know he's back in town," I said.

Mary continued to give the woman that cop stare that always seems to work with people who have something to hide.

"He's in town, but I have no idea where he is."

"Who does?"

She hesitated before turning to Mary.

"You smell like a cop," she said. "Let me see your badge."

The woman's demand told me one of two things. Either she thought I was bluffing, or she was willing to take her chances with the law but not with Malak. I opted to let Mary show the woman her badge and credentials to make it clear we weren't bluffing.

Mary flipped open her bureau-issued leather case and displayed her credentials before flipping it over and showing the woman her badge.

"I think we can approach this in two ways," I said to Athena. "First, we pass on the drug information to the police and wait here until they arrive. That ought to get you into a cell, at least for a while. Then, we can get the bureau going through your stuff here and see if you're cheating on other things too. Like your taxes, for instance. That'll get the IRS involved."

Mary shuddered for effect.

"And then," I said, "when I do find Malak, I can let him know how I found him. From what I hear, his reach can even extend into the penal system."

The woman's angry expression fell as she looked from me to Mary and back to me.

"I'm dead either way then," she said.

I shook my head. "No, not if you work with me. Like I told you before, I'm looking for my daughter. When I find her, I'm out of your life. But I *am* going to find her, and I'll do anything to anybody to do that."

The woman sighed.

"Where can I find him, Athena?" I said.

The woman's shaking hand and trembling voice gave her away. Devlin had her scared.

"I don't know where he is, but I know someone who might."

"Give me a name," I said, "and we walk away. But set us up, and we're coming back."

"And next time, it'll be personal," Mary said.

CHAPTER
FIFTY-FIVE

We left the Fountain of Wisdom with a name. A familiar name.

"He hangs out at the Esparanda," I said. "It's a casino that's located off The Strip. Roper and his guys picked him up just a few minutes after Marty's murder."

"He must have had an alibi."

"Airtight. The casino's camera picked him up at the bar. He was there before the murder, and he was there after the murder."

"Hard to be in two places at once," Mary said.

We turned east and drove to a small complex that probably would have been condemned if it weren't for the fact that people were still willing to pay rent to live there.

"Kind of rough," Mary said as we drove through the main entrance.

"Beats the streets," I said.

We drove to the address Athena had given us. It was as dilapidated and as nondescript as the others and was located near the front of the complex. The apartments within each building didn't share a common foyer, and each building faced another. A common courtyard separated each pair of buildings.

"This is it," I said, parking a couple of buildings away from Max's.

"How do you want to play this?" Mary asked.

"I'm not playing."

We got out of the car and walked to the building. When we reached Minor's apartment, I knocked on the door. Mary had her gun in hand.

"She may have tipped him off," she said.

"Maybe. But she'd have to be certain that he'd kill both of us, because if he didn't—"

Max opened the door. His wide-eyed stare made clear that Athena had not called him.

I shoved him back into the apartment. Mary followed, kicking the door closed behind her.

Max started to speak, and I hit him with a left hook that was as solid as any I had ever delivered. He fell to the floor, starry-eyed.

"Colton," Mary said. "If I knew you were going—"

I pulled Max to his feet by the front of his shirt.

"You made a gesture to me at the police station," I said. "You want to do that again?"

He tried to speak but couldn't seem to form the words. I hit him again.

"Colton!" Mary grabbed my arm and began to pull me off the kid.

I yielded, allowing her to drag me away.

Max groaned and rolled on the floor as he struggled to pull himself to his feet. His eyes were as glazed as an Alaskan highway in mid-January. His face was beginning to swell.

"I want Malak," I said. "And I want him now."

He shook his head. Not as an act of defiance, but to clear the bells.

"I'm going to get him a glass of water," Mary said to me. "You stay right here and leave him alone." There was anger in her eyes.

She went into the kitchen, and I watched as Max slowly pulled himself to the sofa, with one hand on his swollen face. Mary returned with a glass of water and handed it to him.

"What do you think you're doing?" she said to me, under her breath.

"I told you I wasn't playing. I'm going to find Callie, and I'll do whatever it takes."

"Not like this," she said through gritting teeth. "You're not going to do it like this."

I wasn't sure I'd have to. As long as he hadn't heard Mary scold me, he could never be sure what would happen next. And as long as Mary was with me, nothing else would. But I made a vow to myself. If he didn't give us what he could, I'd be back. And next time, I'd come alone.

"How's that feel, Maxey?" I asked. "Am I going to have to get it on with you, or will you tell us what we need to know?"

He shook his head again.

"I can't hold him off forever," Mary said, playing along despite her anger. "And I won't be party to a murder. If he starts on you again, I'll wait in the car until it's over."

He looked at Mary and then me. His eyes were still glassy but more focused.

I sat on the sofa next to him. Mary stood nearby, keeping the distance between herself and me to a minimum.

"You're crazy," Max said to me. "And you're as nuts as he is," he said to Mary.

"You had something to do with Marty's death," I said.

"I was at the casino."

"I don't care where you were," I said. "You're involved. And that means you have to pay. But if you give me Malak, your debt with me is cleared."

"Malak?"

I rose off the couch, and he cowered.

"Colton," Mary said again, grabbing my arm.

I sighed and sat down again. "Tell me where I can find Malak," I said. "He has my daughter, and I want her back."

"I told you the other night that I didn't—"

"You lied," I said.

He looked at Mary. "You a cop?"

"Federal," she said.

"Then you can't let him do this. I'll have your badge for this."

"No problem."

"There isn't?"

"No. I'll gladly give up my badge for the girl."

The kid's eyes revealed his dismay. "I didn't kill anyone," he said.

"There are a lot of ways of killing someone," I said. "You don't always have to be present, and you don't always have to be the one who pulls the trigger."

"But you're guilty just the same," Mary said.

"I'm going to find him," I said, "and I'm going to take him down. And when I do, I will take out anyone who gets in my way. And I do mean *anyone*. Malak will let you have as much of the heat as you're willing to take. You'll pay the price for him. You'll be the one to take the fall." I leaned closer to him as he slid farther away. "And your fall won't happen in court. It'll be with me. Understand?"

The kid fingered the pentagram that still hung around his neck. "I don't know where he is," he said. "I—"

"Yes you do," I said. "You not only know, you're going to take us there."

Max's face continued to swell as a dark bruise began to form. A strong indicator that I had broken his jaw. He was finding it harder to speak.

"My face hurts," he said. "Can I have some aspirin or something?" He started to rise off the sofa. I shoved him down again.

"Mary, can you get it?"

She gave me the look.

"He'll be okay," I said, playfully slapping him on the swollen jaw. "I'll wait until you're back."

Max grimaced and held a hand to his face. His eyes still had the glassy look.

"Stay put," Mary said to me before leaving to rummage around the kid's medicine cabinet.

As soon as Mary was out of earshot, I took advantage of the

temporary reprieve and grabbed Max by the hair, pulling his face closer to mine.

"I'm going to kill you," I said. "I'm not going to do it in front of my friend here, but I am going to do it. You've got to pay for what happened to Marty. You've got to pay for Malak's sins. And if someone's blood has to flow to free my daughter, it'll begin with yours."

I shoved him back into place.

"Nothing," Mary said, coming back into the room. "I didn't find anything except this bag of stuff."

She handed me a transparent bag of white powder.

"Drugs?" I asked, turning to Max. "Say it ain't so, Maxey."

"Hey," he said, wincing with pain. "That's mine."

Mary smiled as she looked at me. "Looks like we have an admission."

"How much do you think that's worth?" I asked.

Mary shrugged. "Ten, fifteen thousand. Maybe a little more."

"You selling this stuff?" I asked.

He slumped in his chair. His swollen face had grown considerably larger. "I ain't sayin' nothing."

"Okay," Mary said. "Let's just haul him to Central Division and let them deal with it. We can find Malak another way."

The pain in Max's eyes deepened.

"I don't know," I said. "It seems to me we've roughed up our friend enough. Roper and his guys might even take offense at what we've done. Besides, what'll happen? Most likely some judge will just toss the charges out since we didn't exactly have a warrant when we came in here."

"Yeah," Max said. "That's right."

Mary seemed confused. It was a look Max probably didn't see.

"Chances are our friend here isn't using the stuff anyway." I turned to him. "You're selling it, right? And I'll bet if we toss this place, we're going to find a lot more of it."

He slumped in his seat.

"Shall we?" I said, to Mary.

For the next thirty minutes, we searched the man's apartment, taking turns watching him lest he should decide to leave.

We began our search in the usual places. I checked the undersides of drawers, the kitchen cabinets, the refrigerator, and a canister set. I found bags of cocaine in most of the places I searched.

Mary spelled me for a while and began looking inside his closets. She found another bag in a pair of shoes and another inside the pocket of a jacket. After finding the extra contraband, I brought a knife from the kitchen and began slicing through his sofa and cushions. We found five more bags of cocaine. When it was over, we had more than thirty bags of coke stacked in neat piles on the coffee table. We were tired.

Max was angry.

"How much?" I asked.

Mary shook her head. "If I had to guess, I'd say a quarter of a million."

I looked at Max with a grin.

"That's how he can afford to hang at the casino all day instead of punching a clock," Mary said.

"He's punching a clock," I said. "It's just not the kind that we're used to. Right, Maxey?"

He said nothing.

"Who're you working for?" I asked. "Who're you selling this stuff for?"

He continued to glare but said nothing.

I looked at Mary and could see that our minds had once again bridged the neuron gap.

"This stuff belong to Malak?" I asked.

Nothing.

I reached to the coffee table and picked up one of the bags. Using the knife I had taken from the kitchen, I cut the bag open and poured the contents onto Max's well-worn carpet.

"Hey!"

"You're selling this junk for Malak. If it was yours, you wouldn't be living here," I said.

"Is that true, Max?" Mary asked.

I opened another bag and dumped the powder onto the floor before I ground it underfoot.

Max's face changed. He was no longer angry. Now he was concerned. Very concerned.

"You know what I think, Special Agent Christopher?"

"Do tell," she said.

"I think that Maxey here isn't afraid of the police. He thinks he's safer with them than he is out here. And I'll bet that if he loses all of Malak's product, no place will be safe. Not jail, and certainly not here."

She nodded. "Yes. I think you may be right."

I opened another bag.

Max began to cry.

"What's wrong, Max?" Mary asked with the most motherly tone she could muster.

I poured another bag onto the floor and ground it into the carpet with my other foot.

"I don't know where he is!" Max shouted, trying to stifle his sobbing.

"No problem," I said. "If you keep losing his coke like this, we can wait until he finds you."

I opened another bag. My guess was that I had already destroyed fifty thousand dollars worth of drugs.

"He'll kill me. He'll kill me if you don't stop."

I dumped the contents of the bag. "How do I find him, Max?"

"He has people around him."

"Go on," I said.

"He lives in the mountains. He has his own…commune. He has followers, and there are guards. Everyone works to serve him, 'cause he's getting ready for the war."

"The war?" Mary asked.

The kid nodded. The bruise on his jaw had expanded.

"A cleansing war." Max looked at me. "He says Satan is going to return, and only the strong will be allowed to survive."

"Does he have guns?" Mary asked.

Max nodded. "Yes."

I turned to Mary. "He's paying for them with drugs and women. It's why he had Binky killed, and then Marty, and Lucinda. They threatened him."

"I've got to call this in," Mary said. "The bureau's going to have an interest in this."

"Max," I asked, "who is closest to Malak?"

He gave me a name.

"Thank you," I said, standing.

"What're you going to do?" Max asked.

"We're going to do you a favor. We're going to call the police."

CHAPTER FIFTY-SIX

W e left Max's apartment and drove back to the hotel as we called the police. Mary also called a car rental service and asked for a car to be delivered. She charged it on the FBI's card.

"My annual leave just turned into bureau time," she said.

We knew that from this point on, we'd have to split up. Mary would contact the Vegas office of the FBI and tell them everything she knew. How she got the information would come up, and she would likely be reprimanded. But with Malak's plans to launch a full-scale "war" against unsuspecting people, she had no alternative.

"You going to check out the name he gave you?" she asked.

"Yep." I steered the car onto Las Vegas Boulevard and began heading for the hotel.

"You know," she said, "with the bureau and Vegas PD involved in this thing, we're going to find her."

"Yep."

"But that isn't enough, is it?"

"No."

"You want to kill the man responsible."

"Yes. Very much."

"You'll lose everything."

"I probably already have."

She shook her head.

"No. Callie called you. She called *you* and no one else. She wants help. She's fighting a war within herself. She wants to do right, but the allure of doing wrong is too strong."

Traffic on The Strip began to thicken again, and my pace began to slow. I cursed.

"Is your goal to save Callie? Or kill the man who defiled her?"

I didn't say anything.

"Colton, if this Malak has lured Callie into his cult, the battle isn't with him. It's in her. There will always be another Malak. There will always be another…someone who is willing to tempt her into something she knows to be wrong. Killing this man isn't going to solve the problem."

"It'll solve one," I said. "He won't harm anyone else."

"He'll have done more than harm. He will have destroyed all of us. You, Callie, and me."

I saw tears in her eyes. The same tears I saw in Anna's the last night of her life.

"What will the justice system do with him?" I asked.

"Whatever we can make it do."

"He could walk."

"No."

"Yes, Mary. He could."

"*You* won't. Not if you kill this man. And what will happen to Callie then? What happens when the next source of evil comes along? Who will protect her then?"

I didn't have an answer. I wasn't capable of thinking beyond my own rage.

"I can't let him get away with this," I said. "I wouldn't be who I am." I snorted. "I wouldn't be able to live with myself."

"Is that what this is all about?" Mary asked.

I said nothing as I continued to drive. The street where the hotel was located was within view.

"This isn't about you, Colton," Mary said. "It's about Callie. It's about doing the right thing."

I said nothing as I wheeled the car off of Las Vegas Boulevard and toward the hotel.

"If she's truly the reason for doing all of this, at least consider what I've said. Sometimes you have to sacrifice for the ones you love."

"I'm willing to kill for her," I said. "I'm willing to go to jail if that's what it takes."

"No. You're willing to go to jail if that's what it takes to show everyone that you're a good father. You're too concerned with the appearance of what is right to consider what actually is."

I was getting angry. She was beginning to hit all the buttons Anna had hit the night we argued. The night she died.

I pulled the car into the garage of the Eureka and parked next to the door that led into the hotel.

Mary got out of the car, pausing before she closed the door. "You can't free her from whatever is eating at her by killing one man. You'll have to slay a dragon. And you can't do that with a gun."

CHAPTER FIFTY-SEVEN

I left Mary at the hotel and drove back onto The Strip as I began working my way north again. By the time I reached the area where the boulevard veers northeast, I was vibrating with adrenalin.

Max had given us the name of a man Marty and I had met with already. And we had disliked him from the start. But little things about him were beginning to add up, and they were things I should have noticed from the start—if I hadn't been so blind with rage.

I turned onto the same dusty road Marty and I had taken the last time we were at the Club Harem. Overhead, I could again hear the whine of another military plane, but the sound this time was more lumbering and less high-pitched.

"Definitely not a jet," I said to myself as I pulled into the parking lot and killed the engine.

The last time I had visited, Marty had watched my back. His vigilance had kept me from getting a knife in my belly. But Marty wasn't here now, and I wasn't armed, thanks to Roper. But I was closing in on Callie and wasn't about to stop now.

I got out of the car.

The interior of the club was as dark as it was the last time I visited and almost as empty. I expected to see more servicemen in the place and was surprised that I didn't. *Probably in the casinos,* I thought. Or

239

worse. Probably in parts of Nevada where the company of a woman-for-hire was legal.

I approached the bar, where a young woman was pouring a drink for a round-bellied cowboy. Except for the man's poor hygiene, weight, height, dress, and smell, he was a dead ringer for Marty. They wore the same style of hat.

"Excuse me," I said to the woman. "Is Jerry Thom around?"

This girl wasn't the same one who had been behind the bar the last time I was here. She continued pouring the man's drink.

"Who wants to know?" she asked.

"Colton Parker. I'm a friend, and I told him I'd stop by to say hi if I ever got out this way."

She finished the drink, told the man the price, and set the bottle back in its place on the bar. After collecting his money, she went to the cash register to ring up the man's libation.

"He's in the office," she said, nodding toward a door that was off to the right of the bar. "You can go on back if you want. He ain't doing anything anyway."

The fat man chuckled.

She counted out the man's change and gave him the balance of his money.

I walked to the office and went in.

Thom was sitting with his feet on his desk, watching TV and drinking a beer. He was wearing an orange T-shirt, jeans, and New Balance shoes. His long black hair was pulled into a ponytail and anchored with a rubber band. He seemed surprised to see me.

"What're you doing here?"

I smacked his feet off the desk. The move was unexpected, and his feet landed on the floor with a thud.

"You got a problem?"

"Yep. And that means you have one too."

He slid one of his desk drawers open and jammed his hand inside. I kicked the drawer closed on his hand, and he yelled.

"What've you got there, Jerry?" I asked, pushing his chair back and opening the drawer.

I extracted a nine millimeter.

"Well, well," I said. "Is this any way to welcome a—"

I heard the click of a knife and felt the sharp cutting motion of the blade as it dragged across my upper right arm. The sudden attack caused me to drop the gun. I stepped back from the desk just in time to avoid another swipe of the blade.

Thom slashed a third time, catching me again on my right arm. This time the cut was on the bicep.

I swung at him reflexively with my right arm in a backhand motion but only connected with him lightly on the point of the chin. He was unfazed and came at me again with the knife.

I spun in the tight office and hit him with a left hook. Although the punch connected, I was unable to get the momentum behind it that I needed. It did little good.

He came at me again, slicing me across the abdomen. The blade cut more deeply this time, and blood began to trickle. He slashed at me again, catching my right hand.

I backed into the open doorway, trying to maneuver myself into a position where I would have more room to respond. As I moved backward, Thom came at me in a slow, methodical approach. His dark eyes were alive with excitement.

I continued to back into the larger barroom, drawing him into the open area, when I suddenly bumped into the cowboy who had been sitting at the bar.

He wrapped his beefy arms around my chest. His action allowed Thom to come at me unabated.

Using the cowboy's bulk for support, I leaned backward and kicked at Thom as he slashed at me again. I connected with his midsection and drove the wind out of him but wasn't able to keep the knife from slicing through my lower leg. Blood began to flow.

"You okay, Jerry?" the cowboy asked.

Thom was doubled over, gasping as he fought to regain his breath.

I tried to take advantage of Thom's temporary incapacity and free myself from the cowboy's grip. But he lifted me off the floor and slammed me into the door frame.

I responded by driving my elbow into his ribs, but it had little effect.

He drove me into the door frame again. And again.

I drove my head backward and into the man's face. He groaned but maintained his grip. He slammed me into the door frame again before throwing me to the floor, where I landed with a thud.

Before I could get to my feet, the rotund rodeo rider began kicking me in the ribs. The first blow caught me off guard, driving my breath from me. The second one nearly lifted me off the floor. The third one drove me across the room, where the cowboy then sat on me as I lay facedown. His weight and the attack made it difficult to breathe.

"Enough of this," Thom said, barely able to get the words out. "Ice this guy."

He kicked the knife to the cowboy.

As the fat man lifted his weight off me to reach for the knife, I was able to turn and drive my fist into his ample belly. The blow caught him off guard and bought me time. I struggled for another breath and hit him again. And again.

Thom rose to his feet and began to move toward the knife.

The cowboy was struggling to breathe and raised even further off me to allow his diaphragm room to expand. His action gave me the space I needed, and I was able to wiggle out from under him. I was on my feet just as Thom reached to pick up the knife. I kicked him under the chin, driving his head backward. He landed on his back.

I knelt to pick up the knife and saw that the fat man was having more difficulty breathing than my blows could have caused. His eyes were wide, and he was clutching at his chest.

I ignored his distress and moved to where Thom was lying faceup. I straddled him and put the point of the blade into his neck. My hand was covered in blood.

"Malak has my daughter."

He was breathing rapidly. The cowboy was laying on the floor, gasping.

"I am willing to kill for her. Are you willing to die for him?" I had begun to push the blade when I heard the click of a gun. I looked up to see the young bartender standing over us with a revolver. The hammer was drawn back, and she held the weapon in her trembling hands.

"Enough," she said. "All of you. Enough." She looked at the fat man. "Morgan, you okay?"

He tried to speak but couldn't.

"He needs an ambulance," I said.

The girl looked at Thom. "Jerry, what do you want me to do?"

Thom tried to turn his head and look at the hurting cowboy, but the point of the knife wouldn't permit it.

"Jerry?" she asked again.

I slid forward on Thom's body and put my center of gravity over the knife. If the girl shot me, my collapsing corpse would drive the knife into Thom, and he knew it.

"Who's your daughter?" he asked.

"Callie Parker."

He licked his parched lips. Blood dripped from my abdominal wound onto his chest.

"I don't know her. Where is she from?"

"Indianapolis."

His eyes revealed recognition.

"Jerry?" the girl asked. "Morgan isn't looking so good."

The cowboy gasped and tried in vain to speak.

Thom's dark eyes revealed his soul. People were nothing to him. He followed an errant leader whose plans, if successful, would lead to the deaths of hundreds. School children, the elderly, the infirmed, none of them mattered to Thom or to the man he followed. The only thing that mattered to either one of them was power. The chance to exert their will over others. The belief that might makes right.

"Jerry?" the girl asked, more frantic this time. "What do you want me to do?"

"Put the gun down, Brandi," he said. "Put it down."

The girl hesitated for a moment before easing the hammer back into place and lowering the revolver.

"Tell her to empty the shells."

He didn't need to say anything. The girl opened the cylinder and pushed the plunger, ejecting six cartridges to the floor.

"Now drop it and back away," I said.

She did as she was told.

"My brother needs an ambulance," Thom said.

"Brother?" I looked at the fat man. His breathing was becoming more rapid. His face was growing purple.

"Take me with you," Thom said, "but let her call an ambulance. He isn't part of this."

I looked at the girl. There was no malice in her face, only concern for the ailing cowboy.

"Okay," I said, easing off Thom. "But you tell me what I need to know, or I'm going to bury this thing in you so deep that the Army Corps of Engineers won't be able to find it."

He rose to his feet.

I knew I was taking a chance. I knew that once Thom and I cleared the building and an ambulance was called, he would no longer have any impetus for helping me. But I couldn't let the fat man die. Not like that. Not like an animal.

I grabbed Thom by the shirt and shoved him through the barroom ahead of me. We paused at the door.

"If anyone comes after us," I said to the girl, "he's dead."

I pushed him through the door with the knife at his back.

CHAPTER FIFTY-EIGHT

We left Club Harem and got on Las Vegas Boulevard, heading northeast. Thom was driving the Camry. The temperature was becoming increasingly hotter, and the air conditioner seemed to have trouble keeping up.

We continued past the Las Vegas Motor Speedway and Nellis Air Force Base until we found an abandoned gas station on a side road, less than a hundred yards off the boulevard.

"Pull in there," I said to Thom, indicating an area behind the building.

He did as he was told, and we were soon out of sight of any prying eyes that might happen to wander past.

I reached across him and turned off the engine, pocketing the keys. "Get out of the car."

He got out, and we walked toward the abandoned building and through a decaying door that had no lock and only one hinge. We were soon standing in what appeared to have been the office. Some counters were still in place but little else.

"Sit," I said, gesturing toward one of them.

He sat.

"Start talking," I said.

He told me where I should go. I rapped him across the mouth. "Start talking," I said again.

"You're taking a chance. How do you know I'll tell you anything?"

"I don't. But I couldn't let him just lay there and die."

He ran a hand over his head. "If I tell you how to find Malak, what will you do?"

"Find him. Then get my daughter out. Kill him if he's hurt her."

"He'll kill me when he figures it out."

"You're putting the bang before the spark. He may not be in a position to kill anyone."

"You either, if I get out of here." He eyed the knife in my hand. Years of back-alley chases, street confrontations, and barroom brawls had given me an innate ability to know when someone didn't like me. I was getting that feeling from Thom. His eyes shifted to the knife in my hand. His body language said he was planning on a way to take it away from me.

I rapped him across the mouth again. "I took you once today already. I can do it again."

He wiped a trickle of blood from his lower lip with the back of his hand. "You ain't nothin' without that knife."

I flipped the blade closed and slid his knife into my pocket. He grinned and slid off the table.

Thom was a man used to slapping young girls. His toughness was self-perceived and not supported by any true skill. As he began to circle to my left, his guard was too low, his feet too heavy. I hit him with a straight left.

"See?" I said. "Knife or no, I'll take you every time."

He swung with a sloppy roundhouse that I easily ducked. I came back at him with a straight left to his gut, followed by a right hook to the side of his head.

He stumbled but came at me again with another roundhouse that caught me on the left elbow.

I drove another right hook into the back of his head, followed by a left uppercut against his chin. This time he went down.

I moved to the counter and sat where he had been sitting just a few moments before. I waited while he flopped into a sitting position on the floor and shook his head, trying to clear his belfry.

"Don't shake your head," I said. "It only adds to the confusion. Trust me on this. I know. Breathe."

He wiggled a finger in one ear before beginning to breathe deeply. It was a few minutes more before he could talk.

"You got me good," he said.

"Not good enough," I said. "I was trying to take your head off."

He shook his head and moaned.

"Sooner you tell me what I want to know, sooner you can find out how your brother's doing."

He remained in his position on the floor and pulled his knees up under his chin. He wrapped his arms around his legs. "Morgan's not very smart."

"And you are?"

He shook his head. "No, I mean he's not…very intelligent. His IQ is lower than most. He's all brawn and no brains."

"Sure. Where's Malak?"

He paused to scratch his head. "Malak is a genius. Way ahead of his time. He has the opportunity to make things right."

"By triggering a war? Killing innocent people?"

"Who among us is innocent, man? Huh? You? Me?" He shook his head again. "Malak has built a following. Most of us would die for him."

I would be happy to oblige them.

"But I couldn't let Morgan die," he said. He lowered his head. "I guess that means I'm weak."

"Gee, that's too bad," I said. "Where is he?"

"He and his followers live in a place up in the mountains. A big two-story building that's backed up against the bottom of a cliff." He grinned. "Makes it easier to protect. You only have to worry about who's coming from the front."

"Is it guarded?"

He ran a hand over his face again. "Yeah."

I showed him a picture of Callie.

"I know her. I knew who she was when you said she came from Indianapolis. Malak was in Indianapolis to meet with Mason. Malak recruited him to begin running girls so we could buy the protection, guns, and other stuff we needed. But then Mason ran into trouble with Binky, and the whole thing just came crumbling down."

"So you killed Binky?"

"Yeah. Malak ordered it, and Mason set it up."

Thom fit the general description I had given to IPD detectives—tall, with long dark hair. It was the best I had. I had been too far away and it had been too dark for me to see his face.

"What were the plans for Mason?"

"He had real potential. He was very committed to Malak. But when he began to mess up, he began to draw the heat. So we passed a tip to that chick's dad."

"Her name was Wendy," I said.

"Yeah, right. We knew the old man would do Mason when he found him because he had been hanging around the pool hall." He shook his head. "That old dude was tough. He wanted Mason bad. Real bad."

I recalled that Anderson said he "found out where he lived." Now I knew how.

"So Wendy's dad knew where Mason lived because you told him. Except he wasn't there, and Anderson followed him home from the pool hall."

Thom nodded, as he scratched his head again. "Yeah. We even told the old man that Mason was at the pool hall that night. I was with him when he left."

"Did you do Lucinda?"

"No. Malak did her. Max used her to set you guys up, and then Malak iced her so she wouldn't talk." He shrugged. "She was starting to fall apart anyway. Malak saw it coming, so after Max used her, Malak decided to get rid of her." He looked at me. "You was supposed to get it too. You was causing too much grief." He lowered his head.

"You missed."

"Yeah. I guess we did."

I held up the knife I had taken from him. "Did you kill Marty?"

"No. That was Malak. Soon as the guy was dead, Malak left to get Lucinda out of there. He knew the cops would be along soon, so he wanted to clean up." He looked at me again. "You were supposed to be there, man. You were supposed to die too."

"Wendy?" I asked, ignoring his regret.

"No. But I was there. It was right before we sicced her old man on Mason. She was having second thoughts. The lifestyle was just a fad for her. Not a real commitment. So Mason set it up, and she got it. She got it good."

"Why are you telling me all this?"

He licked his parched lips. "I guess I owe it to you for not letting Morgan die."

"That's it? A big man like you going sentimental?"

He shrugged. "I'm not going to live anyway."

His comment didn't make sense until I thought it through.

"You could go to the police," I said. "Tell them what you know."

He shook his head. "You found me. That means if you can put pressure on me, so can anyone else. Malak won't accept that. Either way I go, I'm dead." He lowered his voice. "Malak can reach me almost anywhere. Almost."

The balance of his thought—the next logical comment—didn't need to be said. Malak couldn't reach Thom in the grave. And that was where he planned to go.

"How do I know you won't call Malak?"

He snorted. "You don't. But I won't. If you can get Malak, he can't get Morgan. But if you can't get Malak...I won't know about it anyway."

I was struck by the irony of the man's belief system. He seemed to exude a sense of selfless devotion to a man and a cause, even to the point of killing on command. And yet, despite his profession, he was unwilling to die for the man. In fact, when the chips were down, he was willing to cut and run, leaving those whom he left behind to deal with Malak's wrath any way they could.

"How many guards?"

"It varies. Not everyone lives at the compound. But there are enough people there. They won't let him be taken without a fight. They've been preparing for it for a long time." He stood up. "How much more, man? What else do you need to know?"

"How is my daughter?"

"I don't know, man. I really don't. Malak is quite taken with her. He likes her innocence. She'll support the cause."

"You still don't get it, do you?" I said. "Malak's a user. He's surrounded himself with so many gullible people like you that he's beginning to believe his own press. He really thinks he's powerful. He thinks he's above the law."

Thom grinned. "He is the law. And you better be careful if you approach him the wrong way. If the guards see you approaching, they won't hesitate to open up. And he won't hesitate to kill your daughter."

"Is that what happened to Leah?"

He frowned, cocking his head to one side. "Who?"

"The cop's daughter. The one that initiated the road-rage incident."

"Oh, yeah," he said. "He's got her in a lockbox in Seattle. That chick messed up when her old man got on us."

"It wasn't her fault," I said.

He shrugged. "Doesn't matter. She's the one that has to pay."

The blood had ceased to trickle. The wounds on my hands and body were beginning to burn with an intensity that was second only to my determination to find Callie.

"Enough talk," I said. "Tell me how to get there."

CHAPTER
FIFTY-NINE

With several hours of daylight left, I decided to scout Devlin's place and prepare to make a nighttime assault.

I parked the Camry a half mile from the compound and hoofed it the rest of the way, crossing over the rocky terrain. After leaving Thom, I had stopped at a store to purchase a pair of binoculars and some bandages for my wounds. As I climbed through the rocks with the glasses in my hand, the unyielding sun didn't give an inch, and the unseasonably warm temperature began to take its toll. By the time I reached a spot that was overlooking what I knew to be the main building in the compound, I was exhausted. I settled in among some rock formations to escape the heat and get a vulture's perspective on the buildings below.

The main building was a hodgepodge of smaller ones that had been connected to create a larger, more dominant structure. It was a jagged, ramshackle piece of architecture that would have been razed if it were located anywhere else but the nearly isolated mountains of Nevada.

It was also heavily guarded. People milling around the grounds, seemingly involved in various yard projects, were scattered in a defensive formation. Unless rattlesnakes were planning an all-out assault, I could think of no reason why a man who was pruning trees would

251

need to have a rifle jammed into the trash can that he hauled around with him.

And he wasn't alone. I counted five others, all of them covertly armed and all of them facing outward toward the area from which any attack must come.

I swung the binoculars from left to right. There were two other buildings. One housed several vehicles. The other served as a garden shed.

I took time to study the layout, beginning by mentally measuring the distance between the road and the main building, and between the building and the makeshift garage. I counted the number of windows and doors, the number of people I could see, and the weapons they had nearby. When I was through, I removed the binoculars from around my neck and recapped the lenses.

Devlin was as nutty as a can of Planters. But he was a good general. His choice of location made an attack on his compound difficult. With the mountain at his back, the rocky terrain in front, and two neighborhoods nearby, the authorities wouldn't chance a confrontation with him unless they had solid evidence of criminal dealings. And that was not likely as long as he eliminated those who threatened him and continued to keep a low profile—as least as far as the police were concerned—by remaining underground.

I was beginning to understand why Thom knew he couldn't remain alive for very long. He was a threat to this operation. He had been compromised. And once that happened, he, like others before him, became expendable.

I descended from my perch and walked back to my car. The time to cash in the chips on Leroy Devlin was near.

CHAPTER SIXTY

The hike in the mountains and the fight with Thom and his brother were beginning to take their toll. I drove back to the hotel to get some rest. I was going to need it.

But I also needed a plan. If Thom was right, an open attack—especially the kind that the police or the FBI would mount—would trigger a shootout and mean almost certain death for Callie and several officers. And of course, I was concerned about Mary. I didn't want her in harm's way when I took Devlin down.

Cult leaders like Devlin were nothing new. Charles Manson, Jim Jones, David Koresh, and others had all sprung up from time to time with one goal in mind—to sway as many as possible.

I supposed they honestly believed the tripe they espoused, but I couldn't help but wonder why seemingly normal men and women would fall for their lies and walk away from everything they had known to be true. But of course, many had. And disaster ensued, engulfing the innocent in the schemes of the evil.

I didn't want that happening to Callie—or Mary. I loved them both. And I would do whatever I needed to do to protect them.

Once I was in my room, I flicked on the television and ordered room service. I hadn't eaten since breakfast, and I was beginning to feel the effects. It would also be a while before I would eat again, and I wanted to go into the compound as armed as possible, even if that meant walking into hell with nothing more than Thom's knife and a full stomach.

I ended the call with room service and decided to take a shower, pausing long enough to study my battered reflection in the mirror.

My face was swollen and bruised, and my nose was askew. Morgan had probably broken it. My lips were swollen, my forehead was cut, and I had two black eyes.

"Well, big guy," I said, looking at my face from different angles, "I don't think you're going to be a threat to Brad Pitt anytime soon."

I showered and tried to cleanse the knife wounds as best I could. The gash that ran across my abdomen was deep but no longer bleeding. The cuts on my hands and leg were equally deep—and jagged. The rudimentary bandages I had applied earlier were fully red.

After showering, I wrapped a towel around my waist and flopped down in the chair next to the bed. Room service hadn't arrived, so I decided to use the time to formulate an approach to the compound. The problem was unlike any I had ever faced, and I would have to face it alone. I could certainly call the police and have scores of officers at the scene, but I wasn't sure they could do the job adequately.

During the raid on the Branch Davidian compound in Waco, the authorities had bungled the job badly. Fire had erupted, officers and innocents had been killed, and investigations into what went wrong dragged on for months. And Waco wasn't the first bungled job.

During the bureau's attempt to nab John Dillinger at the Little Bohemia lodge, overzealous agents had fired on civilians. Dillinger got away, and innocent people died.

And during the search for newspaper heiress Patty Hearst, a raid had been conducted on the house of Donald DeFreeze, the mastermind behind the heiress' disappearance. As at Waco, the FBI had underestimated the degree of DeFreeze's conviction. The result was a bloody shoot-out that triggered a house fire and left several dead.

Then, of course, the assault on Randy Weaver left his wife, one of his children, and even the family dog dead.

I wasn't faulting the bureau or other police agencies for doing the job they were charged with doing, but I knew that things never go according to plan. When the adrenalin is rushing and the lead is flying, personal survival becomes paramount for all involved. That often means the potential victims can take a backseat, and that was something I couldn't afford.

I began to make a mental map of the layout I had noted while perched high in the rocks. Several people had been in front, and I assumed more were inside. How *many* were inside was anyone's guess.

From what I could tell, the mountains abutted the back of the building, forming a sort of backdrop that provided a sense of security and outright physical protection. The face of the rock behind them was sheer, and only a highly skilled team would be able to insert themselves by way of the mountains. I wasn't a highly skilled team, so that approach was out.

On the other hand, a single individual, coming from behind, wasn't something they would be expecting. All of their security was thus directed toward the front of the compound.

I needed to sketch the layout of the compound so I could plan various scenarios for the assault. I had just risen off the chair to get a notepad when a knock came at the door.

I opened it and allowed the server to set the dinner tray on the table, near the chair in which I had been sitting. After signing for the tray, I abandoned any thoughts of maps and sat down to eat. When I was finished, I fell quickly asleep with any plans I had for the assault drifting away with me.

I slept soundly but woke on my own volition. The television was still on but muted. Evening was beginning to settle over the city that never sleeps, and a crescent-shaped swath of rose-violet color highlighted the desert's western sky.

I pushed aside the tray that had carried what could be my last supper and began dressing for the evening's events. A black polo shirt, jeans, and New Balance cross trainers. I wouldn't need a jacket.

I had pulled the binoculars from the bag and was about to turn off the TV when I did a double take—the silent picture revealed a shot of Malak's compound. An attractive yet generic-looking reporter was standing in front of the camera with a hand-held microphone. The look on her face was grim.

I turned up the volume.

> "The officer was gunned down the minute he stepped out of his car. His partner, a man who the police have yet to identify, contacted the Central Division of the Las Vegas Police Department, and other officers soon converged on the scene. We also have agents from the FBI, ATF, and United States Marshall Service. The SWAT team has also been called.
>
> I spoke with Detective Michael Collins, who had this to say…"

The scene shifted to a taped interview with a balding, middle-aged man who looked like a hundred cops in a hundred different cities. A cluster of microphones were stuck in the man's face, each of them prominently bearing its station's logo.

> "Officer Melvin Smith, a twenty-one year veteran of the Las Vegas Police Department, was shot and killed this evening as he tried to serve a warrant in conjunction with agents of the FBI and ATF.

An off-camera voice asked, "Who is inside the house?"

> "We are seeking a suspect named Leroy Devlin. We have reason to believe that Mr. Devlin is involved in two recent homicides in the city and is dealing in illegal arms, drugs, and prostitution. Officer Smith and the federal agents with him were attempting to serve both state and federal warrants."

Another voice asked, "When were those warrants issued?"
It didn't matter. I flicked off the set and left for the compound.

CHAPTER SIXTY-ONE

I was able to get within a half mile of the area, which was surprising given the extent of police presence. I parked the Camry and walked the remainder of the distance before I was stopped by a yellow Crime Scene ribbon.

The mob that had accumulated was impressive, and police had their hands full trying to keep spectators, news media, and other gawkers from getting in the way or getting hurt. An officer approached me.

"You're going to have to move back, sir," he said. "You can't come any closer than—"

"My daughter is in the house," I said.

"I don't care. You've got to move back to the—"

"I care," I said. "She's in that house, and—"

He slipped under the yellow cordon and began moving me backward by putting his hand on my chest and pushing. The look on his face said he was tired and had been pushed to his limit.

I knew exactly how he felt.

"I told you to stay back behind the line up there, and I mean what I say."

Behind me was an invisible line that most of the others had seemed to recognize. I hadn't noticed that the spectators were clumped together some fifty yards from the Crime Scene tape.

"My daughter's—"

"And I told you that I don't care. We'll take care of—"

I grabbed the hand he had placed on my chest and twisted it at the wrist. He went down but began to pull a canister of pepperspray from his belt. I kicked the can out of his hand as I continued to subdue him.

Before long, two other officers slid under the yellow barricade and came at me. We began to tussle, and the officers forced me to the ground. A plainclothes officer come running over. It was Roper.

The three uniformed officers from the Vegas PD were beginning to cuff me. One of them had his knee in my back. They stopped to look at Roper as he approached with his badge in hand.

"I'm Todd Roper." He showed them his badge. "Let him up."

An officer whom I assumed to be the senior of the three said, "He assaulted Doyle. He—"

"I'll take responsibility for him," Roper said. "Let me have him, and I'll see that you get him back later if you still want him."

The officer who had his knee on my back said nothing as the three of them seemed to mentally weigh their options.

"Okay," the senior man said. "But we want him. He's not going to assault one of us and walk away from it."

Roper thanked them, and the man got off my back.

I stood and dusted off dirt and debris. The officers glared at me as they walked away.

"What are you doing here?" Roper asked, clearly upset with me.

"I saw this thing on the news," I said. "Where would you expect me to be?"

He sighed. "Okay, you can go through the line with me. But stay with me. If you wander off again, I'll let those guys rubber hose you all night long. Understand?"

I agreed, and Roper led me past the yellow ribbon and into the thick of things.

Two helicopters were flying overhead. One appeared to belong to the LVPD and the other to a news outlet. Several squad cars were parked on the lawn of the compound along with a few police vans and several unmarked cars. A few klieg lights rimmed the front of the grounds. The lights were focused on the house but provided enough light for the officers to conduct their work around the property.

"The FBI is here," Roper said. "I think one of them is a friend of yours." He led me to a cluster of plainclothes standing behind a row of unmarked cars. It was dark now, and I couldn't see Mary until we came up on her.

"Agent Christopher?" Roper asked. "Does this belong to you?"

Mary had been talking to several other agents and turned to face me.

"Colton?"

"Sorry," I said. "But I saw this on the news, and—"

"I had hoped you wouldn't," she said.

"You set this in motion, didn't you?"

Mary nodded.

"Callie's in there," I said.

"We don't know that."

"All the more reason to assume she is."

One of the agents approached me. He was about my age, tall, slender, and dressed in a dark business suit. He had the Efrem Zimbalist look that had once been the norm for FBI special agents.

"You know anything about this guy?" he asked, nodding toward the house.

I told him everything I knew.

"That's pretty much what you said," the man said, looking at Mary.

"We learned through ATF that a significant number of firearms have been purchased with this address attached to the paperwork," Mary said. "Nothing illegal, and nothing that would have attracted attention if it weren't for what we learned from Max."

"And we've had several burglaries of local gun stores," the other agent said.

"And some not so local," Mary added.

Roper said, "We got a judge to give us a warrant on Lucinda's killing. The girl had been assaulted before she died, and we found

Devlin's prints in the camper. You might also be interested in knowing that his prints were found in the apartment where Marty died."

"I already knew that," I said.

Roper frowned. "How did you know that?"

"I talked to a guy named Thom. He used to be one of Devlin's henchmen."

"Gerald Thom," Roper said. "Goes by Jerry." He leaned closer to look at my face. "What happened to you?"

Mary leaned forward to study me.

"I said Thom and I talked. I didn't say we had a pleasant conversation."

"Where is he, Colton?" Mary asked. Her voice was tinged with concern that I had stepped over the line again.

"He's probably at a place called Club Harem. It's a few miles northeast of Vegas." I knew I needed to assuage her concerns. "He was fine when I left him."

Her pursed lips told me she wasn't sure.

"But I don't think he intended to stay that way," I said, telling her about our conversation.

"We'll get someone to go out that way. Bring him in if he's alive," Roper said.

Mary was about to speak, when a bullhorn interrupted her.

"Devlin, this is the FBI. We have the place surrounded. Come out with your hands in the air, and no one will get hurt."

There was no response.

A second attempt by the FBI also brought no response.

"Do you have a negotiator on hand?" I asked.

The other agent nodded to a slender man who was clustered together with the other agents.

"He's the best in the business," the agent said. "We're going to try to call the house now."

I had noticed the compound was dark as soon as I arrived. Closing off the power was standard procedure and an easy, non-threatening way to get the attention of those inside. Although I still had visions of Waco dancing in my head, I felt more at ease. The negotiator did indeed know his stuff.

I waited with Mary and Roper as the agent left us to go to a group that stood near the rear of a car. They had a map spread over the vehicle's trunk and were trying to read it with the aid of several flashlights. All of the agents were wearing blue nylon windbreakers with FBI stenciled in gold lettering across the back.

"Relax, Colton," Mary said. "We know our job. If she's in there, we'll get her out."

"I was with the bureau, remember? I'm not worried about you getting her out. I'm worried about her condition when you do."

Mary put her hand on my shoulder. "I love her too, Colton."

CHAPTER SIXTY-TWO

The night began to drag on, and around midnight, some additional officers came to the scene with a coffee setup. It was a welcomed sight, not only to ward off the desert chill but also for something to do. Mary and I had a cup and remained near the cluster of FBI agents who had made little progress in their talks with Devlin. He had hung up on them twice.

After getting a cup of coffee and taking a call, Roper walked over to where Mary and I were standing.

"Thom's dead," he said. "He made it back to the bar and shot himself in front of customers."

"Any word on his brother?"

Roper furrowed his brow.

"He had a brother named Morgan. Big guy, probably well over three hundred pounds. He had a heart attack earlier this evening in the bar."

"I'll look into it if you really want to know."

"I do," I said.

For the next hour, we milled about, drinking coffee in silence while the FBI made repeated attempts to get Devlin to come out of the house or talk on the phone. The drone of the helicopters overhead was becoming annoying.

"Any progress?" I asked the agent I talked with earlier. I had learned

from Mary that he was the ASAC—assistant special agent in charge—
of the Las Vegas office. The SAC was apparently on vacation.

"None. But we can't let this thing go on for very long. There
are a couple of residential areas around here that have too many
schoolkids. They'll be out and about soon." He looked at the sky.
Daylight would begin to break in a few hours, and that would up
the risk for nearby civilians.

"You've vacated the residences that are nearby?"

"Yeah, but people aren't going to stay out of their homes for long.
This thing is going to have to wrap up soon."

As long as lead wasn't being exchanged and the fireworks weren't
happening, I knew that Callie would be safe. But the ASAC was
right. Something would have to break soon.

"You need a warm-up?" Mary asked, nodding toward my near
empty cup.

"In a bit," I said.

"How long did you two work together?" the ASAC asked.

Before I could answer Mary said, "I told him all about you."

It explained why the ASAC had been as open with me as he
had. Once again, the brotherhood of the badge had worked in my
favor.

"A while," I said.

He grinned. "You work together well. Too bad it had to end."

I looked at Mary. She was looking back with no attempt to hide
her feelings.

I was about to speak when the bureau's hostage negotiator came
to where the three of us were standing.

"Boss, we got a problem. The ATF guys are saying that by their
estimate, these guys have a couple hundred thousand rounds of
ammunition. If they decide to open up, this is going to get very
messy."

The ASAC massaged the back of his neck. "Try again, Mike. Try
connecting with Devlin again."

The negotiator went back to the car, which was serving as a sort of rallying point for the FBI, and took a cell phone from one of the other agents. Mary, the ASAC, and I followed.

"Leroy? How we doing in there?" the negotiator asked in his we're-just-friends tone.

I glanced at Mary. Although she appeared confident, I knew she was as uncertain as me.

"Leroy, no one wants this thing to end badly. I know we don't, and I'm sure you don't either. What do you say we turn the power back on if you send out a few of your people with their hands in the air?"

There was a pause.

"Okay then, how about you send out some of the other people you have?"

He paused again but looked at the ASAC with an expression of resignation.

My anemic hope for a successful outcome began its death rattle.

"Hello? Hello?" The negotiator disconnected. "He's not going to deal. Says he's never going to give in." The negotiator shook his head. "He warned me to not force his hand."

No sooner had the negotiator spoken than a single rifle shot was fired from a second-story window. The bullet struck an LVPD squad car, shattering the windshield and forcing us all to duck.

After the echo from the rifle shot died, the ASAC slowly rose to his feet, as did the rest of us.

"This has to end," he said. "Get some tear gas and smoke canisters ready."

"Hold on," I said. "If you push this guy, he's going to start pushing back."

"He's pushing already," the ASAC said. He cursed. "We can't wait forever. We've shut off the man's power, we've cut off his water, and yet nothing's happened. We don't know how much food he has stored away, which means we really don't know how long he can hold out. And don't forget," he said, "one officer is dead already."

"My daughter's in there," I said for what had to have been the hundredth time.

"I know," he said. "And I'll do my best. But I have a lot of innocent people I need to think about. Your daughter is one of them."

I was about to protest when Mary gently pulled me away by grabbing my arm.

"Come on," she said. "Let's go get some more coffee."

We walked to the coffee table, and she poured a cup for me.

As I started to drink, I heard the *whump-whump* sound of the canisters as they were fired into the house. Before long, I could see smoke drifting from the second-floor windows.

"When this thing opens up," Mary said, "I want you to trust us. And I want you to get over there." She nodded to an area behind the yellow line.

"You want me to run?"

"I want you to be safe."

The helicopters were beginning to buzz nearer the house. I looked overhead and watched as they circled above, with the LVPD chopper flying closer to the compound. I recalled Waco and Ruby Ridge again.

"What's the ASAC doing?" I asked. "He knows they're too close."

I was cut off by the sound of another rifle shot. The police chopper was hit in the tail rotor. The aircraft began to spin violently out of control as it dropped to the earth. It hit the ground a hundred yards away with a sickening thud and exploded.

Things began to move.

Mary began shoving me toward the yellow tape. I dropped my coffee. Agents and police officers began scurrying around with renewed vigor.

"Go, Colton. Get out of here."

I watched as another canister was propelled into another second-floor window. Then another.

A fire erupted, igniting the roof and most of the west end of the second floor. A thick sheet of lead began to come from the house as gunfire began. We all ducked, and the police began to fire back.

My fears were realized. Things had gotten out of control.

"Go, Colton," Mary yelled with her gun drawn. "Get behind the line."

I did as I was told and ran as fast as I could toward my car.

When I reached the Camry, I climbed behind the wheel and started the engine. I floored the accelerator and drove toward the compound.

I steered the car around the growing crowds and then past them and through the yellow tape.

I picked up speed as I went around the phalanx of squad cars, marked and otherwise, and past the throng of police officers and federal agents.

I continued to press the accelerator to the floor as I began to head for the house. I could hear gunfire and the yelling of the officers over the whine of the engine. Behind me, the shooting ceased as I moved ahead of them and into the curtain of lead that was coming from the house. Several rounds struck the car with violent force. In my rearview mirror, I could see the glow of the burning chopper. But it didn't matter. None of it did. I no longer cared about what was behind me. I focused on what was ahead and propelled the Camry through the front door.

CHAPTER SIXTY-THREE

I must have momentarily lost consciousness because I didn't feel the impact. When I came to, the rear of the car was elevated, and the accelerator was stuck. The engine was revving, but the vehicle wasn't moving. The air bag had deployed, and I had fresh blood on my face again. I turned the key, killing the engine.

I tried to open the door, but the crash had crumpled the front of the car. The door wouldn't open.

I moved toward the other side and was able to push open that door. I got out.

The place was in chaos. Smoke filled the interior of the living area where I was located, and I could hear yelling and screaming from various areas of the building. Not screams of fear, but commands to an organized army that's committed to victory. I hoped their commitment in the battle with the police outside would keep them at their posts until I could find Callie.

I began to limp away and glanced around the room. The car was hung up on a desk I had hit when I rocketed through the door. The remainder of the room seemed to be very large and minimally furnished. The floor was concrete with no carpeting, and two staircases fed into the room. One was partially lit from the klieg lights outside. The other was in darker shadows.

Blood trickled from my scalp and into my eyes. I wiped it clear with the back of my hand as I began my search of the first floor.

From outside, the building had looked like a jumble of smaller buildings that had been joined together to make larger quarters with no concern for aesthetics. Once inside, I saw that I had been right.

I cautiously began to move along the first hallway I came to, trying hard to hear over the sounds of the gunfire coming from the building. I knew that the agents and officers outside were regrouping for an assault. That meant I wouldn't have long to find Callie.

The first door I came to was locked. I kicked the door open and saw the room was furnished but empty.

I moved to the next room and found the same thing.

I was about to enter the last room in the hall when I felt a sudden sting on the back of my left leg. I turned to see a young man standing not more than ten feet away. He had a pistol in his hand and an unworldly look on his face.

I charged him.

He fired again and hit me again, but my momentum carried me forward, and I tackled him to the floor.

The man was surprisingly strong. Whether it came from his youth, his motivation, or some sense of possession, he was difficult to subdue. But I did. I put Thom's knife into him and took his gun.

I rose off the man's body and began to resume my search of the first floor when I saw another man coming from the room where my car had landed. He had an automatic weapon in his hand and was beginning to level it at me when I fired, hitting him in the chest.

I knelt to take the man's automatic weapon, an Uzi, and tucked the pistol in my rear waistband.

The gunfire suddenly stopped, and the house was relatively silent. I took the opportunity to listen.

Above me, I could hear the muffled sound of hurried footsteps. I decided to move upstairs, choosing the partially lit steps over the darker ones. The cult members would expect the officers outside to mount an assault, using the darker staircase for the stealth it would provide.

I moved upward as quickly as I could. My left leg was beginning to throb, but I could hear a wave of agents coming, and I knew I needed to keep moving.

Time was running out.

The smoke was thick upstairs, but the glow of the growing fire illuminated more resistance at the top of the steps. I saw a woman dressed in an army-green tank top and battle fatigues. Her hair was pulled tightly back, and she had a semiautomatic pistol in her hand. She pointed the weapon at me, but I fired the Uzi before she could pull the trigger.

I eased myself to the top of the landing and stood flush against the wall to my right. I coughed as the tear gas wafted through the hallway. Although the agents outside had ceased firing more canisters into the compound after I entered the building, the few they did manage to launch were making it difficult to breathe. I tried to clear my throat and then paused to listen. Judging from the sound of the voices and hurried activity inside, the assault from outside was in motion. I heard someone yell for Malak. His response told me where he was.

CHAPTER
SIXTY-FOUR

I moved to my right, staying along the wall as I moved down the hallway toward the voice. There was less tear gas accumulation at that end of the hall, and as I progressed, I was able to breathe more easily. I paused long enough to look to my left for any more resistance, but all I could see was a cloud of black smoke that partially obscured the glimmer of a fire from that end of the hall. I could hear coughing as someone struggled to put out the fire.

I turned back to my right and tried to see how many rooms there were. The light from outside had done a credible job of lighting some areas of the house but had almost no effect on the interior hallway where I was now standing. I decided to move along, trying each door until I found the one where Malak was hiding.

The first door I came to was unlocked. I opened it, prepared to spray the room with lead, but it was empty. I moved to the next door. It too was unlocked. When I opened it, I saw a young girl in a black halter, black leather skirt, and black boots. Her hair was black, and she wore black lipstick and eye shadow. It was Callie.

She was standing next to a very tall, solidly built man dressed in a black shirt with flowing sleeves, black pants, and black riding boots. Standing next to him was a taller, younger man who wore a holstered .38 on his hip. As soon as I entered the room, he drew the pistol.

I fired, and Callie screamed as the man went down, dropping

the gun on the floor, less than three feet from where she and Malak stood.

"Come here," I said to Callie. "Let's get out of here."

She didn't move. The look on her face was blank. She seemed neither pleased nor angered to see me.

"Stay where you are," Malak instructed her.

I raised the gun.

"No!" Callie said, still standing in front of him.

"Callie, get out of the way," I said.

"No!"

"The place is on fire. I have to get you out of here."

She shook her head but said nothing.

"Don't listen to him," Malak said. "He drove your mother away, didn't he?"

She nodded.

I wanted to shoot Malak, but I hesitated for fear of hitting Callie. "Don't listen to him, honey," I said. "He's bad. All bad."

"Bad according to who?" Malak asked Callie. "They always attack people like us. They do it in numbers because by themselves, they're weak."

"Mary is with me," I said, looking directly at Callie. "She's outside. She wants to see you."

Callie said nothing.

"Pastor Millikin wants to see you," I continued. "He's concerned about you. We all love you. We all want you to come home."

"Love? Don't listen to his lies. They only love themselves," Malak said. "They want you only for what you can do for them. They want to control you."

"No," I said. "You know that's not true."

"They want to tell you how to live your life," Malak said. "They don't think you can make your own judgments. They fear your independence, your strength."

Callie backed up toward Malak, shielding him all the more. She still said nothing, but the flat look in her eyes spoke volumes.

"Callie," I said, trying again, "I'm your father. I've been searching for you for days. I want you to come home."

"Listen to him," Malak said, standing behind Callie. "Everything he says begins with 'I want.'"

"Your mother wouldn't want this for you," I said. "She wouldn't want you to live like this."

Callie's face began to contort. From the distance, I could hear gunfire as agents and police officers began to storm the building. I wanted to get Callie on the floor before she got hit by a piece of shrapnel or flying lead.

"He's bad, Callie," I said. "He's killed girls like you. Your friend Wendy is dead. He sells them and makes—"

"She was turning away. She didn't believe, but you do, don't you?"

Callie nodded.

I kept the muzzle of the Uzi leveled at Malak.

"He's got you dependent on him," I said to Callie. "He won't let you leave." I was beginning to grow weak. "He doesn't love you," I went on. "Mary and I love you. We want you home. Callie, he's a liar. A deceiver. A murderer."

"He killed your mother," Malak said. "He wants to kill me too."

"No!" Callie said.

"Look at him, Callie," Malak continued. "Look at him. He hates your commitment. He hates what you are. He wants to kill me the way he killed your mother. He thinks he's strong because he has a gun. Don't give in."

"I won't give in," she said.

Her statements didn't have the robotic quality I had always expected cultists to have. Instead, she seemed genuinely convinced.

"They can kill us, but they can't defeat us," he said. "If I die, you must live. You have to carry on."

"Your mother died, wanting you to carry on," I said. "She didn't want this for you. She wanted you to have the life you wanted. We both did. Since you were a baby, we loved you. We stood over your crib every night. We stood over your high chair every day. You—"

"Listen to the weakness in his voice," Malak said.

"I love you, honey," I said. "We all want you to come home." My hand began to tremble. My vision began to darken.

"He wants, he wants," Malak said. "What about what *you* want? You have to choose your own destiny."

Millikin, Mary, and Marty had been right all along. The war wasn't for Callie's freedom. It was for her soul.

"Callie, you can have the kind of life you want. And we can help you," I said.

Dark smoke was beginning to billow through the doorway. Heavy gunfire was coming closer.

"He's lying, Callie. He wants you to come home for his own selfishness. He needs to have a daughter. He only wants you to live your life *his* way."

"I want you to live life *God's* way, the way He intended it," I said, startled by the words that had come from me. "This man is a deceiver, Callie. You can't live life your way. None of us can. I ought to know. I've been doing it for years, and look where it has gotten me."

A puzzled look crossed her face.

"And now he wants to help you live your life?" Malak said. "He can't even live his own."

"I can with God's help. And yours, honey. We can help each other."

My vision was beginning to narrow. My legs were beginning to tremble.

"Listen to him," Malak said. "He needs you to *help* him. He only wants you for what you can do. You're strong, but he is weak. And the strong will survive."

"No one is strong," I said. "None of us can take our next breath if God doesn't permit it." I coughed. The smoke was growing thicker. From outside the room, I could hear agents kicking in doors and firing as they searched the building room by room.

"He wants to kill me," Malak said. "He wants to take me from you. Look at the fear in his eyes. He knows you're willing to die for me. To sacrifice yourself for me, and he can't fight that."

He was right. I couldn't fight it in the traditional sense. But I had a new weapon now. One that I had not had before. I was seeing things as they really were.

I wouldn't win Callie unless I won her heart. And I couldn't make her love me. I could only give her the chance to choose. And that chance was all she would need, if only she would take it.

"He has deceived you, honey," I said. "I'm your *father*. You're part of me, and I love you. I want you to live with me. It's your choice."

I dropped the Uzi.

"Choose, honey," I said. "Choose where you will live."

Malak lunged for the gun on the floor. My wounds and the trauma I had experienced prevented me from reacting in time. Malak picked up the gun.

"Here," he said, handing her the pistol. "End it, Callie. End his control over your life."

The loss of blood took their toll. I collapsed, landing on the floor with a jarring thud.

I looked up at Callie. She pointed the gun at me, her finger on the trigger, her hand visibly trembling.

A moment passed.

"Callie," Malak said. *"Now."*

Another moment passed. I felt darkness. I kept my eyes on Callie.

She slowly released her grip on the gun, and the weapon fell to the floor. Callie rushed to where I was lying and knelt by my side.

"Daddy!" she sobbed. "Daddy!"

My breathing was becoming labored.

Malak cursed as he knelt to pick up the gun. He walked toward us, slowly, confidently. "You're weak," he said to Callie. "You could have ruled with us…"

Callie rose and turned to face Malak.

"I'm disappointed in you," he said, staring at her. "So very disappointed." He raised the gun and aimed at Callie's head.

His attention to Callie gave me the diversion I needed. I reached for the gun in my waistband.

Malak caught the movement from the corner of his eye and brought his gun to bear on me just as I pulled the pistol forward and fired.

The first shot drove him backwards, causing him to drop his gun. A stunned expression creased his face.

I fired again. And again. And I kept firing until everything went dark.

CHAPTER
SIXTY-FIVE

"Colton?"

I struggled to rise from a pit of darkness.

"Colton?"

The voice was pleasant. Soothing.

"Colton?"

My eyes fluttered and closed. Fluttered again. And closed again.

"Daddy?"

My eyes opened.

Mary and Callie were standing bedside. Roper was in the background.

I focused on Mary and managed a weak smile.

"You're in Desert Springs Hospital," she said.

"If it hadn't been for Callie," Roper said, stepping forward, "we probably wouldn't have found you in time. The house was so thick with smoke, we were afraid we'd shoot each other."

"The doctor said you came through surgery fine," Mary said. "And that—"

"Surgery?" I looked at my arms. I had an IV line in one.

"Yes, Colton," she said, smiling. "You had surgery. The doctor said you did fine and that you should make a full recovery."

"Lost a lot of blood, though," Roper said. "They had to give you a full charge."

276

I sighed. I felt weak. Nauseated.

"One shot got you in the leg but only tore some muscle and nicked a bone," Roper said. "But the other got you in the gut and nicked a...a..."

"Renal artery," Mary said. "The damage to the artery caused you to lose a lot of blood."

"You were in surgery quite a while," Roper said. "You started coming around, so they moved you up here to ICU. You'll be here a while, and then they're going to move you to another room."

"And then home," Mary said, leaning forward to kiss my cheek.

"After we deal with all the problems you caused," Roper added.

"Later," Mary said. "The legal stuff can wait."

"All right folks, everyone out. The man's got to rest." A large black woman in green surgical scrubs was standing at the curtain that served as a door to my cubicle. Although she was smiling, it was clear that she meant business.

Roper slapped me gently on the leg and winked as he left.

Mary kissed me again. "Wilkins said their lab techs have finished going over Mason's computer, and they've collected all kinds of information from his hard drive. Apparently, Malak and Mason had connected through some websites, and Malak wanted him to help build a new enclave. Some of their messages seem to indicate that Malak was also trying to move into Cleveland, Chicago, New York, and Tampa."

"Is the bureau going to look into it?" I asked.

She smiled. "They are now." She turned to follow the nurse and then paused. "Oh, yeah. Wilkins also wanted me to tell you that he found some information on the location of some lockboxes. Does that make sense to you?"

"Perfect," I said.

Callie stepped forward. She hesitated a moment, knelt over my bed, and hugged me as she began to cry softly.

I told her that I loved her and that everything would be okay.

Before ushering everyone out, the nurse asked me if I needed anything. I told her I didn't. But I was wrong. I did need something, and I had needed it for a long time.

After she closed the curtain and left, I was alone again, just as I had been in Wilkins' squad room a lifetime ago. But a lot had changed.

For the first time, I began to understand the kind of love that expresses itself in sacrifice. I had seen it in Marty. And I had felt it while trying to free Callie from the grip of a madman.

And I even began to develop a new appreciation for Millikin.

He's an expert at finding lost sheep, Colton.

Yes, I thought. And no one was more lost than me.

I closed my eyes and began to pray. I didn't know where it would all lead, but that didn't matter. It was the right road to take. And it was the right time to take it.

IF YOU ENJOYED *THE LOST SHEEP*, BE SURE AND READ THE THREE PREVIOUS COLTON PARKER MYSTERIES

Original Sin

ISBN-13: 978-0-7369-1809-1
ISBN-10: 0-7369-1809-4

Colton Parker was just fired from the FBI and has a teenage daughter who blames him for her mother's death. Now that he's hung out his shingle as a PI, his first paying client—Angie Howe—has enough money for only one day's worth of investigating. But Angie looks like she could use a friend, so Colton has his first case.

When the mystery is resolved, Colton is resigned to improve his parenting skills with his daughter—and while the pair still struggle, hope finally gets a chance to grow.

Seventy Times Seven

ISBN-13: 978-0-7369-1810-7
ISBN-10: 0-7369-1810-8

Lester Cheek had everything a man could want. A beautiful home, thriving business, and money to burn. But he was alone—very alone. Until he met Claudia.

The attractive and effervescent Claudia was everything that Lester could hope for. But then she mysteriously disappears, and Colton Parker is hired to find her.

Suspense…intrigue…drama in the tradition of Dashiell Hammett and Raymond Chandler.

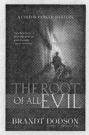

The Root of All Evil

ISBN-13: 978-0-7369-1811-4
ISBN-10: 0-7369-1811-6

Wealthy businessman Berger Hume is dying. And the one thing he wants most is the one thing his millions cannot buy—a relationship with the son he has never met. As Colton Parker searches to locate the son, he finds himself the target of threats from a powerful gang with ties that extend to high-level government.

The twists of this case cause Colton to question his own values. Will he risk the one thing that matters most? And will this race against time become a race for his own life?

© Susan Gerth 2005

MEET
BRANDT
DODSON

Brandt Dodson was born and raised in Indianapolis, where he graduated from Ben Davis High School and Indiana Central University (now known as the University of Indianapolis). During a creative writing course in college, a professor said, "You're a good writer. With a little effort and work, you could be a very good writer." That comment, and the support offered by a good teacher, set Brandt on a course that would eventually lead to the Colton Parker Mystery series.

A committed Christian, Brandt combined his love for the work of writers like Raymond Chandler and Dashiell Hammett with his love for God's Word. The result was Colton Parker.

"I wanted Colton to be an 'every man.' A decent guy who tries his best. He is flawed and makes mistakes, but he learns from them and moves on. And, of course, he gets away with saying and doing things the rest of us never could."

Brandt comes from several generations of police officers and was employed by the FBI before leaving to pursue his education.

A former United States Naval Reserve officer, Brandt is a Board Certified Podiatrist and past president of the Indiana Podiatric Medical Association. He is a recipient of the association's highest honor, the Theodore H. Clark Award.

He currently resides in southwestern Indiana with his wife and two sons and is at work on his next novel.

INTRODUCING RACHAEL FLYNN, ATTORNEY AND SLEUTH EXTRAORDINAIRE... MYSTERIES BY SUSAN MEISSNER

Widows and Orphans

ISBN-13: 978-0-7369-1914-2
ISBN-10: 0-7369-1914-7

Widows and Orphans is the debut novel in the new Rachael Flynn Mystery series by critically acclaimed author Susan Meissner. The perfect new series for readers who enjoy CBA authors Dee Henderson, Angela Hunt, and Brandilyn Collins.

When her ultra-ministry-minded brother, Joshua, confesses to murder, lawyer Rachael Flynn begs him to let her represent him, certain that he is innocent. But Joshua refuses her offer of counsel.

As Rachael works on the case, she begins to suspect that Josh knows who the real killer is, but she is unable to get him to cooperate with his defense. Why won't he talk to her? What is Josh hiding?

The answer is revealed in a stunning conclusion that will have readers eager for the second book in this gripping new series.

Sticks and Stones

ISBN-13: 978-0-7369-1915-9
ISBN-10: 0-7369-1915-5

Critically acclaimed author Susan Meissner's Rachael Flynn Mystery series started with the popular *Widows and Orphans*. In the second serving of intrigue, *Sticks and Stones,* lawyer Rachael Flynn receives an unsigned, heart-stopping letter:

They're going to find a body at the Prairie Bluff construction site. He deserved what he got, but it wasn't supposed to happen. It was an accident.

When the body is uncovered, Rachael and detective Will Pendleton discover that the fifteen-year-old victim, Randall Buckett, had been buried twenty-five years before. Are the letter writer and the killer the same person? Why would someone speak up now? And why are they telling Rachael?

The Trouble with Tulip

ISBN-13: 978-0-7369-1485-7
ISBN-10: 0-7369-1485-4

Josephine Tulip is definitely a smart chick, a twenty-first-century female MacGyver who writes a helpful-hints column and solves mysteries in her spare time. Her best friend, Danny, is a talented photographer who longs to succeed in his career...perhaps a cover photo on *National Geographic?*

When Jo's neighbor is accused of murder, Jo realizes the police have the wrong suspect. As she and Danny analyze clues, follow leads, and fall in and out of trouble, she recovers from a broken heart, and he discovers that he has feelings for her. Will Danny have the courage to reveal them, or will he continue to hide them behind a facade of friendship?

Blind Dates Can Be Murder

ISBN-13: 978-0-7369-1486-4
ISBN-10: 0-7369-1486-2

Blind dates give everyone the shivers...with or without a murder attached to them. Jo Tulip is a sassy single woman full of household hints and handy advice for every situation. Her first romantic outing in months is a blind date—okay, the Hall of Fame of Awful Blind Dates—but things go from bad to worse when the date drops dead and Jo finds herself smack in the middle of a murder investigation.

With the help of her best friend, Danny, and faith in God, Jo attempts to solve one exciting mystery while facing another: Why is love always so complicated?

Elementary, My Dear Watkins

ISBN-13: 978-0-7369-1487-1
ISBN-10: 0-7369-1487-0

Mindy Starns Clark's first two books in the Smart Chick Mystery series—*The Trouble with Tulip* and *Blind Dates Can Be Murder*—are followed with more love and adventure in this final, suspense-filled book.

When someone tries to push Jo Tulip in front of a New York train, her ex-fiance, Bradford, suffers an injury while saving her—and the unintentional sleuth is thrown onto the tracks of a very personal mystery.

Jo's boyfriend, Danny Watkins, is away in Paris, so she begins a solo investigation of her near-murder. What secret was Bradford about to share before he took the fall? And when Jo uncovers clues tied to Europe, can she and Danny work together in time to save her life?

THE CHAMBERS OF JUSTICE SERIES
BY CRAIG PARSHALL

The Resurrection File

When Reverend Angus MacCameron asks attorney Will Chambers to defend him against accusations that could discredit the Gospels, Will's unbelieving heart says "run." But conspiracy and intrigue—and the presence of MacCameron's lovely and successful daughter, Fiona—draw him deep into the case...toward a destination he could never have imagined.

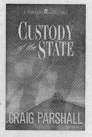

Custody of the State

Attorney Will Chambers reluctantly agrees to defend a young mother from Georgia and her farmer husband, suspected of committing the unthinkable against their own child. Encountering small-town secrets, big-time corruption, and a government system that's destroying the little family, Chambers himself is thrown into the custody of the state.

The Accused

Enjoying a Cancún honeymoon with his wife, Fiona, attorney Will Chambers is ambushed by two unexpected events: a terrorist kidnapping of a U.S. official...and the news that a link has been found to the previously unidentified murderer of Will's first wife. The kidnapping pulls him into the case of Marine colonel Caleb Marlowe. When treachery drags both Will and his client toward vengeance, they must ask—Is forgiveness real?

Missing Witness

A relaxing North Carolina vacation for attorney Will Chambers? Not likely. When Will investigates a local inheritance case, the long arm of the law reaches out of the distant past to cast a shadow over his client's life...and the life of his own family. As the attorney's legal battle uncovers corruption, piracy, the deadly grip of greed, and the haunting sins of a man's past, the true question must be faced—Can a person ever really run away from God?

The Last Judgment

A mysterious religious cult plans to spark an "Armageddon" in the Middle East. Suddenly, a huge explosion blasts the top of the Jerusalem Temple Mount into rubble, with hundreds of Muslim casualties. And attorney Will Chambers' client, Gilead Amahn, a convert to Christianity from Islam, becomes the prime suspect. In his harrowing pursuit of the truth, Will must face the greatest threat yet to his marriage, his family, and his faith, while cataclysmic events plunge the world closer to the last judgment.

To learn more about books by Brandt Dodson
or to read sample chapters, log on to our website:

www.harvesthousepublishers.com

HARVEST HOUSE PUBLISHERS

EUGENE, OREGON